Contentment Cove

Also from Islandport Press

Stealing History
by William D. Andrews

Windswept
by Mary Ellen Chase

Shoutin' into the Fog
by Thomas Hanna

down the road a piece: A Storyteller's Guide to Maine
by John McDonald

A Moose and a Lobster Walk into a Bar
by John McDonald

Mary Peters
by Mary Ellen Chase

Silas Crockett
by Mary Ellen Chase

Nine Mile Bridge
by Helen Hamlin

Titus Tidewater
by Suzy Verrier

When I'm With You
by Elizabeth Elder and Leslie Mansmann

In Maine
by John N. Cole

The Cows Are Out! Two Decades on a Maine Dairy Farm
by Trudy Chambers Price

These and other Maine books are available at:
www.islandportpress.com.

Contentment Cove
By Miriam Colwell

ISLANDPORT PRESS

ISLANDPORT PRESS • FRENCHBORO • NEW GLOUCESTER

Islandport Press
P.O. Box 10
Yarmouth, Maine 04096
www.islandportpress.com

First Islandport Press Edition, June 2007
Contentment Cove was originally published by
Puckerbrush Press in 2006.
This Islandport Press edition is published by arrangement
with the author.

ISBN: 1-934031-04-6
Library of Congress Card Number: 2007923158

Book jacket design by Karen F. Hoots / Hoots Design
Cover image by Dean Lunt
Book design by Michelle A. Lunt / Islandport Press

With thanks to Cynthia,
who spoke at the right time to the right person.

Also by Miriam Colwell

Wind off the Water

Day of the Trumpet

Young

About the Author
Miriam Colwell

If ever a writer could write authentically about what it was like to grow up, live, and work in a Maine coastal village, appreciate its heritage and recognize the changes brought by time, it would be Miriam Colwell. As postmistress for more than thirty years in Prospect Harbor—the Down East town where she was born and raised and that her ancestors helped settle—she watched the daily comings and goings of townsfolk and visitors, and was witness to the events, issues and emotions that shaped their lives. Her observations combined with what Maine author Sanford Phippen calls Colwell's "authentic Down East voice and dry, subtle sense of humor," shaped her four novels and forged them into a testament of coastal life and change in the 1940s and 1950s.

Her voice, however, was not fashioned solely in Maine. She spent a few years amongst the literary and fine arts crowd of New York City and then brought a bit of that world home to Prospect Harbor. The mixture of those perspectives and her innate writing talent helped create a voice that captured the time and still resonates in many ways today.

Courtesy of Miriam Colwell
Miriam Colwell, 1950s

"Everyone who wants to get acquainted with the whole body of Maine literature in the twentieth century should read Miriam Colwell," wrote Betsy Graves in *The Puckerbrush*

Review. "She represents an important piece in the body, an authentic voice of Maine."

Miriam Colwell was born in 1917 in Prospect Harbor. She has lived there most of her life, save for a year at college and her time in New York City. In the later '70s through the 1980s she lived in Georgia for six months of the year. Today, she lives in the lovely large farmhouse where she was born, a house built by her great-great-great-grandfather in 1817.

In the late eighteenth century, Colwell's mother's family, the Coles, moved from Massachusetts to help settle the town, building a sawmill in Prospect Harbor on the Schoodic Peninsula. Her father's family also made their way Down East, coming from Nova Scotia and settling first on Petit Manan Point before moving to the village as well. Her grandfather, George Colwell, was a pioneer in the growth of the lobster industry.

When Miriam Colwell was but two years old, her mother, Genevieve, died in the Spanish influenza epidemic that swept the nation. The epidemic had already claimed the life of Colwell's only sister. Meanwhile, her father, Clarence, suffered from tuberculosis and was forced to live in near seclusion with his parents, leaving Miriam's maternal grandparents to raise her. She saw her father often, though, visiting him when his health permitted at her paternal grandparents' home on the other side of the village. Despite the loss of her mother and her father's illness, Colwell recalls her childhood fondly. Both sides of her family provided a "very warm, supportive childhood. There is no question . . . I was so spoiled, I was never asked to do anything or taught to do any cooking or cleaning or bed making or dishwashing or anything. I never was expected to do anything except play," she said in a 2005 interview for the Smithsonian *Archives of American Art.*

Grandfather Louis Ponvert Cole ran a general store and served as the village postmaster as his ancestors did. Grandmother Susan Blance Cole served meals during the summer for a few regular patrons, perhaps as much for the social benefits as for the added income. Her grandmother also surrounded herself with books, which Miriam Colwell, a voracious reader, appreciated greatly.

Colwell attended a one-room schoolhouse in Prospect Harbor until she was old enough for high school, where—although shy and quite "an innocent"—she won prizes in public speaking contests and began to write poetry. She graduated from Winter Harbor High School in 1935 as class valedictorian and, using some money left to her by her mother, she headed for the University of Maine in Orono. However, after only a year at the university, she decided it was not for her. She returned home and went to work at her grandfather's store.

Meanwhile, her poetry would soon garner attention from some important corners. Sometime after returning home from Orono, Colwell received an invitation from her high school friend, Louise Young, to come to Corea to meet some of her new acquaintances. Young's mother had opened a small summer eatery, Katie's Restaurant, which very quickly became popular with all the summer visitors. Young, as an ebullient seventeen-year-old waitress, became equally popular. During Colwell's visit, which was to change her life, Young introduced her to two New York City schoolteachers and to Chenoweth Hall, with whom Colwell would eventually share her life and travels.

"They were completely exotic to me and I was exotic to them . . . They treated me as this exotic object, this tall, blonde Maine Down East girl who was writing poetry, a budding Millay," she told her 2005 interviewer. She blossomed under the admiration.

Hall, who came to be renowned for her music, paintings, sculpture, and writing, was then working at a New York City advertising agency. Though very different in some ways, Hall and Colwell struck up an immediate friendship, and soon Colwell was driving down to the city for visits, eventually moving there in the late 1930s. The two women lived in an apartment in Manhattan, a long way from Prospect Harbor. Colwell passed her time exploring the city, writing freelance advertising copy, peddling an exercise gizmo called Trimtummy, conducting market research surveys, and, most importantly, enjoying the artistic milieu of Hall and her circle of friends. Soon, Colwell established herself as part of that circle.

However, after two years in the city, Colwell learned that Grandfather Cole had reached the mandatory postmaster retirement age of seventy. The job always had been held by someone in the family, and her grandmother was anxious for Colwell to return home to be near her family. Colwell reluctantly agreed, and Hall was ready to relocate with her. And so at age twenty-three, Colwell left New York City and returned to Prospect Harbor where she became the youngest postmaster in the country. Fortunately, it was a relatively easy job that gave her time to pursue other interests—and to begin writing. With a growing network of friends, writers and artists, life in Prospect Harbor was from the beginning a blend of two worlds. Marsden Hartley, Berenice Abbott, Ruth Moore, Katharine Butler Hathaway, and John Marin were among the well-known writers and artists of the time that Colwell and Hall (who passed away in 1999) entertained in Prospect Harbor. They also traveled extensively, both in the U.S. and abroad.

Yet, when Colwell began writing her novels, she wrote not about the "exotic" life of which she had become a part, but rather drew inspiration from her Maine heritage and the lives of all the people she knew growing up and with whom she still spoke every day as she handed out their mail. She did not write with an intellectual view, as did Hall, but took a more realistic and grounded approach. Her first effort was *Wind off the Water,* published by Random House in 1945. The book tells the story of three brothers in a Maine fishing village, two content and one decidedly not.

"*Wind off the Water* was an attempt to portray the life of a small rural fishing community," she said. "In one's early twenties there seems to be the confidence that your particular insight may be illuminating enough to warrant exposure."

Critics offered their praise.

"Its distinction lies in its firm sense of the seasons and the life of the village, and in its authentic Yankee talk. It cuts deep. Miss Colwell is a youngster to watch," said *The Providence Journal.*

Colwell quickly followed *Wind* in 1947 with *Day of the Trumpet*, a fictional tale loosely based on her grandfather's experience in the fledgling Maine lobster industry. Eight years later, and after a few years working on another novel that went unpublished "for good reason," she wrote *Young*, the story of a day in the life of two small-town Maine girls who have just graduated from high school. Colwell said this was the most enjoyable book to write and the only one that was in any way autobiographical.

Once again, critics praised Colwell. Robert Linder said *Young* was "[an] amazingly perceptive study of the modern girl in her late adolescence. What J. D. Salinger did for the [American] male, Miriam Colwell has done for the [American] female."

And finally during the 1950s, she wrote *Contentment Cove* (which she originally titled *Plus and Minus*). However, the book went unpublished and she filed it in the chicken house behind her home. After about fifteen years of writing, with three published novels and two unpublished, she stopped writing for reasons unclear to her even today. "Perhaps feeling I had said what I had to say, perhaps because life was too engaging," she said recently. She moved on to other pursuits.

But she would be published again. Some fifty years later, while sorting through the contents of the chicken house file, she came across her forgotten manuscript. She reread it and enjoyed every word. This time it found a publisher and was released by Puckerbrush Press in 2006.

Contentment Cove is set in a picturesque Down East village of the same name during the 1950s. The story takes place over a matter of days one summer, and is told from the illuminating perspectives of three women—a local shopkeeper, an artist, and a wealthy retiree—whose lives become entwined, pleasantly at first and then tragically. The novel is "a gently satirical treatment of summer people and natives . . . We are dealing with the same things now as in the '50s and '60s," Colwell said in the 2005 Smithsonian interview. With *Contentment Cove* as with each of her novels, she said, "I was trying to present a true look at the world around me."

Bangor Daily News *photo by Linda Coan O'Kresik*

Miriam Colwell, 2006

Says Phippen: "The novel was way before its time with its depiction of well-to-do newcomers who pick a small Maine village for their year-round living, only to become terribly disenchanted with the place. Colwell, with her wit and sharp, cold eye, does a very nice job revealing *Contentment Cove*."

Burton Hatlen, English professor and director of the National Poetry Foundation in Orono, called the book "nasty, funny, witty, biting, perceptive" in a 2006 article in the *Bangor Daily News*. "The themes recall *The Great Gatsby* and the whole issue of class in America. A major theme is that the very rich or the moderately rich are different from you and me, that wealth and money inspire a certain kind of carelessness. Miriam has a definite eye to class gradations within that community," Hatlen said.

Colwell believes that within the fifteen-year span of time during which *Wind off the Water, Young,* and *Contentment Cove* are set, the changing coast is clearly reflected. *Wind off the Water* is about an isolated community dependent on lobster fishing and the sardine industry. There are no summer people mentioned. In *Young,* one of the characters spends some time working for a summer visitor, and a few other summer folks are mentioned. By the time of *Contentment Cove,* the "folks from away" are having a greater impact and the conflicts are building.

"In their own small way," Colwell said, "I think these three books bear witness to and portray the changing demographics and changing culture that has taken place along coastal areas over the last fifty years."

And Colwell, who has closely watched that change for nearly ninety years, should know as well as anyone.

Part I
Dot-Fran

Part II
Hilary

Part III
Mina

The Town

(in the late 1950s)

The town lies along the sea, around the fingers of land to east and west, and up the sloping hill.

In the winter, on cold sunny days, the bay has streaks like curving, satiny hair ribbons from shore to shore, and fishing boats loom on the horizon like the pasteboard cutouts of a child, stiff and unmoving.

Wild ducks fly in from the offshore islands in December, and in the late afternoon, when the breeze has died, dippers swim along the edge of the sandy beach with their straight, rapid wakes giving way as they dive, one here, one there, leaving the water tranquil and unmarked.

By four o'clock, on those clear days, the sea begins to steal the spreading color from the sky, like a giant prankish chameleon. The ruffled, deep blue beyond the islands burns a light, luminous pink.

The low-storied, old white houses; the high Victorians painted cream or brown; the Cape Cod type with the shallow roof and the too-large chimney; the new summer cottage like a Howard Johnson's, with venetian blinds drawn at the picture windows; the stores; the fish houses along the rocks; the spider-legged wharves; the restaurant; Hamburger Heaven; the small, brick branch of the Guarantee Trust; across the causeway, the island summer colony of turreted gray-shingled mammoths with fieldstone fireplaces and enormous vases of lilies and delphinium, each guarded by its porte cochère; the Coast Guard station, with radio towers blossoming amongst the heath cranberries: this is the town, in winter, in spring, in summer, and fall.

Through equinox gales that churn the bay to froth, break windows in the summer cottages, and sweep a spindle-legged bait house off the ledge that it has rested on for thirty-five odiferous years.

In autumn, when the swamp mulberries turn gold, and the maples drop their leaves, when the mountain ash hang heavy with berries; when the hurricanes come; when school opens, and the streets are quiet after the rumble of the big, yellow school bus fades away at eight each morning.

This is the town in August, swelled by the retired plumbers, certified public accountants, and schoolteachers, the retired generals and chief petty officers who come hurrying north from Brookline, East Orange, Fort Lauderdale, and St. Pete.

PART I

Dot-Fran

DOT-FRAN said:

It was a lovely day, the morning of Hilary's party, with bright sunshine and a clear blue sky, and just enough breeze to keep it from being too hot.

The party was the first thing I thought of when I woke up. Stan and I were going, just like summer people! And it was a perfect day. I could wear my navy sheer, with the pleated skirt.

Dad had breakfast ready when I came downstairs. The bacon smelled so good, and the whole house was full of sunshine, and Dave Garroway talking away to himself on the television in the den. Beulah was purring around Dad's feet, everything so dear, and familiar, and everyday, and, lying underneath, was the wonderful thought of the party to look forward to. It was one of those times when you just feel like singing!

I gave Dad a hug while he was trying to slide my egg onto the plate without breaking it.

"Well, well," he said, with his pleased little grin, "somebody's happy today! What's up?"

"Oh, nothing, just that it's so nice out, and this afternoon is Mrs. Wister's party!"

"So that's it."

He leaned down and gave Beulah her strip of bacon. No one had any peace in the morning until she got it.

"This is the shindig Stan's coming down from Center City for, is it? The bank certainly gets its money's worth out of him. Having to drive a hundred miles every time one of their customers gives a cocktail party."

My brother Stan's coming had nothing to do with the bank, but I hoped Dad really believed it did. You never knew whether he was being fooled or not.

Dad had angina. He couldn't go to the drugstore since his last bad attack, but he did all the bookkeeping in the den at home. He had to be quiet, and not get nervous or upset.

"I hope he gets a babysitter for the boys, and brings Beulah along with him this time," he said. "That's a long drive to make all alone."

Our cat, Beulah, was named for Stan's Beulah, because the way she loved anything new reminded us of her. The minute anything new came into the house, from a refrigerator to a new chair cover, our Beulah had to jump up on it, sharpen her claws on it, and take a nap on it straight off the reel.

Of course Stan had no intention of bringing Beulah to the party.

It was just as well that I had to hurry along and open the drugstore, because Dad had been making remarks like that lately, and he could usually tell if I was trying to hide something.

Alfeus was sweeping the Post Office lobby when I got there.

"*Good* morning, Blondie!" he said.

Alfeus was no relation, but he seemed like an older brother. He was forty-one his last birthday, eighteen years older than I was.

We had both lived in Contentment Cove all our lives, and we were together so much in the store and P.O. that he might just as well have been in the family.

My great-grandfather Hathaway divided the store building with a wire partition in 1865, putting the P.O. in on the other side.

That was when his brother, Uncle Jake, was appointed postmaster, after he caught a fever in Barbados, on board his ship, and had to give up going to sea.

It was still divided that way, only the P.O. wasn't in our family anymore. Alfeus had it.

Besides being postmaster, he was the second selectman and the tax collector of Contentment Cove, and after his father died, he was appointed a trustee in his place at the Guarantee Trust Company in Center City, the bank where my brother worked.

Alfeus was a wonderful person. Everyone in town brought him their troubles, even the summer people, but you never would have known it from him. He was as closemouthed as a clam.

But with all his wonderful, intelligent qualities, he was a terrible tease.

"My, my," he said, "aren't we looking bright-eyed and bushy-tailed! What's our glamour girl got on her mind today, I might inquire?"

"Not one single, solitary thing," I said, looking for my feather duster. "You raise more *dust*, Alfeus . . ."

"Don't try to fool your old Uncle Alfeus, I can spot that gleam in your eye. Why, sure! It's Hilary Wister's party. Our little belle is going to hobnob with the elite!"

He held out his broom and waltzed it around the lobby, bowing and smirking. He was a very good dancer.

"You'd better finish sweeping . . ."

The Potters' big Cadillac convertible stopped across the street. The top was down, but I didn't recognize the people with Mrs. Potter.

"Alfeus, who's that with Mrs. Potter? Look, she's coming over."

"Darling!" he said, bowing to his scraggly old broom, "Angel! I want you to meet my New York friends. What's that you say, broom? You want to know where New York is? My God, you're a dumb stick!"

Mrs. Potter had told us about the friends she was expecting from New York City for a visit. She had been afraid that they would miss the Contentment Cove road and get lost.

One was a very unusual, brilliant woman she had met on a cruise in the Caribbean, who used to have a very important job on *Life* magazine, and her husband who was a zipper manufacturer, and a professor who was with them.

She left them sitting across the street in the car, and came hurrying up the steps all out of breath. She was short-winded from being so plump.

I liked Mr. and Mrs. Potter a lot. Everyone did. They were the nicest kind of people, friendly to everyone, not the least bit stand-offish as you might have expected from having so much money.

"Dot-Fran? Dot-Fran?" she called through the screen. "Oh, *there* you are! My dear, I simply had to come flying in this morning to tell you that my son, Gus Junior, is definitely arriving! *Today!* At last! We've had a telegram. He'll be here in time for the big party. Isn't that simply *grand!* Won't Hilary be surprised! Oh, my!

"Aren't you excited, Alfeus? My son's arriving in time for Mrs. Wister's lovely cocktail party this afternoon."

She looked very nice in a lavender angora sweater and a white flannel skirt, with her beautiful triple string of pearls that Mr. Potter had given her on her birthday. He bought them at Tiffany and Company in New York.

"My, my, yes!" Alfeus said. "Just a jiffy while I finish sweeping and I'll go raise the flag."

He could say anything with that grin.

"It's supposed to be out right *now,*" I said.

Sometimes I could kill him for saying things like that to someone like Mrs. Potter. But, of course, as long as it was Alfeus, she loved it.

"Oh, you old tease!" she laughed. "Now I really must go bring my friends to meet you. I have *so* many things on the agenda this morning. But they're such charming people, and I so want them to meet you two dears . . ."

Along with all of Alfeus's wonderful characteristics, you could depend on him like you could on a rock; he did sometimes show an unpredictable streak, like his mother.

He was the one who gave Mr. and Mrs. Potter that nickname, though I guess he would have thought twice if he had ever imagined that everyone, all over town, would start using it. I would have curled up and died if the Potters ever heard it.

It came about after they had finished remodeling the old Harvey Place. Of course the selectmen raised the taxes. That was to be expected after all the improvements they made: insulation blown in all the walls, and under the roof, a big picture window put into every room that faced the water, as well as a hot water heating system, for which they had to dig out the cellar and cement it—that alone was a major operation—and three new bathrooms with tubs and showers in all of them, not to mention rebuilding the fireplace to install a Heatilator.

But, naturally, from three hundred dollars in valuation to fifteen thousand is quite a jump in taxes.

Mr. Potter's first name was Augustus, Gus, for short. Mrs. Potter's was Mina. I still called them Mr. and Mrs. Potter, but their close friends like the Pecks and the Elliotts and Hilary called them Gus and Mina.

The selectmen thought fifteen thousand dollars wasn't too high an evaluation for their house, but Mr. Potter was so upset that he called the state tax assessors to come down.

The day Alfeus and the other selectmen met the state assessors, Admiral Peck waited around at the soda fountain all afternoon to hear what happened.

It was almost four o'clock when Alfeus got back and the Admiral had him by the arm before he got up the steps.

"Damn it, Mayor, come in here and I'll stand you to a root beer! Did you get Gus quieted down? He ought to have his head examined for getting those state men down here. Be one hell of a mess if they called for a whole town assessment."

Alfeus pretended to wipe sweat off his forehead. He was wearing one of those sheer dark blue Orlon shirts,and with his suntan, looked very nice. "You're telling me, Admiral! Oh, I guess things will straighten out all right now. One of those state guys was in my class at the university. He's a good scout."

The Admiral passed him a cigar and put another one in his own mouth. He had already smoked two. "Well, give us the dope. Loosen up that old New England jib, Mayor! You going to lower the taxes on Gus and Mina's place or not?"

"That's the stickler! Of course your aim is to keep everybody happy in Contentment Cove, Admiral! But it wouldn't seem hardly fair to lower that evaluation, everything considered."

The Admiral held out his lighter, and Alfeus made a face at me while he puffed. He didn't like cigars much, even the Admiral's. Then he said, "No, Admiral, I guess the taxes on Plus and Minus's place are about right the way they are."

Admiral Peck might not have laughed so hard if he had known what people called him and his wife. Mrs. Bushel and her Peck.

It wasn't that Alfeus disliked the Potters; he didn't have any reason in the world not to like them. They were always doing nice things. Every Christmas they sent him a big bushel basket of oranges and grapefruit from Florida, they sent Dad and me one too, and they made a big donation, a hundred dollars, toward the new church organ, mostly because Elsie was on the committee. It was just his disposition to make jokes like that.

Mrs. Potter was shooing her friends out of the car. Alfeus poked his broom in the office out of sight and said, "Now, Marilyn Monroe, honey, do me a favor; pry open those big blue eyes and try to look reasonably intelligent. If that's too much, at least stay *awake*! Damned if I feel up to being folksy for both of us."

"You're so funny, why don't you go on television?"

It was too nice a day to be cooped up inside an old drugstore or anywhere else, with that beautiful big Cadillac sitting out there with the top down. It wouldn't matter whether you had any place to go or not if you had a car like that to go in. I could have ridden around all day long, as happy as a lark, and not even wanted to eat. Queen for a Day!

The woman with Mrs. Potter didn't resemble her at all. She was tall and very imposing, with a lovely feather curl hairdo and wearing big silver earrings in the shape of lobsters. I wanted to run and hide, until I had a chance to comb my hair and put on some lipstick. She had wonderful posture, like Loretta Young, only she was much bigger and bustier and older, about Mrs. Potter's age. She was wearing narrow-legged black slacks that looked like a million dollars, and a black low-cut sweater covered with rhinestones.

Mrs. Potter made me think of a Boston Bull, in a lavender sweater, escorting a big Irish wolfhound. I couldn't decide what the men were.

"Dot-Fran! Here are my dear friends whom I'm dying to have you meet. They've come all the way from New York, isn't that flattering? But we'll make it worth every mile, won't we? Oh, they just love it already, they really *do*, I think. You should have heard dear Greta at Bluff Rocks last night, and of course we must ride around the island too, where all the rich summer people live! Greta darling, this is the beautiful little village girl that Gus and I are so crazy about!"

She came in behind the counter, and made me come out with her, keeping her arm around me. Mr. and Mrs. Potter were wonderful for your ego. They really let you know how they felt about you.

"Gus and I have practically adopted this child, haven't we, darling? She runs this store single-handed, since her father's bad heart attack. He's such a charming man—how is he, dear?

"This store has been in their family for years, you can *see*, can't you? Isn't it fascinating? Those old bottles up there, look at them, Greta, had you noticed, and those glass cases, completely unspoiled. Isn't it priceless!

"Their deed is signed by the King of England, Greta. Imagine! Dotty, I want you to meet Greta Van Buran Chubb Pearl, formerly of *Life* magazine. She won't let me utter a word about her really *big* position, but we *all* know what being with *Life* means! Oh, Greta, just let me brag the teeniest bit to Dot-Fran. I want her to know what important, famous, stimulating guests we have visiting us!"

How I wished I had put on something beside my faded old jeans. But it didn't seem to matter to Mrs. Van Buran Chubb Pearl a bit. She had the nicest smile, and a way of looking at you very intently, as though you were the only person for miles around that she was interested in.

"Dot-Fran, I'm simply thrilled to meet you. I couldn't be more enchanted!" she said, as though she really meant it.

Alfeus was outside cranking up the awning, and talking to Jerry Jacobs who ran the hardware store across the street. I'm sure I don't know when he went out there.

"Your town!" Mrs. Van Buran Chubb Pearl said. "My dear, I'm absolutely *dedicated* to it already! Your store is a love. And ages old, of course, you can tell from the atmosphere. Oh, if I were only an artist, I'd paint you beautiful, honest, true people. Don't blush, my dear, it's true, you're one! Yes, Mina, darling, you told me I'd fall madly in love with this place. Lover, Lover! Mr. Pearl, where are you? Come here, love, and meet this darling child."

When I take the trouble to wear a dress, no one comes in but people I can see twelve months out of the year.

Mr. Pearl was a beagle, with a long, tired face and sad eyes behind heavy-rimmed glasses. He smiled, but he looked as though he hadn't slept for a month. He wasn't at all like his wife.

"Yes, dear, lovely little town, delighted to meet you, Miss Dot-Fran. Beautiful child, Greta, beautiful," he said, and rubbed his nose as though saying that much had tired him all out.

"Alfeus, Alfeus!" Mrs. Potter called. "Come in here this minute and be introduced. Alfeus is one of the Cove's big wheels, I'll have you know! He's our postmaster and selectman, and he has a lovely little wife, Elsie, who sings at church, and two darling boys. I fell for this man at first sight, and then what did the naughty boy do? Alfeus, you wretched man! He raised our taxes to a staggering amount! Really, we were heartsick, it was so unexpected. Gus was almost wild, he's so crazy about this place, you know. But I said, be philosophical, take the bitter with the sweet. What place in the world is perfect, I asked him? Isn't that true, Mr. Pearl? And it's all blown over, hasn't it, Alfeus darling? We're one happy family again, and I think, I have the tiniest little suspicion that when we get to be old residents instead of 'furriners,' he'll take pity on us, because he's really a *love*."

She pulled his arm around her and he shook hands with Mrs. Van Buran Chubb Pearl and Mr. Pearl with the other hand. Mrs. Pearl took a long holder out of her handbag and started feeling around for her cigarettes, never taking her eyes off Alfeus. I was just as glad he didn't have on his navy blue shirt that morning, considering the effect he was making without it.

"You can't know what being in this heavenly place does for me, Alfeus," she said, smiling at him. "I've never been more enchanted. You have another convert, oh, you do. I must live here, I simply must, I shall die if I don't live here, it's sheer heaven on earth. All the precious houses, so sweet and unpretentious, that glorious, fabulous ocean at your feet . . ." She paused, looking at him in that intent way, "and, my dear, such handsome people!"

Naturally he lapped that up; what man wouldn't? He loved big women anyway, the bigger they were, the more he flirted with them. In a perfectly harmless way. The world would come to an end sooner than he would ever look at another woman than Elsie.

"Oh, we natives *are* a handsome lot," he said, grinning back at her, "we don't deny it!"

Alfeus wasn't what I called handsome, but he was certainly attractive in a bony way. Plenty of the summer women thought so. They came in for sodas and sat around giggling and nudging each other, and whispering about his lovely brown eyes and the dimple in his cheek, until I felt like reminding them that they had better think about their husbands just for a change.

He still had his arm around Mrs. Potter.

"Mina," he said, "there's something that's been worrying me, preying on my mind, you know! If our Dotty here goes to this fancy party of Mrs. Wister's this afternoon and starts making eyes at anybody, there's bound to be trouble! Dotty has a heavy romance, you know!"

"I'd like to know who with!" I said.

He knew perfectly well that I didn't have any heavy romance.

Ken Hill and I had been going around together for years, off and on, mostly from habit. But it happened to be very embarrassing, because I didn't want Mrs. Potter to think I had any ideas about her son, even if she had talked so much about him to me. I mean, I didn't want her to think I was taking anything for granted.

She pretended to slap him.

"Just you leave Dot-Fran right alone now! I can hardly wait for Gus Junior to meet her."

Gus Junior, their son, had never been to Contentment Cove.

In fact, Mrs. Potter always said that it was only by luck that she and Mr. Potter found it themselves. They had been taking a week's tour around New England, and happened to see a sign for the Sea Breeze Inn. They liked the sound so much, Sea Breeze Inn in Contentment Cove, that they drove down to spend a night.

Twenty-four hours later they bought the old Harvey Place and the next day after that they had hired a carpenter and a plumber to start right in building it over.

That was the way Mr. Potter did things. Grass didn't grow under his feet. I felt that we should be very flattered to have a couple like them with so much money come to the Cove to settle when they could pick and choose and go anywhere. Of course they weren't the only ones who had done it. Admiral Peck and his wife came back to live after he retired from the navy, and there was Florence and the Elliotts and the Spindles, but I think Mr. and Mrs. Potter were better off than any of them.

Their home was in Cincinnati, Ohio, where Mr. Potter owned a big contracting business. After the war, he sold his business and retired, and they moved out to Palo Alto, California, and built a lovely new home out there, with orange and lemon trees growing on the lawn. I saw pictures of Mrs. Potter picking oranges from the trees in their yard.

But Mr. Potter didn't like California. "They brag about what they've got out there," he said, "the biggest strawberries and the biggest oranges, the biggest steaks and the biggest crackpots! But let me tell you what they do: They ship all the big strawberries and oranges and steaks back east, and just keep the crackpots! You can't even tell a Republican from a lousy Democrat out there. No sir, give California back to the Indians for all of me. It's lousy. Contentment Cove is the place for me—God's own country."

Mr. Potter was a good-looking man for his age, with white hair and thin cheeks and snappy brown eyes. They moved from California to San Antonio, Texas.

Mrs. Potter showed the Woman's Club movies of the ranch-type house they owned there. It was modern, with glass all along the front, facing a canal, and lovely hibiscus blooming on both sides of the front walk.

But she told us that it was dreadfully hard to keep all that glass clean, being so close to the water. She said she imagined that may have been why the former owners wanted to sell. Then when they closed the house for a month to go back to Cincinnati on business, buffalo bugs got in all the rugs.

Mr. Potter telephoned to San Antonio from the drugstore the day after they bought the Harvey Place. It was so hot that he left the phone booth door open, so naturally I couldn't help overhearing.

He said, "Hello, hello? Gus Potter here. Right. Oh, feeling great, great, better than I've felt for years. Up here in God's country! Yeah, the way to hell and gone is right! Further the better. Look here, I've found the only place fit for a white man left in this whole damn country. Wipe that lousy Texas dust out of your eyes and come up and see! Look, I want you to put that house up for sale. Yeah . . . "

When people like them, who had lived all those different places, and had plenty of money so they could pick and choose, chose Contentment Cove, it really made you sit up and feel pretty good.

Of course, they didn't have to stay in the winter when it got cold, although their house had a new furnace so they could stay if they wanted to.

But Mrs. Potter didn't want to be referred to as summer people; she wouldn't have it.

"We're not, my dear, not at *all*. Oh, really, it makes me cross to be regarded as part of the 'summer complaint'! I want every soul in Contentment Cove to know that we regard it as our home, our real home. We've made it our legal residence, my dear, we hang our hats here! We pay you our taxes! Oh, Dot-Fran, not that I would for a minute wish to infer that the families who own those lovely summer homes over on the island aren't grand people. I'm *sure* they are, though there hasn't seemed the time nor opportunity to make their acquaintance as yet, but my dear, they can't know and love the Cove as we do, can they? Out there playing golf on their old island! My dear, think how much they miss by not being more a part—but we won't tell them, will we! Gus and I just pray that this marvelous, unspoiled place will always stay just as it is. We're *so* selfish, but after all the places we have lived and given so much of our lives to, I do think God will forgive us. No, Dot-Fran, never, *never* consider Mr. Potter and myself as summer people. We want to be regarded as a real part of the community."

She really meant it, that was the wonderful thing about Mrs. Potter, she never said anything she didn't mean, and as soon as the Woman's Club started meeting in September, she joined. The club didn't meet during the summer because most of us were too busy working.

It gave her a big kick to belong to such a small club after the big city chapters she had known. Ours was the smallest and the most fun, she said. We were certainly lucky to have her to steer us along as we had only been chartered a year. She really knew how to get the ball rolling, and she was very smart about parliamentary procedure and things like that.

But there's always someone in a small town like Contentment Cove who is going to be resentful of any outsider. Like Ella Constant. Ella was recording secretary of the club and she resigned. We could have understood her attitude better if the people who had come to the Cove to live, like Hilary and the Pecks and the Potters, weren't all such lovely people. She would really have had something to gripe over if we had gotten some other kinds moving in.

Her brother had the same exact disposition. And the unfortunate thing was that they owned all of Gooseberry Point, from Sand Cove east to the island, almost five miles of beautiful shoreline.

I don't know how many different people had wanted to buy the Point from them, or even just a lot, but they wouldn't have given up an inch of that land if they had been starving, which they weren't. It had always been in their family, and I guess it always will be.

A man from New Jersey wanted to put up a big motel in the field just above Sand Cove, fifty units, with picture windows looking over the bay. A motel like that would have brought a lot of business through town, but that cut no ice whatsoever with Ella and Harry. The day he called on them was cold and rainy, a southeaster, and he got soaked standing on their porch trying to persuade them to let him in.

All Ella said was, "Our property isn't for sale. Any of it. We have no land for sale."

Harry kept shoving the door shut on the man's foot. He was limping when he came in the drugstore afterward for an Alka-Seltzer.

"You ever going to wake up around here?" he said to me, dripping all over the floor like a Saint Bernard. "I suppose you know those two old mossbacks up on the hill, Blondie? Real screwballs. Characters like them really bitch up the works, huh! Know what I mean, kid? A good motel would put this place on the map, bring in some traffic, see? Gimme a couple of Bufferin, dear. My God, it always rain like this around here?"

That first time Mrs. Potter came to a meeting of our Woman's Club, everyone, or most of us, made her very welcome.

"Oh, *dear* people, don't make any fuss over me," she said, and I could see she meant it. "I just want to fit right in. It's such a *treat* to be here, and that view . . . my dear Miss Constant, that view is worth a *million* dollars! Do you *realize* what a treasure it is!"

We were meeting at Ella's that day, and of course her house on Gooseberry Point was one of the oldest in town.

Ella drew her mouth down the way she had and just gave a polite little sniff.

But later when Mrs. Potter was telling us of some of the lovely projects her Cincinnati Club had sponsored, which most of us were very interested in hearing about, Ella got up and began to pass the refreshments around.

She mentioned having the start of a sick headache to Della, so the meeting broke up early.

As we were driving home, Della said to me, "You and I better go see Ella tomorrow, and try to soothe her down. Golly, I'd certainly miss those crabmeat sandwiches she always makes!"

But we didn't have a chance to do much soothing.

Ella said, "If the rest of you need to be told when to breathe in and when to breathe out, I'm very thankful that you have somebody in Mrs. Potter who will be glad to oblige. Not only when, but how! As far as I'm concerned, girls, Contentment Cove's ways aren't San Antonio, Texas's or Cincinnati, Ohio's, either, and I thank the Lord for it! I hope they never will be no matter how many Potters move in here. Goodbye, Della, goodbye Dotty, thank you both for coming, I'm sure."

In the car, Della and I agreed how awful it must be to feel so crabby at the world. But of course, it must be awful to be getting old like Ella and Harry, and to see things changing all around them from what they've always been used to. But everybody has to give in to progress sooner or later, no matter how they hang back.

"Greta darling," Mrs. Potter said, smiling at me, "my son says that he just feels that he knows Dot-Fran and the Cove just from my enthusiastic letters! I shouldn't tell you this, Dot-Fran, men are *so* awful, but he says after the big buildup I've given you, he just hopes he won't be disappointed! As though he could be! Why, Alfeus, now naturally, I know about Dotty and Ken going on dates, but I'm sure I never thought it was serious! He's a sweet

boy, so quiet and attractive. Greta, you remember Della Hill, that
sweet woman who does our laundry and cleaning, so efficient,
you met her yesterday at the house. Kenny is her son. The
Admiral put him through the university, I'm told, that Admiral
Peck, Greta, remember the lovely house with all the delphiniums.
Della has worked for them for years. You know, several times a
week as she does for us. It was such a generous thing, wasn't it?
They have no children of their own which makes a difference.
Ken teaches now, doesn't he, dear? Alfeus, you are so naughty. We
must just let nature take its course where boys and girls are con-
cerned, so there! And my son has a Jaguar!"

The professor had been strolling around the store while everyone was talking. I think Mrs. Potter had forgotten his name. He
was wearing a gray tweed jacket and a red beret, and he had a nice
figure for a middle-aged man. His shoes were just like a pair Hilary
had given Stan, two-strap leather sandals with thick crepe soles.

Suddenly he came up behind Mrs. Potter and gave her a little
shake. "Does anyone realize that I haven't been introduced?
Doesn't anyone care?"

"Oh darling Eddie, I'm so ashamed!" Mrs. Potter whirled
around and threw both arms around him. "This is Edgar Chubb,
dears. He's a marvelously learned professor, one of those intelligent, intellectual people who just simply frighten little old stupid
me, except that Eddie is a *darling* in spite of all his brain!"

He was bald when he took off his beret, but his head was very
brown and sort of attractive, like Yul Brynner's.

"Dot-Fran, delighted! May I call you that, Miss Hathaway?"

"Shall I call you Edgar, Mr. Chubb?"

I wanted to bite my tongue off the minute it came out, but they
all laughed, except Alfeus, who gave me a look that would kill.

By that time, it was ten-thirty and almost mail time. People had
begun to come in to wait for the mail truck, and I didn't have a
chance to stand around and talk anymore. Sara King wanted a

bottle of aspirin, and Joe Peterson bought a root beer soda with chocolate ice cream.

Alfeus was trying to excuse himself and go back over to the P.O. side where Joe's mother was waiting for him at the money order window. But Mrs. Van Buran Chubb Pearl wouldn't let him go. She was still telling him how beautiful Contentment Cove was. Her voice carried so that everyone in the store was listening. But she had the kind of poise that it didn't bother at all. I certainly wished that I could be sure of myself like that. In a big New York job I guess you develop poise and self-confidence.

Every time I glanced toward the professor he was watching me, whether I was behind the fountain or waiting on someone at the magazine rack. He was leaning against the cigar counter, where Simple Simon was curled up asleep, following my every move. It made me so flustered, and flattered, that I rang up the cash register three times trying to hit twenty-five cents for Joe's soda. His face was so brown that he looked quite young except for the pouches under his eyes.

At quarter of eleven, Hilary came up from the Point for her mail. "Hi there," she said to me behind her hand. "For God's sake, are you holding a convention, duck?"

She had on a white shirt and Bermuda shorts, which looked wonderful on her, and her copper fish earrings from Mexico.

"Well, Mina!" she called, "all set for big doings this afternoon?"

"Hilly darling, how marvelous to run into you here. I was planning to drop over just for an itty minute to introduce some dear, dear friends whom I hope you're going to let me bring along."

"The more the merrier!"

She wasn't pretty or beautiful, but she had the kind of personality that stood out. The minute she came into a room you wondered who she was, and everything seemed more interesting.

My brother, Stan, was in love with her. I couldn't blame him. Anyway, it was partly my fault for taking him to see her that night. She wasn't like anyone either of us had ever known; she was almost like someone from another planet. But Stan had a wife and two children, and Dad's bad heart to think about, as well as his job at the bank. Poor Stan. But when you're really in love, that's all that matters. It's something you just can't help.

It started one night in the winter. Stan came down from Center City on bank business, and stayed for supper. We were sitting in the den with Dad, drinking beer, and watching the state basketball tournament on TV—Center City was playing off in the semifinals—when the phone rang.

It was Hilary out on Marsh Point. She asked me to come out if I wasn't doing anything, and bring her mail.

She had been living out there alone since she and Spencer, her husband, separated in September. No one dreamed she would stay through the winter, but she wasn't nervous about being alone, and she said she liked being able to paint all day without interruptions. A lot of evenings, though, she would get lonesome and call me to drive out for a little while and bring her mail or groceries or whatever she needed. When it was too cold, or if there was a lot of snow, she didn't bother taking her car out at all.

I loved going. I felt like the luckiest person in town to get to be friends that way. She was so understanding and a lot of fun when she liked you, not a bit like some people thought. Her house wasn't a bit like anyone else's, she had so much imagination. There were rugs she had brought from Mexico hanging on the walls instead of on the floor, handwoven by the Indians, and chairs that looked like baskets but were very comfortable. None of the rooms were papered. She liked plain walls for paintings. They were mostly Spencer's.

"He's such a good painter and such a lousy husband," she said, when she was showing one to me.

They came to the Cove back in 1945. I was too young to notice them very much except once in a while getting their mail. They kept mostly to themselves at first, but after a few years everyone got to know them. Abbey Peterson saw them more than anyone else because she did their cleaning.

The day they separated Abbey was so upset she could hardly get to the drugstore to tell me about it. A stranger might have thought her husband had just dropped dead from the way she looked.

"Oh Dot-Fran, Dot-Fran!" she heaved, "I'm so broke up, there, I can hardly talk, I just can't grasp yet that it's true."

I gave her a glass of water and waited until she got her breath. "You're just a child, dear. Oh, you've got no way of knowing . . . and it's just as well . . . oh, dear."

Abbey enjoyed getting wrought-up, like Stella Dallas. I suppose it was mean to say she enjoyed it, because she felt bad at the same time, but in a way she enjoyed sharing other people's troubles. It made her forget her own. And she loved being confided in.

"Nothing's hit me so hard since my brother died, and of course that was a blessing you might as well say with his stomach being eaten away by inches. I had to stop in for something cold to drink or I never would have made it the rest of the way home. It's awful warm walking, even if it is the middle of September. Dot-Fran, I tell you, it don't seem fair nor right, I just cannot reconcile myself to it. There was never a finer, sweeter woman than Mrs. Wister to work for. I would willingly take the rags off my back for that woman if she asked me to, and to have this happen just when she's in the midst of her painting, and needing peace and quiet. A Coca-Cola, please, dear."

"What's happened, Abbey? Is Spencer sick?"

"Sick. He's left!" Abbey said with another deep heave. Abbey was famous for them, she had the disposition and the breastworks. They were kind of a hobby. "He's cleared out, bag and baggage. The poor brave little soul, she drove him to Center City herself to catch the noon train. And do you know that all she said to me was, 'Well, Abbey, now we can air that ghastly smell of rotgut tobacco out of the house.' "

I had never known Spencer very well. He wasn't unfriendly, but he wasn't very talkative. Some people are like that; they come for their mail and leave instead of having a Coke and smoking a cigarette and staying around a little while. He was tall and quite thin, with a small reddish mustache and reddish eyebrows, and he usually wore black corduroy trousers.

His studio was rebuilt from the old henhouse on their property. Hers was upstairs on the south side of the house overlooking the water. In the summers they always had a lot of company, but the only ones I knew were the Balls, who came to the Cape every year for July and August, and the Weavers, who owned a house in Jericho, on the other side of Center City. They had all known each other a long time.

Stan really perked up when he found out who was telephoning. "Well, my quiet little sister getting chummy with a famous artist! What do you think of that, Dad?"

"I think Mrs. Wister's lonesome out there on that godforsaken point," Dad said. "Why wouldn't she be? It's a damned funny place for a woman to live by herself this time of year."

Stan swallowed his beer and jumped up. "I'd better drive you out there. You know, I've never been to Marsh Point since they bought it? Ten to one you'd get stuck on her road with all this snow. Mrs. Wister's a customer of ours at the bank."

"Oh, let Doffy go, if she thinks she's got to. She knows that road down there blindfolded by now," Dad said. "You've got a long drive back to town, boy. The game will be on in just a minute now."

"Gosh, I can't miss a chance like this—to rub shoulders with royalty! It might rate me a raise!"

To tease him I said, "She thinks you're mighty handsome, Stannykins. Last time she saw you at the bank, she said, 'Your brother has certainly gotten to be a stunning hunk of man!' "

He put his suit coat back on, trying not to look pleased. "What are we waiting for, kiddo?"

"You're both of you out of your minds," Dad grumbled, "going out in the cold when you could sit here in comfort and see a good ball game."

It was cold, only two above zero, but one of those lovely, clear, absolutely still winter nights, with the stars shining like cake decorations. The Cove looked like a Christmas picture, lighted windows reflecting on the snow, and the fields so white against the dark water. Everything creaked with frost, the shell ice around the rocks, the car, the trees, the road, though there wasn't a breath of wind stirring.

Out on the Point, we sat around Hilly's fireplace and ate roasted chestnuts and drank bourbon. She played recordings from *My Fair Lady* that Spencer had just sent her, and Stan loosened up after a couple of drinks and sang along with them. She was very quiet, just sat and watched him and ate chestnuts. It was unusual for her to be so quiet.

Later on the moon came up. It seemed to rise straight out of the ocean beyond Calf Island with the dead black water beginning to silver and dance and shimmer like gold lamé. It was so beautiful I couldn't speak.

Hilly said, "Come, children, let's go watch this from the upstairs studio."

The whole end of her studio was glass, with a narrow second-story porch hanging out over the rocks. We didn't need any lights. The walls were white and the whole room was as light as day, with stars shining through the big skylight. Her painting things were arranged very neatly on shelves and in racks along the walls, big stacks of paper and dozens of brushes sticking out of pitchers. The only clutter was on the big table under the skylight. A big piece of burlap was thrown over her easel.

It seemed so odd standing there in that big, bare room with the aluminum chairs glinting and the ocean within reach of your hand. The moon climbed higher and higher, spreading a wide moonpath beyond the islands.

The phonograph still played downstairs. It seemed dreamlike, Stan and I standing there with Hilly watching the moon rise over Calf Island. All the bourbon was making my head spin, but I was so happy, so keyed up and excited, that I unlatched the glass door and stepped out on the porch before I really knew what I was doing.

The air was freezing cold, but it didn't seem to matter. Stan and Hilly were only a foot away inside the glass. They stood very still, with moonlight on their faces, as though they were cast in a spell, not able to move, even to smile.

Stan's eyes shone the way they used to when Dad had promised to take us to Center City for the circus or the ice show. It was as light as day on the porch, but not real. I could hear water slapping against the rocks, and I had the feeling you have when you dive into a big, cold roller and come up without any breath, tingling all over. Hilly's earrings looked like live things, glinting and trembling against her hair.

When I stepped back in they were dancing. The music sounded faint and faraway, and I didn't think they heard me until Hilly said, "Darling, run downstairs and get the bourbon before you have a chill."

The next morning, after she got her mail, she came over to the fountain and ate a dish of chocolate ice cream, though she hates ice cream. I didn't know then that it was going to be serious with her and Stan, but I think she did.

"Sweet of you two to come by last night," she said with a funny little smile, as though she was apologizing for something. "I was damn fed up with my own boring company."

"You couldn't ever be boring."

She laughed and reached over and patted my hand.

"God, what a lift to see you blond, glowing creatures arrive. Darling, Stan's wife never should let him out alone nights, a ravishing male like him. Not when there are lone women like me around!"

Of course I thought she was fooling, but she hardly ever was.

The mail was late, and the drugstore was full of people visiting. It sounded like a henhouse full of broody hens. Joe Peterson finished his soda, and went over to the magazine rack and started reading the last *Confidential*.

When there was a chance, I sailed over and said, "Are you planning to buy that magazine, Joe? It's for sale, you know!"

He turned around as though I had stuck a knife in his ribs. "Hell, no."

At least a thousand times I had wasted my breath telling him not to hang around reading the magazines. Joe was a headache. Of course he got blamed for a lot of things he didn't do, but the way he slouched around with that silly grin and his eyes always trying to see around the corner, he looked like a skinny villain out of a Western movie, when they had run out of grown-ups. He thought he was a tough hombre.

Abbey, his mother, thought he was picked on. When anything was missing in town—a pair of dungarees from a clothesline, or a power lawn mower from the display in front of the hardware store—Joe was blamed for it.

When they went to Abbey, she always gave one of her big sighs and rolled her hands in her apron and said, "Oh, my poor boy, Joe. He gets the blame for everything. He is a sensitive boy, Joe is, and someone is always after him. Maybe he gets into mischief, I don't deny he gets into things he has no call to, but there's plenty of others right along with him. He's no worse than the rest, my boy isn't, but he's the one is blamed. Poor little Joe. All his life has been after him. His father's never had any patience. Some days all I can do is keep them apart. But Joe don't mean any harm, he's a good boy to his mother, and a mother knows her boy's heart."

When Abbey didn't have Joe's stealing or fighting with his father, or the twins throwing tin cans down the neighbor's well to worry about, she could always fall back on Mrs. Peck. Mrs. Peck was worried about the Admiral's drinking which was bad for his high blood pressure, so Abbey worried about Mrs. Peck's being so worried. Or she could worry about dear lonesome Mrs. Wister now that her husband had left her. Dear lonesome Mrs. Wister wasn't so unbearably lonesome that I could see. But Hilly was just as loopy about her.

"Isn't Abbey a marvel?" she said. "There she is with that poop of a husband and a delinquent son, and it never gets her down, it never vanquishes that spirit of hers, bless her. She has such warmth and honest, down-to-earth wisdom, Dot-Fran, under that exterior. It's like telling your troubles to Mother Earth."

It was like telling them to a broadcasting studio, too, but I didn't say so because it would just have made Hilly feel bad, and she probably wouldn't have believed it anyway.

Alfeus finally tore himself away from Mrs. Van Buran Chubb Pearl and went tearing into the P.O. to write Abbey's money order.

The store was buzzing, and the bread truck and the Coca-Cola salesman arrived at the same time, both wanting an order.

Professor Chubb was standing there in the same place, watching me. Whenever I glanced his way he smiled and touched his beret or lifted his eyebrows as though we had some private joke. It was disconcerting in a way, but I guess no one minds being noticed.

"Beautiful, isn't she?" I heard him say to Hilary. "I didn't know there was such fresh, unspoiled beauty left anymore."

Hilly glanced over at me. "Oh, Miss Hathaway is one of the Cove's star attractions, Professor Chubb. Well, I suppose Mina has been taking you on the usual grand tour?"

"Hilly!" Mrs. Potter called. "I *must* ask your advice. Gus and I are positively sick about the way the swimming pool is going."

"Which way is it going? To the dogs with the rest of us?"

Mrs. Potter looked a little annoyed. She was really upset about the swimming pool. "You can joke, my dear, but it's a dreadfully serious matter. I'm in earnest about needing your advice. You've lived here so much longer than we have. My dear, Gus was simply sunk this morning when he went over and saw how little progress they've made."

Sara King was pretending not to listen, but she couldn't hold out. "Why, excuse my saying so, Mrs. Potter, but I think it is just disgraceful that they can't get along any faster, with you and Mr. Potter being so generous as to donate all that money."

"It *is* a disappointment, Mrs. King, when we did so want the community to enjoy it this summer. Mrs. King, do let me introduce my New York friend, Greta Van Buran Chubb Pearl. Greta, this is dear Mrs. King, who raised that delicious corn we ate last night for dinner."

Mrs. Van Buran Chubb Pearl said, "This swimming pool is absolutely the most exciting, the most fabulous thing I've ever heard of in my entire life. Oh, for these two *precious* people to conceive of building such a thing for this darling town, such an asset, such a feather in your caps. Mina, *actually*, I think it's too thrilling! Mrs. King, I *am* delighted to meet you. Lover! Come here and meet Mrs. King."

Mr. Pearl had been leaning against the greeting cards having a nap, though he kept smiling all the time so no one noticed.

"Lover, isn't this swimming pool a fabulous, marvelous philanthropic idea? My husband, Mrs. King. He *gorged* himself on your corn last night, didn't you, love?"

"Melted in your mouth," Mr. Pearl muttered, blinking. "Haven't eaten so much in years. Sea air, I suppose. Fabulous idea, yes, my dear, no question, fabulous, shows real benevolence."

While they were talking, Mrs. Potter pulled Hilary to one side. I was filling the strawberry syrup container behind the fountain and could hear every word they said.

"Now Hilly, just between you and me, because you know I wouldn't want hurt feelings for the world, and dear Mrs. King might misinterpret, you never know how they will react, do you? But now, tell me honestly—do you think Gus should be firmer with Ted Hill and the men? Poor darling, he was *so* enthusiastic when Ted started work on the pool, like a boy with a new toy. *You* know how men are . . . "

"And how they aren't!" Hilly said, with her little lopsided grin.

But Mrs. Potter was too worked up to appreciate Hilly's sense of humor.

"Ted Hill said he couldn't give us an estimate, which naturally we should have insisted on anywhere else, but we understood that this was a new undertaking for him, so that was taken into consideration. Naturally Gus knows roughly what it should cost, he hasn't been a businessman for thirty years for nothing, my dear. But Hilly, you have no idea how *baffling* it is; work goes on, day after day, on and on, with so *little* progress. My dear, there are *ten* men employed. Darling, I need your sincere, honest opinion. You've had dealings with these people, you know them; what would *you* do?"

"The same thing you'd do back home, in Indianapolis, anywhere. Give them hell!"

"Our home was in Cincinnati, dear. But everything is so different here. One feels that one must tread carefully, you *know* how easily their feelings are hurt, and then there's simply *no* way of getting anything done. But Hilary, thank goodness there aren't those awful labor unions to contend with in Contentment Cove. It's simply a question of money and nothing else, once those *unions* get a foothold. Grab, grab, grab. And it's all so different here. We mustn't tread on sensitive toes. It's so difficult knowing *what* to do."

"My God, don't worry about Ted Hill's toes," Hilly said, lighting a cigarette and glancing over to see if I was listening.

"Oh Hilary, you artists!" Mrs. Potter tried to sound light, but it was an effort. "I should have known better than to bother you, dear. You're always so casual, so cynical about things. What a blessing it must be to have that kind of disposition. But darling, you see Gus and I have a large investment tied up in this project, and the summer is simply flying by without the poor townfolk benefiting as we had so hoped . . ."

"They'll worry along," Hilly said. "Better times are coming!" She put her hand on Mrs. Potter's arm. "Look, Mina, here's my advice: Tell Gus to damn well demand to know where he stands on this thing. My sincere, honest advice is to give Ted Hill a good poke in the ass!"

I wish he could have heard that.

The Potters' idea of building a swimming pool for the benefit of the whole town came as a surprise to just about everyone.

They arrived back in the Cove the day before Town Meeting in March, much earlier than they usually came back from Florida. Mrs. Potter had written me every few weeks from Miami, and when they took a cruise through the Bahamas they sent postcards to nearly everyone in town, but it was a complete surprise when they walked in that day, looking so brown from all the Florida sunshine that I felt like a mushroom beside them.

Mr. Potter gave me a big hug and said, "Same old beautiful Dotty! What do we go to Florida for, hey! They can have it, it's strictly for suckers!" He shook hands with Alfeus. "This is the place for me, boy! You look great, both of you. Everything looks great, hey, Mina? God's country. Boy, how I love getting back here where I can breathe white man's air again. What about that mail that's been piling up all winter, Alfeus? You must have a carload in there. Well, I'll take that damn nuisance off your hands. It's Town Meeting day tomorrow, I hear. Big deal! We just made it, didn't we? Any excitement on the agenda tomorrow? Any opposition to you entrenched selectmen?"

It was always wonderful to see the Potters again; they were always so glad to be back in Contentment Cove. They made you forget about the winter days—when the electricity failed and the house was freezing cold and the car wouldn't start and you couldn't stop sneezing and sniffling—and realize that it was a pretty nice place to live in, and that you were pretty lucky.

"I haven't heard of any opposition, Gus. It sounds like a quiet meeting."

"Say, that's too bad," Mr. Potter teased. "I was hoping they'd run you fellers out and elect someone a man could reason with! Well, boy, just between you and me and the lamppost, Mina and I have a little surprise to spring on the folks tomorrow. Yep! Come on, Mina, I want to get this lousy Florida sand out of my shoes and feel like I'm home again."

Alfeus was as nervous as a cat in a gale of wind after they had gone. He had been working on his postal manual, putting in a whole stack of changes that had been piling up for months, things like a raise in the air-mail rate to Tanganyika in yen, or parcel post to the British Camaroons a pfeffing less an ounce, which he usually poked in a drawer when they came, where the postal inspector found them. "Too busy campaigning for that selectman's job to keep up with things here, Alfeus?" he asked.

"Those damn things? It would take a one-armed paper hanger to keep up with all that stuff."

"Cut off an arm then and get busy," the inspector said.

But after the Potters left he just sat there staring at his desk, grunting something unintelligible.

"Are you talking to *me*, Alfeus?"

He didn't even answer, just got up and walked over and stared out the window, looking mad.

"What is the *matter* with you?"

"Now what in hell do you suppose Plus and Minus are going to spring at Town Meeting?"

"Maybe they're going to adopt Joe Peterson!" The things that will pop into your head.

"Sure, that's great," he said sarcastically, opening the partition and coming over to the fountain. "Give me a cup of that stuff you call coffee."

We drank three cups each, trying to guess what the surprise could be, while he got grumpier and grumpier, but we had to wait for Town Meeting to find out.

The meeting began at ten o'clock with Jerry Jacobs elected moderator as usual. It was a lovely warm day for March, with the eaves dripping, and the sun really hot out of the wind, and the seats in the hall were full. A lot of people came for the chicken dinner more than anything else, served by the Eastern Star and the Woman's Society for Christian Service.

The board of selectmen and the tax collector were all reelected by the clerk's casting one ballot, as there was no opposition. The first article that there was any discussion about was number eight: To see if the town would vote to establish and supervise a town dump. We certainly needed one. As it was, garbage and beer cans and bottles were all thrown into the harbor to wash up along the shore, or thrown out of cars on the sides of the road.

Admiral Peck got up and said that he was all in favor of having a town dump, and having it properly taken care of. He said that dumps were unsightly and smelled bad and attracted rats, which attracted little boys with guns they shouldn't be allowed to have, and needed to be burned every day for sanitary and safety reasons, but that the Cove would be better off with one than without one, and he was willing to have his taxes raised to pay for it.

Everyone applauded, but after some discussion about how much it would cost and so on, Bert Namon made a motion to indefinitely postpone the article. All the men in the back row shouted "Aye." The Admiral and quite a lot of others said "No," but it was a vote, and that ended that for another year.

Jerry was reading article thirty-seven when Mr. Potter got up and said, "Mr. Moderator, may I have the floor?"

It took a few minutes for everyone to quiet down so that he could be heard. There was always a gang standing at the back of the hall, smoking, carrying on their own meeting.

"Ladies and gentlemen," Mr. Potter said, standing out in the aisle so everyone could see him, "I don't intend to take up too much of your time, but my wife and I have an idea that we would like to present to this meeting. It seemed to us that a Town Meeting was the place to present it. My name's Gus Potter, in case I'm a stranger to some of you . . . "

"You sure are, Gus," someone snickered back by the door. A few smart alecks thought Town Meeting was an excuse to drink beer and make stupid cracks.

"I'm a property owner and a taxpayer in Contentment Cove. Sometimes when I look at my tax bill, I wonder if I'm the only one they tax! But that's all right, I know when I'm licked. See Alfeus grinning over there. And we just went ahead and reelected the son of a gun!"

"You're not licked," Alfeus called, from where he was sitting on a bench against the wall, "just down for the count!"

Mr. Potter waited for it to quiet down.

"Here is what I came to say to you good people. My wife and I have been residents of Contentment Cove for almost two years now. We've lived all over this country, or enough of it, at one time or another, and I want you to know, friends, that this town right here is the one spot in the one state in the Union where my wife and I have hung up our hats and called home. It's God's country. I want to tell you a little story to go along with that. The day we bought our house a feller came up and said to me, 'Mr. Potter, you'll get along up here if you just take into account that us natives is as independent as hogs on ice!' Say, if he thought that was going to discourage me, he had another think coming! It was music to my ears! I knew right then that Contentment Cove was in a class by itself, and it was sure enough the place I had been looking for, where folks were still thinking for themselves and didn't need a damn union or the federal government horning in, trying to do it for them.

"Yes sir, this is the place for us. This winter we began saying to ourselves, what can we do to give the town a boost? What can the Potters provide in the nature of an improvement, a benefit for all, a step forward for the good people who live here? Because, folks, let me tell you, we want to put something on the record, something lasting, from Gus and Mina Potter, for the reason that old Contentment Cove is *one* spot left on God's green earth where you can live without being crowded off the sidewalks by inferior races, and dictated every move to by the lousy socialists in control of Washington, D.C."

Mr. Elliott, Ted Hill, and a few others clapped.

"Thanks," Mr. Potter said, smiling, "I see there's some others shares my sentiments along those lines. Well, ladies and gentlemen, to be brief, I want you all to know how much we appreciate your making us welcome here, making us feel at home, and this winter while we've been away . . . "

"What they'd go away for if it's so all-fired wonderful here?" someone muttered in the row behind me. Two or three women tittered, and I could have murdered them all. Jerry rapped his gavel.

"This winter while we were away," Mr. Potter went on, "my wife and I decided we had reached a milestone, friends. We were all done roving. From here on in, it was going to be Contentment Cove for us . . ."

"Oh, for God's sake, give us the million dollars and get it over with," the same voice behind said.

I could have cried I was so thankful that Mr. Potter didn't hear. Jerry rapped his gavel again. "Let's have it quiet, please."

"My wife and I have given this thing a lot of thought, and it seemed to us that one great lack in Contentment Cove was a place of recreation, a community center where the young folks and the old folks, *everybody*, could get together and have a whale of a time. Well, folks, in a nutshell, that's what the Potters want to prove. We hope you're going to like our idea. We hope you're going to agree with us that our little project is going to give this little town a big boost."

He wiped his forehead, and walked over to put his hand on Mrs. Potter's shoulder. "My wife and I propose to build Contentment Cove a community swimming pool!"

"Oh my God!" the voice behind said.

The hall began buzzing like a beehive. It took Jerry almost ten minutes to get the meeting back to order. Then Ted Hill made a speech thanking the Potters on behalf of everyone, and as far as most of us were concerned, the meeting was over.

The drugstore was crowded for the rest of the afternoon, with the children racing around, screaming and whooping as though it was Christmas.

Ted Hill was the center of attention. Della and Ken's father, a brother to Ted, were there, and Lister and Abbey Peterson, and Sara King, among others. Trust Sara to be Johnny-on-the-spot.

"I hope you'll have a job for me, Ted?" Lister said.

Abbey bought the twins each an ice cream cone to keep them quiet for five minutes. "Aren't the Potters lovely people? Imagine their being so taken with Contentment Cove. They want to improve it, don't they? It just shows what generous, kind, fine people there is in the world. I said to Lister when they first bought the Harvey Place, I said, 'Lister, Mr. and Mrs. Potter are the loveliest kind of pleasant people. They aren't above passing the time of day with anybody.' "

Della was edging over. Her expression said as plain as day that she had the first and last word on Mr. and Mrs. Potter because *she* worked for them.

Abbey saw the expression all right, she was far from blind, and gave a deep sigh. "Hello, Della dear. My, you must be some proud to be working for people like them. Their kind is the real salt of the earth, aren't they? But Della, you know something that struck me right off quick? I said to Lister, soon after they settled here, I said, 'Lister, these two is never known right down deep in their hearts what it is to have a home.' I said, 'Ours may not be much to look at, but it's a *home*. We've never lived nowhere else and we've got neighbors that cares if we live or die, and when we're gone, some of the kids will carry on, under the same old leaky roof.' Money ain't all there is in this world, Della, isn't that a fact? I said, 'Mrs. Potter has got a look in her eyes that says a lot. She may be a good deal better off than we are most ways, and wear expensive clothes and drive a big car and lack for nothing money can buy, but all the money there is can't buy some things, you know that as well as I do.' Sometimes, Della, I have seen a sad and lonesome look in that poor woman's face."

Della's eyes were snapping like sparks. She turned on me, marking time while she got up a head of steam. "Ken will be home tomorrow." That was anything but a surprise. He came home every weekend while he was teaching at Jericho High because coming home saved paying board for two days. He was a born and bred Hill. We usually went out Saturday night to the movies or a dance somewhere.

"With all their money," Abbey said, sighing—nothing pleased her more than getting Della's goat—"it's still my humble opinion that they *envy* us people here in Contentment Cove, and that's why they've set out to do this wonderful, kind, generous thing for us . . ."

Della took a deep breath and clicked her teeth, smiling her Hold Off and Watch Out smile. "I can't truthfully say that I ever considered Mrs. Potter as a sad and lonesome-looking woman, Abbey, but then I'm not the kind that goes around looking for such things. Of course no one sees her any oftener than I do, working right in her house two and three times a week, so I suppose I would be in more of a position to know than *most*. But it's not my nature to be hashing, hashing every minute of the day. I'm just thankful we've got people that wants to spend all that money in the Cove, and is concerned enough to want us to have a lovely community center like that. We better thank God we got that kind moving in here and not some other kinds."

Ken's father chimed in. "This'll be a godsend to this town, having rich people like them interested in making improvements." He had a year-round job as caretaker and gardener of one of the big cottages on the island. "Say, Ted, how many will you need for a crew on this swimming pool job—twenty-five or thirty?"

Ted was being as casual as though he had known about the whole thing for months. Now that all the summer people hired him, he could hardly be bothered to do repairs for the hoi polloi anymore. The summer people might not have thought he was so wonderful if they had known he couldn't read their blueprints to save his life.

"Oh, we won't need more than ten or fifteen," he said, rubbing his whiskers. "Mrs. Potter tells me they're planning a combination clubhouse and bathhouse at one end of the pool. She's even talking about having a little kitchenette."

"A kitchenette!" Sara King cried. "Put just a little more marshmallow on this ice cream, Dot-Fran, please. Why, we ought to get right down on our knees to those people, every single one of us. Did you ever hear of such a public-spirited thing in all your *life*?"

I didn't have a chance to talk to Alfeus until we were walking home that night.

"Wasn't that the most *wonderful* surprise! Golly, I never *dreamed*. Won't it be grand having a pool just like they have over on the island?"

"It was certainly quite a surprise."

"Did you hear Ted? It must be going to cost a fortune. Imagine having enough money to be able to do things like that? Isn't it *wonderful*, Alfeus, for them to *want* to?"

"Great, just great," he said, grinning.

He made me want to spit, sometimes, when he refused to get excited.

"Can't you say any more than *that*, for heaven's sake! It's a big thing, for the town and for everyone . . ."

"It must be if you say so, honey."

"Oh Alfeus, honestly, what's the matter with you? Everyone else thinks it's just wonderful. And you do too. How could you help it?"

"Sure, sure I do. It's a damn public-spirited thing for the Potters to think of. "

"It certainly *is*."

"But Franny, use your head a minute. For instance, who is elected to pay for repairs and upkeep year after year? What are the operating expenses likely to be? Is the town going to have to ante up for those items? A swimming pool like the one they're talking about is an expensive plaything to maintain, in a little one-horse town like this. It will mean higher taxes, you can bet on that."

"Oh, for heaven's *sake*."

"Think it over, Franny; you're a big girl, you're running a business. You've got an idea what another sizable item in the town budget will do to your tax bill. All I'm saying is let's not go off half-cocked; let's get a few details worked out first. There's a little doubt in my mind as to whether a place this size can maintain or *needs* . . ."

"They're *giving* us a big elegant swimming pool, like they have over on the island, and all you can think about is whether it will cost *us* something."

"That's right, I'm just an old spoilsport," he said, giving my hair a ruffle as he turned into his yard. "Comes of being old, and poor, and crotchety! See you tomorrow, honey."

He didn't say much about it after that. All over town there was talk of the extra jobs it would give the men in the spring, and how grand it was going to be for the children all summer, and people were arguing about how warm the temperature of the water should be, which was very funny after being used to the Atlantic Ocean, and making jokes about not allowing any of the islanders near it because natives had never been allowed to use theirs.

Work started the middle of April. Mr. and Mrs. Potter gave a piece of their land for the pool to be built on, out of sight of their house, but not very far away. For the first few weeks Ted and his crew did so much blasting that I got to the point of not even jumping when a charge went off.

Mr. and Mrs. Potter had expected it to be ready by the middle of the summer, but Ted didn't get along as fast as they had planned. I knew they were upset about it, because I had over-heard Mr. Potter talking to Alfeus.

"If this wasn't Contentment Cove," he said, "I'd think these fellers were playing me for a sucker, Alfeus. Now, here's the situation in a nutshell. We've earmarked a certain amount for this thing, Mrs. Potter and myself have, and that's what is forthcoming, no more nor less. It looks as though it may run over what we had planned. Let me make myself clear here, Alfeus: I looked into the whole deal pretty thoroughly before we went ahead with this thing. I've got estimates from three of the best contractors in Cincinnati as to the cost of this pool, and the largest of those three estimates is the amount Mrs. Potter and I earmarked. Now considering—I hate to say this, Alfeus boy, but it's better to spit it than to swallow it—considering that local lack of know-how is playing hell with our budget, I'm wondering if you selectmen wouldn't want to step in and help get this thing in shape where it's going to be a definite addition to the town. Oh, I know I'm bringing up a ticklish matter, for you fellers to monkey with town funds without authorization, but considering that the town is going to be served thereby, it seems to me in this case you would be justified. My God, Alfeus, we wouldn't want to lose what is potentially one of the town's biggest assets, vacationwise, for lack of a few thousand dollars, but as far as Mrs. Potter and myself are concerned, we've drawn the line, and I think anyone would agree it's a damn generous one, but it has to stop somewhere. That's the situation. I'm frankly up a tree on this thing."

"It's a hell of a shame," Alfeus said, rubbing his hand back and forth over the top of his crew cut. It's the only way to tell that he's upset. "I'm certainly sorry to hear this, Gus. Elsie and I drove by there last Sunday and it looked like it's going to be a beautiful layout. But, my God, Gus, the selectmen can't do anything like you suggest. We've got no right or way of spending money unless it's authorized by a legal meeting of the townspeople."

A customer came in, and Alfeus walked out to the car with Mr. Potter so I missed the rest of the conversation, but it certainly sounded as though Ted Hill was dragging his feet, or feathering his nest for all he was worth. That just bore out my private opinion of Mr. Big Deal Hill, but it seemed awful that the Potters had to be mixed in it, when their only thought was giving.

If there was anything that burned me up it was to see Ted tearing around town looking like a big, harried businessman, when actually he didn't do a hand's turn anymore, just stood around and palavered. To him, being a contractor instead of a plain carpenter, meant never doing anything yourself, or never using one man when you could use two and take a cut out of both their wages. He was born for it.

Last spring when Admiral Peck and his wife were in California, he wrote Ted to fix his driveway before they got home, hoe out the weeds and rake on a fresh load of gravel. Ted had been sitting on his hands most of the winter, drawing unemployment insurance; just the exercise would have been good for him, taken down his beer belly a little. But no, he hired Angel Colonier and Mike Masefield, the two laziest men in town, and showed up himself every morning to hand them each a hoe. The rest of the day he rode back and forth to Bluff Rocks with a bottle of beer, waiting for four o'clock when he could take the hoes away from them.

That made two men and a foreman. He paid Angel and Mike a dollar an hour, and charged the Admiral a dollar and a half for them, so besides his own pay he collected eight dollars a day just on them. It took three days and a half.

Admiral Peck got the bill in his mail about a week after they got home. He always ripped his letters open in the P.O. and read them on the spot. Then he would sit out in his car and read his newspaper.

When he opened that bill from Ted, I thought he was going to have a stroke. "Alfeus, do I look to you like a total damn fool?" he shouted, glaring at me over the tops of his glasses.

"I never thought so, Admiral."

"How long is my driveway, Goddamnit?"

"Two hundred feet, for a guess."

"Look at this bill," he growled, pushing it through the money order window. "It's outright robbery. I could have done that job on my hands and knees in less time than that. Three men!"

"It doesn't seem as though they hurried, Admiral."

"Well, I've laid *their* last golden egg," Admiral Peck said. "They've killed this goose. I didn't expect to get my throat cut. Goddamnit, I could have hired Gramp Bradley, but I thought Hill needed the job."

"Gramp's a good man," Alfeus said. "Didn't he do your driveway a couple of years ago?"

"Sure he did, in a day and a half, and a damn good job. Alfeus, I'd hate to give Hill a blank check and tell him to clean out the septic tank!"

"It wouldn't pay to gamble on what was left either way, Admiral."

Fifteen minutes after Randall got to the Post Office with the mail, the letters would be sorted, everyone would be gone, and it would be as quiet as a tomb. But beforehand, it was a small bedlam.

To add to the confusion, the Peterson twins came galloping in. They could always be counted on to find a nice mud hole to play in, even during a dry summer, and they were a sight.

Mrs. Van Buran Chubb Pearl was talking to Hilly, but when she saw the twins she stopped and clapped her hands. "The precious *urch*ins! Did you *ever* see anything so picturesque, their darling, dirty *faces!*"

"She's been on *Life* magazine, dear," Mrs. Potter whispered to Hilly. "Isn't that enthusiasm of hers con*tag*ious? *Such* eagerness, about *every*thing!"

"God, her poor husband!" Hilly muttered.

It always sounded funny when she said things like that, so deadpan, but often I wished she wouldn't, because when you thought it over sometimes it sounded more as though she was sort of jealous of people like Mrs. Potter and her friend who could be so outspoken and enthusiastic about things, which wasn't in her nature.

"Mina, aren't they priceless?" Mrs. Pearl called. Everyone was listening and smiling. "Have you ever, ever seen such absolutely blank, priceless little faces? Ravishing! And so gloriously filthy! How old are you, lambs? Tell the nice lady how old you are. Mina darling, they're struck dumb! They don't know what to make of the city lady, do they? Isn't it priceless! You divine, *divine* little creatures. They're not able to utter a *single* word."

Usually they didn't bother with uttering single words, they shouted at the top of their lungs, but now they just stood staring at Mrs. Van Buran Chubb Pearl. Bobby began to suck his thumb.

"Lover, come here and give them an ice cream cone. Buy those adorable urchins something. Look at them taking the city lady all in, they're so devastating, utterly blank! Will you eat some ice cream, angels?"

"Sure," Billy said, "Tawberry."

Joe came loping over, hoping he would get in on the treat. "What you kids doing in here—you looking for your big brother?"

"Naw," Billy said, giving him a scornful look. "Lemme have tawberry, him too."

43

Joe hung over the fountain with his mouth open watching me scoop it out, and finally Hilly threw him a dime and said, "For God's sake, you're drooling on the potato chips, Joe. Buy yourself one."

"Gee thanks. You want one too, Mrs. Wister?"

"I'd rather die," Hilly said, making a sour face. All the kids thought that was hilarious.

"They're *angelic* under the grime," Mrs. Van Buran Chubb Pearl said. "They have that wonderful *some*thing that all these marvelous people have, Mrs. Wister, that fresh, unspoiled, *inno*cent *some*thing. Like this darling girl," she looked over the fountain at me. "Yes, darling, these babies positively remind me of you, and you *all* have that same incredibly marvelous speech."

Hilly looked amused. "I suspect bifocals aren't the answer, Mrs. Pearl, but they might help."

"My dear, *I'll* never wear bifocals, *never*. Oh, but you're joking . . ."

Mr. Pearl handed me a twenty-dollar bill just as the mail truck arrived.

Randall loved having a crowd waiting. "Gang's all here!" he shouted, throwing mail sacks into the P.O.

Sara leaned over and hissed, "Special handling!" She always said that, or sometimes "Handle with care!" If he knew she was there, Randall heaved them extra hard for her benefit. Half of the P.O. business came from sending back merchandise that arrived broken.

"Come on, people," Mrs. Potter called to her friends, "we'll go over to the Post Office side now. 'Bye, dears; see you at the party."

The professor walked by me and whispered, "This afternoon, then!" He had a polka dot blue scarf tucked inside his shirt collar.

Sara watched him go down the steps. "Well, aren't you moving in high society these days! I suppose *Stanley* is going to the party too! Haven't you two made a hit with the summer people!"

That made me furious. I slammed the ice cream scoop full of chocolate ice cream into the bowl of water where it's kept, and while I was cleaning up that mess the telephone rang.

"Dot-Fran? This's Bud. There's a fire back of Petersons' house, in the bushes. Tell Alfeus he better get down here quick with some men and Indian pumps." The receiver banged in my ear.

"It's a fire back of Abbey's. Bud was all out of breath, he said to get pumps over there quick."

"Abbey's? My God . . . " Hilly cried.

There were Indian pumps in the shed back of the store, and Randall went lumbering out after them at full speed, he weighed three hundred, with Joe jabbering a mile a minute at his heels. I flew in to get Alfeus.

"Finish sorting this mail," he said. Just like that. Alfeus was wonderful in an emergency, though. He never got the least bit upset. "Abbey, there's a brush fire back of your house. Better send someone after Lister down at the swimming pool. Come on, Sam, you can lend a hand, anybody, come on, jump in Ran's truck out there."

Five minutes later, they took off in a spray of gravel up the hill. All the women were babbling, the kids were slamming in and out of the screen doors, and I was stuck in the P.O. with all that mail.

"My dear, what *is* it? *What* has happened?" Mrs. Potter rapped on first the money order window and then the parcel post window—they were kept closed while the mail was being sorted— trying to get my attention. "Dot-Fran, darling, do open this blind for just a minute. *What* is all the excitement? Where has Alfeus gone?"

Across the lobby I heard Abbey sobbing, "It's all we got in the world, all we got . . ."

Hilly had both arms around her, holding her up. The twins were crowded around their knees, bawling, and dripping ice cream all over everything.

"Dot-Fran, is it a fire?" Mrs. Potter called, thumping on the blind. "How perfectly dreadful. At the Petersons'? Where do they live, dear? Dot-Fran, can you hear me?"

I pulled back the blind. "The Mill Pond Road, Mrs. Potter." I was so nervous, trying to hurry, and upset, that it was a wonder any of the letters went in the right boxes. "Up the hill on the right," I stuttered.

"The Mill Pond Road? Oh, of course, yes. Darlings, we simply must tear home for Gus or he would be furious. Ohhh, dear, and it's so near lunchtime . . ."

Poor Abbey was wailing and the twins were bellowing. Even Mr. Pearl finally looked wide awake.

"Food at a time like this, Mina! My dear, don't give it a thought. I'm so fearfully excited."

Mrs. Potter poked her head through the crack in the window. "Darling, we'll be back for the mail. Poor dear Mrs. Peterson, no wonder she's hysterical. Hilly is being so marvelous with her. If only we could help . . . Darling, we're off, oh, I'm *such* a nuisance, forgive me, darling, but those Deerfoot sausages should be in the mail today. Could you just set them where it's cool? Oh, and darling, *could* you tell Della when she comes that I need her day after tomorrow, it's her day at Peck's, but Hazel will understand, I know. If only there was something I could do for that *poor* soul. 'Bye, dear."

They were down the steps before I came to. "Mrs. Potter, you could get Lister at the pool," I shouted, but she didn't hear and before I could reach the door, the Cadillac went roaring off down the street.

"Goddamnit," Hilly said over her shoulder to the twins, "stop that racket! Run outside and I'll give you a treat later, understand. Go on with you now. Come on, Abbey, try your pins like a good girl."

"My legs are weak as water," Abbey groaned. "Oh, I can't stand to see it, I can't stand to go look. All we got in the living world is that house . . . " She began to cry again.

"Franny, chuck the mail for a minute and bring me some spirits of ammonia." Hilly was as calm as though something like this happened every day, and when I came rushing back with the bottle she patted my shoulder. "This should do the trick. Thanks, kid. A good sniff, now, Abbey."

Right away Abbey began to shake her head, and her eyes cleared. "Oh Lord, oh Lord, has someone gone to fetch Lister?"

Then I suddenly realized that everyone had gone, except Sara, and she had varicose veins. "There wasn't anyone here with a car except Mrs. Potter," I said.

Hilly glanced quickly around. "Damn it, has she gone?"

"They went to the fire." It came out before I thought.

Abbey stared over at me, the pupils of her eyes as big as fifty cent pieces.

"The fire!" she cried. "The fire! She took her company to see the fire, you hear, Mrs. Wister? They've gone to stand around and watch while we lose every stitch we own, like it's an entertainment. I heard her, I heard her pounding on the window for you to tell her how to get there, don't think I didn't. I wasn't deaf. Poor Mrs. Wister was holding me up, but I wasn't deaf just the same. Did they have one thought except for their pleasure and entertainment? Something to watch? Before they go home and set down and eat their lunch! Not one thought but Number One, you hear that?"

"Oh no, Abbey, she wanted to help. She said so."

She pushed me away, so hard that I stumbled. "Don't you try to tell *me*. You're nothing but a child, having your head turned with talk about your looks. Oh, you'll be all right, you'll be flying high till the novelty wears off your pretty face, and then you'll be cropped back into the puddle with the rest of us. Don't you know what we are to people like *them*? All but Mrs. Wister, God bless her. I'll tell you what the natives are—we're cheap entertainment, and cheap help. We're good for scrubbing their floors. We're good for catering to them and scraping and making them feel like Lords of the Manor, which they ain't by a long shot, none of them, and our kids are good for being insulted because they been playing in the dirt, and when a house catches afire it's something to treat their company to . . . ohhh." The anger went out of her voice, and she began to sob again.

Hilly tried to quiet her. "All right, all right, now, Abbey."

As upset as I was, I couldn't help thinking what a funny pair they made, Abbey, short and fat in her short-sleeved cotton dress, with her face red and streaked from crying, and Hilly looking as slim as a boy, with her short hair and nice legs.

"We're going after Lister right now. Come on, steady on, old girl, your house is all right. Alfeus knows how to handle fire. He'll have that out long before we get there. Come on now, Abbey, steady as we go."

She motioned for me to take her other arm and between us we got her into Hilly's car. Abbey didn't say another word, but she looked as though she was on the verge of having a stroke.

Sara was waiting for me in the P.O. "Mrs. Wister's got a crazy woman on her hands. If she had asked I would have been willing enough to get in with them, but I wasn't going to *push* in. Abbey's that emotional kind, awful emotional. I hate to think what she may do up there if her house is burning up. I remember when old lady Springer's house burned years ago; it took four men, and my husband was one of them, to keep that deaf and dumb daughter of hers from running into it and being burnt up. She was real hysterical, wasn't she, going on that way about the summer people? I'm sure I don't know what she'd do without them. I don't believe she had any idea what she was saying, do you? Of course that old house is all the poor soul's got between her and the weather but my land, to lash out at poor Mrs. Potter, as generous and sweet, thoughtful woman as ever lived. Can't I help you in there with that mail, Dot-Fran?"

She knew that no one was allowed to touch the United States mail unless they had taken the oath. It was all sorted except for a big bundle of magazines, which was lucky, because I felt as though I had been pulled through a clothes wringer.

A few minutes later, the gypsy painter came walking in. He was wearing khaki shorts, and dark glasses, and looked more like a prizefighter than a painter.

"Good morning," he said to Sara, then he looked in the Post Office window. "Why, hello. I've been trying to decide whether to stop over here or not. Now I've made up my mind!"

48

He was attractive in a stocky, heavy-shouldered way, and his smile was nice, but I didn't like him right from that minute. Perhaps it was his way of talking, so self-confident, or perhaps it was because I was tired and upset to start with.

"Ladies, let me introduce myself. I'm a painter. My name is Chauncey Humber. Is it your opinion that I could stir up an art-loving public if I stayed around a few days?"

"A painter?" Sara repeated. "We've got a painter living right here in Contentment Cove the year round. You probably know her name—Mrs. Wister?' "

"No, I guess not."

"She's just left here to a fire. That's where everyone is."

"Is that so?" He grinned and leaned his elbow on the P.O. shelf, looking in at me. "So this is Contentment Cove! Who runs the drugstore when there are any customers?"

"I do."

"*You* do!" He had thick-lashed, wise, gray eyes, and a way of looking as though he knew what you were thinking. "Well, fine, then we can talk turkey. I can tell right off that you'd like to be a patron of the arts, now wouldn't you? What I'm going to do is bring in some of my things and make a nice display over there in the middle of the floor. OK? And when a customer wants some toothpaste you can wind up selling him a painting! For a com-mission, of course."

"No, you can't . . ."

Sara was so intrigued by his smile that she forgot all about the fire and everything else. "Why, now, maybe she could!"

"Wait till we get this place fixed up in here!" he said to Sara, and ran outside to his car, a 1950 Ford, with a small, faded-blue house trailer hitched on behind. He opened the trailer door and began lifting out paintings, leaning them against the wheel.

"Why, you're going to turn into a picture gallery!" Sara said, watching. "Hasn't this been a *day*! What more do you suppose will happen before night? He's a real nice-looking man, isn't he, and he's got a lovely manner. Most men that wear shorts don't have the legs for it, like him."

"Oh Lord, he can't do *that*." I left the bundle of magazines and went tearing across the lobby and out after him. "You . . . you can't bring those in the store. There isn't enough room."

"No?" His ears were small and set close to his head. "No, Miss Storekeeper?"

I shook my head and wished Dad was there.

But he didn't argue, or even look annoyed. Instead, he began setting the paintings all along the side of the trailer facing the sidewalk.

"I'm afraid you're another Philistine, after all," he said, "but a pretty one, for a change, thank God. Well, take a look, baby, while you're out here. They won't bite you."

Sara came hurrying out after us. "They are *some* beautiful! That surf rolling, and see those gulls! Isn't that one *hand*some? And so lifelike. Look at that old fish house! I can all but smell the fish heads."

As much as I hated to, I agreed with her; they were very good. I could have looked at them all afternoon, but I wasn't going to give him the satisfaction of admitting it.

"Well, baby, what do you say!"

"They're very good," I said coolly. "You have wonderful technical ability."

I had heard Jules Balls say that about someone. Jules and Hilary argued about painting and other painters all the time, as well as about everything else. Hilly wouldn't have liked these because you could recognize everything. She would have waved her hand and said, "More representational crap!" but I really liked them better than her kind, which I couldn't make head nor tails of.

There were fish houses and seining boats and waves breaking on the rocks, and one was just beach grass with a dory hauled up. Any other time I could have enjoyed looking and looking.

He looked pleased but a little startled. "Good, fine. Now, the next question is, where am I going to park my house on wheels and set up housekeeping? I'll bet you've got a nice, big yard at your house, Goldilocks? With an electric line I could plug into? Then you can introduce me to all the summer people, and to this

Mrs. What's-Her-Name, the painter. Or maybe she won't be happy about having competition? What do you say, dear? Which way to your house?" He winked at Sara. "She's a lovely girl. Tell you what, in exchange for a parking space, I'll paint your portrait while I'm here. Is that a fair bargain?"

"My, I should think so!" Sara tittered.

I felt so dead tired all at once that I just wanted to cry. Having to say no, no, no, while he laughed at me.

"Paint Sara. She's got plenty of room in her backyard."

Because I still didn't know whether Abbey's house had burned flat, and I couldn't forget the way she had pushed me away, and the things she had said. If any of it got back to the Potters, Lister would have to give up his job. I couldn't blame Abbey for being worried crazy, but Mrs. Potter wasn't like that. I think she would have gone for Lister in a minute if she had known. Of course she had been right there in the P.O. when Alfeus mentioned it, that was the trouble.

I had just finished sorting the magazines when their big convertible came purring down the hill, and stopped behind the trailer. They all spotted the paintings lined up along the sidewalk first thing.

"Did they stop the fire, Mrs. Potter?" I called.

"Darling, they saved the house. Oh, it was so exciting. Some outbuildings burned, but the house was *saved*. I'll be right in, dear. Look at the lovely paintings! Oils, aren't they? Greta, aren't they *charming*!"

"*You're* charming!" The professor called softly through the screen. "I'd rather feast my eyes on you, Miss Dot-Fran, than on fires, *or* paintings!"

Mrs. Van Buran Chubb Pearl slapped his arm. "Isn't he a monstrous flirt! You're really dreadful, darling. And is the handsome young man here the artist? How perfectly enchanting! Your work is divine, absolutely di*vine*."

More cars were driving down the hill. Everyone was getting back. Mrs. Potter hurried in for her mail. I was glad she was too rushed to notice me much.

"Gus is ready to kill me, Dotty. You *know* how he hates having meals delayed. And Gus Junior will no doubt have arrived when we get home. What a *day*! See you at the party, dear."

Outside, I heard her talking to the painter. "Mr. Humber, you must let us see these all again when we can really *look*. But we're all simply starving at the moment. Shall you be here at the Cove for a while? Oh, how grand, then we *will* see you. And has Dot-Fran told you of *our* artist, Mrs. Wister? You *must* meet her, of course. She lives on Marsh Point, beyond the Sand Cove. We're all going there for cocktails this afternoon."

Everyone began to stream in, hot, and smelling of smoke, and wanting their mail, cigarettes, candy, and Cokes. When I had the chance to notice again, the trailer had gone.

Hilary gave a big party every summer. She pretended that it was a bore and a nuisance and that she only did it to pay back hospitality, but she always had a wonderful time at parties. It was true that she hated to owe anyone anything, even hospitality. "No strings!" she always said.

Her friend Jules Balls said she was neurotic about it. "It's very serious, old dear," he said, "especially for an artist."

It was hard to know when they meant what they said to each other, and when they were just being clever. A lot of times I don't think they knew themselves, especially after a few drinks.

"My God, don't give me that old saw about the artist's debt to society," Hilly said. "An artist's only responsibility is to be free, completely, unencumberally free. He should be responsible to nothing, and to no one."

"Christ, girl, what crap—an artist isn't free!" Jules shouted. They always shouted; it didn't mean anything except that they were having a good time, but I could see Stan getting uneasy. It was the first time he had met the Balls. "He's the least free of God's creatures. Where did you pick up this mishmash about no responsibility? You don't think you're encumbered? You're as bound by custom as any bank clerk. An artist's *primary* responsibility is to lead his time, and not tag along on its coattails."

"Oh, Balls!" Hilly said, pouring herself another drink, and grinning at him. "What do you know about artists, anyway?"

"I know plenty about you, dear!"

Stan got up. "Listen, Hilary, I think we'll push along."

"Hey, kids!" Jules said, looking around, "my wife's passed out."

He always acted surprised, but she went off and went to sleep somewhere sooner or later, every time they came.

Hilly put her arm around Stan. "You are certainly *not* pushing along. Poor darling, have we shocked you? Don't mind Jules, he's really not as bad as he sounds, thank God! And anyway, darling, I can't break with him because he knows far too much about me!"

"You're quite right there, sweetheart," Jules said, with his wide grin. "Look at Lucy! We ought to take her picture sometime. She looks like a witch."

"Oh, take your drunken wife and go on home," Hilly said. "You've drunk up all my liquor, and shocked these two young, wholesome things with your crudities. Who needs intellectual friends, anyway!"

"Come on, wake up, Lucy, the booze's all gone!"

He finished his glass in one swallow, and got up and kissed Hilly very affectionately, and then woke up Lucy, his wife, and Hilly kissed her very affectionately, and they went home.

Just before I left the drugstore to go home and get dressed for the party, Ken came in from the golf links on the island. He had charge of them every summer. Della was with him.

"Hi, Dot," he said. "How about a Coke? And don't forget our date tonight."

He needed a haircut, and looked much better that way, but the first chance he would go to the barbershop and get skinned like a convict again.

"Have we got one?"

"Sure, we got one. What's the matter—did that fire this morning addle *your* brain? I hear poor old Abbey almost lost her marbles."

Della was wearing her snippy smile. "I *told* you she was going to Mrs. Wister's party. My goodness, Ken, what would she want with you, when she's flirting around with all the summer people!"

Della just couldn't get used to my being invited to things like that.

"My, my!" she said, "it must be real thrilling for a young girl like you after the Admiral and Gus Potter have soaked up about four martinis! I'd rather be out in the kitchen myself, where it's safe, and sane."

"Come on, Ma," Ken said, with a disgusted look, "let's go on home. I'll pick you up at Mrs. Wister's then, Dot. About seven-thirty."

Alfeus was tapping away on his typewriter in the office.

"Don't forget Mrs. P's message for Della," he called.

"Oh yes—Mrs. Potter wants you day after tomorrow."

"Day after tomorrow? That's Pecking day."

"Never mind that," Alfeus said. "Plus and Minus have company. That adds ten points."

"I've met the company," Della said. "They're lovely people. Mrs. Pearl asked me to press her a dress, and gave me five dollars. If you please! It's too bad Mrs. Minus isn't more inclined in that direction. But she's all right to scrub for. Mr. Pearl drove me home in that lovely big car of theirs. Except for a big, expensive car it's got the homeliest upholstery I ever in my life laid eyes on. I wanted to tell him it looked for all the world like the old deer's hide that was nailed up on our shed all winter!"

Stan's car was parked out front when I got home.

He looked a little tired, but very handsome in a new pair of dark brown slacks, and an oyster white jacket without any collar.

"Sharp, boy, sharp!" I said, whistling at him.

"Look at the circles under his eyes!" Dad grumbled.

Stan groaned, and put his glasses on. He thought they made him look more like a banker. "Beulah thinks we need a new Bendix, that's all. I was just telling Dad."

"For heaven's sake, you bought a new washing machine last year."

"That was last year, and it wasn't a Bendix."

Dad swished the beer around in his glass. There was a ball game on the television screen, but no sound.

"Beulah's a hard little worker. She works mighty hard making you that nice home, son, don't forget it. Why didn't you find a babysitter, and bring her along with you tonight?"

Stan pretended to be watching the game. "Don't worry, Dad, I'm not forgetting anything. She doesn't like parties where there are a lot of strangers."

Beulah and I had never been close friends, though I was a bridesmaid at her wedding. She was pretty, with a soft voice and a nice-nice manner, but once she set her mind on something you could have argued better with a steamroller. And she always had her mind set on something. I don't know whether she was keeping up with the Joneses, or the last issue of *The American Home*, but every time we went to Center City she had something new—ruffled nylon curtains, venetian blinds for the boys' room, a new Hoover vacuum cleaner, or a clutch cape to wear to the annual bank dinner out at the country club. Or a Capeheart phonograph, or *some*thing.

Of course Stan should have put his foot down, but actually he was just as bad about the house as she was. They couldn't let it alone. One week, they had to have new inlaid linoleum for the kitchen, and the next, a new portable TV for their bedroom.

Now that she had Hilary Wister to hold over his head, it was a new Bendix washer and dryer. No wonder he had circles. On his salary?

When I came downstairs, Dad got up and kissed me. Then he turned and gave Stan a hug. He never said anything, but I know he was proud of the way we looked, and I think he was a little pleased, too, that we were invited to the party.

"Behave yourselves, and remember you're Hathaways. It's nothing to be ashamed of."

Stan didn't have a word to say the whole six and a half miles to the Point.

The Potters' convertible, and Admiral Peck's Chrysler Imperial were already there; Jules Balls's station wagon, the Spindles' Jeep—meaning that their lane was still too rutted for their Buick—and three or four other cars.

"It looks like a used car lot," I said, trying to cheer him up.

Hilary came dashing across the terrace. "Darlings, where have you been? My God, Stan, you look marvelous in that rag. I knew it was for you, lamb. Franny, darling, you too, what a sweet frock. Come in, come in, and let me show you off to these old has-beens."

She looked very exotic in black velvet slacks, with a tight white shirt with stand-up collar, and her long turquoise earrings set in silver. Her hands were covered with turquoise rings. She had a perfect figure for clothes like that.

Going upstairs to the studio, she said, "Franny, this horrid man named Chubb insisted on telling me what an unspoiled gem of womanhood you are. As though I didn't know. Don't for an instant let him back you into a corner. I know the type!"

At the top of the stairs, she gave me a push inside the studio. "Just see who I found this time!"

Mrs. Van Buran Chubb Pearl and the professor were talking with the Spindles; Jules waved from the big table under the skylight where he was mixing martinis. The canapes were spread out on one end. Hilly could make even raw carrots and sour pickles look good.

Jules was very tall and thin, with a pockmarked complexion, and curly gray hair. He wore dark tortoise-shell rimmed glasses, and I thought he looked distinguished, but Mrs. Potter once remarked that he was the homeliest man she had ever seen, though I think that was partly because they disagreed about politics.

His wife, Lucy, was out on the porch with some other people, and Admiral Peck and Mr. Pearl were exchanging cigars.

Mrs. Van Buran Chubb Pearl and the professor came right over where we were. She was wearing a beautiful green taffeta cocktail dress, with straps over the shoulders, which showed off her wonderful mahogany tan.

"My dear, we thought you would *never* get here! Do leave her with us, Mrs. Wister, don't dare take them away. Who is this simply *stun*ning young man? Your brother, child? Mrs. Wister, have you ever, ever, *ever* in your life seen two handsomer creatures! Completely glorious, both of them, and born and brought up here in this adorable, unspoiled gem of a town. Introduce me, introduce me by *all* means to this ravishing young man!"

Hilly winked at us. "This ravishing young man is Stanley Hathaway. Promise me not to eat them while my back is turned, Mrs. Pearl! They're good, tough New England gristle under the surface, you know!"

The Weavers were coming in. The studio looked like a movie scene of a party, with pretty dresses and bare shoulders, and lovely jewelry, and the men in light suits and sports jackets. Even though I recognized most of the people, I got that shivery, scared, excited feeling.

"What a charmer Mrs. Wister is, such a sparkling, sharp wit. Rather bohemian for this part of the world, wouldn't you say, Mr. Hathaway?"

Stan just grinned.

Professor Chubb whispered in my ear, "Do you know how young it makes me feel, Miss Dot-Fran, meeting someone as fresh and lovely as you? Please, *please* don't mind my telling you so. Why should you mind when it gives such pleasure? But you have nothing to drink, my dear. Bourbon, scotch, martini? And your brother?"

"Martinis, for both of us, thanks."

Admiral Peck was booming away on the divan, in a cloud of cigar smoke, and Mr. Pearl was smiling and trying hard to keep his eyes open. He must have been a terrible victim of insomnia.

Mrs. Van Buran Chubb Pearl watched the professor go off after the martinis. "Dear Eddie used to teach at the Hill School, you know, frightfully exclusive and all that, my dear. He's a superb teacher, of course, he's so genuinely devoted to things of the intellect. Poor Eddie, we were married, you know. Oh yes, darling, didn't Mina tell you? He was my previous husband. Chubb is one of the best Long Island names, my dear, but the tragic thing was— no money. And a teacher's salary, well, my dear, it was just one of those youthful tragedies, we were so young and foolish! Darlings, I have a simply fabulous notion! You two angels must come to us for a visit. On Long Island. Pearl would love it. I can't *wait* to show you off to my friends. Come to our summer place at Montauk. Do you know where Montauk Point is, loves?"

I was so stunned at hearing about her and the professor that I couldn't utter a word.

Admiral Peck came up and put his arm around me. "Hi Dotty, Stan. How's the boy? Mrs. Pearl. Somebody mention Montauk Point? No, where is it?"

The Admiral loved loud clothes, even though he was inclined to stoutness. For the party, he had on a bright red tennis blazer, trimmed with white braid, and gray English flannels. He ordered his trousers from England by postcard—he never wrote anything but postcards—so Alfeus always knew when he was getting a new pair.

He waved his glass. "But who in God's name would *want* to know where Montauk was? A hotter, more forsaken, less inviting neck of the woods it has never been my pleasure to stay away from. Oh, excuse me, somebody around here mention Montauk?"

Mrs. Van Buran Chubb Pearl gave him a very cold smile. "It just happens, Admiral, that my husband and I have a little summer cottage there."

The Admiral bowed very politely. "Rum go. Put my bloody foot in it, eh what!"

Mrs. Van Buran Chubb Pearl turned her back and said to Stan, "We intended just a shack for weekends, but, my dear, you know how those things go; before we knew it, a $40,000 *show*place. But Pearl is such a dear man. Money means nothing to him if it's my happiness. Where is he? *Where* is my lover boy?"

I said, "He's sitting over there on the divan."

The Admiral squeezed my shoulder. "Steady on, and never expose the flank," he said, and moved away.

"The Admiral seems quite shaky, child," Mrs. Van Buran Chubb Pearl remarked. She didn't know him very well, or she would never have thought *that*! "Who would ever dream such as he held an important naval post, and knew state secrets? But Mina would have me believe it's true. Angels, *what* was I saying? Oh, of course, about your coming to visit. We should simply adore it, simply *adore* it. Perhaps your famous Mrs. Wister would come too."

The professor came strolling back with our drinks, making a detour around the Admiral and Dido Weaver. The sun was shining on Dido's hair, and I wanted all of a sudden to laugh, for no reason at all, except that it was such fun to be there in the middle of the studio with all those people chattering, and the sunlight flashing on the aluminum chairs, and someone I didn't know offering me a plate of crackers and cheese dip.

"Eddie, it's all been settled while you were gone. These two precious babes in the wood are coming to Montauk to visit. Won't that be heavenly fun?"

"Splendid!"

I felt myself blushing, when he looked at me that way.

"Perfectly splendid. When?"

Stan shook his head, looking disappointed. "It's certainly wonderful of you to ask us, Mrs. Pearl, but we couldn't very well get away, especially in the summer."

"Darling, you've simply *got* to manage it. I won't let you out of sight, now that I've discovered you. Oh, Pearl and I have fallen in love with this angelic town, *help*lessly in love. And have you heard about the dreadful fire this morning, Mr. Hathaway? Oh, it was fearfully exciting. I nearly died dashing around with my camera, trying to get pictures. Alfeus, that darling man, rescued an armload of chickens, all flapping and crowing, and trying to get away, *price*less. I shall send him a print, of course, if anything comes out. I'm simply *mad* about Alfeus. The postmaster, you know? But you must know him."

Stan was trying to look around for Hilary without seeming to. "Since I was knee-high to a grasshopper, Mrs. Pearl!"

"Darling, what *fun*. My dear, we intend to buy here. I promise you. Last night I made Pearl promise to look around and see what the prospects are."

Stan said, "Contentment Cove's quite a town. So many new families are moving in that I hardly know the place anymore."

"Lamb, what do *you* do? You're not in real estate?"

Stan smiled at her. "I work at the Guarantee Trust in Center City. Ask for me when you come in to open your account!"

She almost hugged him. "How *utterly* marvelous."

She waved at Mr. Pearl across the room, pointing at Stan, trying to tell him that Stan worked at a bank. Mr. Pearl kept nodding and smiling and puffing on his cigar.

More people kept coming upstairs. The studio was growing noisy.

Professor Chubb took my hand and pulled me away. "I am a connoisseur of three things," he whispered. "Plato, Plotinus, and feminine beauty. My dear, you are the freshest thing to cross my vision in a long time. Do you mind so much being extravagantly admired, Dot-Fran?"

I minded his whispering—his breath was bad—and his standing so close, but I guess everyone likes to be admired, so I just shook my head.

Stan was making another customer for the bank. Perhaps they would give him a raise, and that would certainly help.

"Darling, I shall come see you at the bank *tomorrow*," Mrs. Van Buran Chubb Pearl was saying. "Will that make Mrs. Wister too furious? Do you know that my friends are going to positively *faint*, positively *die* when I introduce you as my banker!"

She reached behind Stan and took Professor Chubb's arm. "Eddie dear, I have to drag you away now. You can't monopolize this pretty girl the *whole* afternoon, it's not proper. We must go talk to that fascinating Mr. Balls, he looks so suave and charming and he makes such elegant martinis. Don't go 'way, dears, we'll be right back."

Mrs. Elliott was smiling and beckoning, but I pretended not to notice. Hilly was showing off the phonograph loudspeaker that Spencer had built into the wall beside the fireplace, to a woman in a wide-brimmed black hat, carrying a Pekinese dog under her arm.

"Who's Mrs. Pearl visiting?" Stan muttered. "Boy, she's got plenty on the ball, hasn't she? Maybe her husband will let me invest a couple of million for him, Doffy!"

"She's visiting the Potters, but my goodness, Stan, did you hear her say that about Professor Chubb's being her ex-husband? I thought they were brother and sister."

He raised his eyebrows. "Don't ever try to keep up with them. People like that are out of our class, Doffy."

All at once I remembered Abbey.

"Stan, Abbey had a regular tirade this morning in the P.O. when she thought her house was on fire."

"Someone said they lost some chickens. Wait here, I'll get us a refill . . . "

Out of the gabble of talk, I heard, "We use nothing but fitted sheets. Neither Harry nor I can abide anything else. Isn't that extravagance? But what is more important than your own comfort when you've reached our age? I have twenty pairs of fitted silk sheets in pastels . . . "

"Yes, darling, a swimming pool! The Potters. All it takes is money!"

"They'll just take it off their income tax . . . "

". . . isn't she a perfect horror? No, I do *not* know her name."

Mr. Potter was headed for me with his son. It couldn't have been anyone else. He was very brown, about my height, with dark hair, and a mouth like Wyatt Earp's.

I felt like an actress standing there waiting for them. It seemed like make-believe: the studio with the sun slatting through the venetian blinds, the big table under the skylight covered with trays and bottles and glasses, the chatter and milling around, and laughter, and my being right in the midst of it.

"Young lady, you're the one I'm looking for. Here's a feller I've been wanting to introduce for a long time. All he needs is someone like you to straighten him out!"

Gus Junior looked embarrassed, and I couldn't help blushing. Mr. Potter was so sweet, always saying complimentary things like that.

"Cut it out, Dad. I'm happy to meet you, Dot-Fran. I feel like we're acquainted already from my mother's letters."

"Son, now listen to me." Mr. Potter winked at me. He was one of the nicest-looking older men I had ever seen, with his wavy white hair. "This is the place right *here* where they really breed 'em. Ever see a prettier sight in your life than my Dotty? You know what, Dotty? This here son of mine has been hanging around those lousy cities so long, he's forgotten what living is like, that's his trouble! Hanging around down there with all the rest of the suckers!"

Gus Junior had a nice shy smile. He didn't seem like either his father or mother. I couldn't think of a word to say, but Mr. Potter went right on.

Stan was across the room with the woman with the big hat and the dog. He looked as though he was feeling a lot better, even if it took two martinis.

"Hey, Hilly," Mr. Potter called, "come over here with those martinis—we need a toast. Look! I got the two of them together. What I wouldn't give to be his age, hey!"

Hilly laughed, and her earrings waved back and forth, making a tinkling sound. "Hold out your glass, Advice-to-the-Lovelorn. If you keep this up, Gus, you'll have them forming a suicide pact before they're properly introduced."

While we were all laughing, Gus Junior offered me an L&M, and lit it with his lighter. We were the only two quiet people in the room; everyone else was talking, or shouting, or giggling like Mrs. Spindle.

She giggled even when she said good morning. Hilary said that she would giggle when old Ned Spindle passed to his reward and she had to call the undertaker. She giggled when Gus Junior held his lighter for her.

He had awfully nice manners. Ken would have stood around trying to be inconspicuous. That was the difference between a summer boy and a native—their manners, and their clothes, even the way they stood around. You could always tell.

"Hilly, I've been dying to see you," Maizie Spindle said, giggling again. "*I* had drinks at the Yacht Club yesterday, on the island yet. You may touch my hem, all you commoners!"

The summer people on the island were always asking Hilly for cocktails and dinners, because she was such a famous painter, but she hardly ever went.

"Bully for our side," she said. "Are they still serving straight formaldehyde at the Yacht Club?"

Even through the cigarette smoke, I could smell wisteria blossoms from the vine outside the window. Out over the bay the water was blinding bright with the sun glare on it.

Mrs. Van Buran Chubb Pearl's voice carried through all the others. Her former husband was talking with Stan, and the woman in the hat.

"Why don't we go over there and sit down?" Gus Junior said.

I felt like a horrible stick, not being able to think of a single word of conversation. He would think I was the dumbest girl he had ever met. "Smell the wisteria?"

"Oh, is that what it is?"

We sat down on the divan, and he smiled at me. Suddenly I knew that he didn't care whether I made conversation, because he was the same way.

I felt so happy that I could have floated. Everything was perfect—the sunny, blue day, the party, all the wonderful people there, Jules mixing more martinis and waving at me, Stan across the studio, looking so handsome in his new jacket, Gus Junior smiling because he couldn't think of anything to say either, and it didn't matter.

It seemed like the happiest moment of my life, being there in the middle of Hilly's wonderful party. No one could have told that I wasn't summer people too, not that I wanted to be, but no one could have told the difference.

Gus Junior's father had gotten into a friendly argument with Mrs. Spindle about her having a drink at the Yacht Club, and we sat there, with our martinis, listening.

He said she, his wife, Hazel Peck, and all the other women made him sick and tired yakey-yaking about the Yacht Club, and the golf pro, and the this, and the that, over on the island.

He said that he wouldn't give a dime for their lousy Yacht Club, or their hotel either, or their tennis tournament, for a lot of lousy rich kids. Ten to one, he said, that he had as much income to get along on as they did, and what did they have over there besides those big houses, that only a sucker would want, costing a fortune in taxes every year, the way the town gouged suckers.

He said that if he wanted to pay twenty dollars for dinner, he would take Mrs. Potter and go down to Atlantic City or some-place like that where you got something for your money, instead of an old-fashioned that was mostly water, and a lousy piece of fried ham and some pickles that they served at the hotel over on the island and called a meal. Just because three or four bus boys were prancing around with the pickles to impress the suckers didn't make it anything but a lousy meal.

Hilly came flying by and handed me the empty martini pitcher. I loved the perfume she was wearing. Just then in that minute I wished she could know how much I admired the glamorous way she looked, and the way she smiled and threw back her head, everything that made her the way she was. It was the most wonderful and unbelievable thing in the world that I was her close friend, that I felt closer to her than to anyone in that whole room, except my brother, Stan.

"Fill this up like a lamb, will you? Four to one, and plenty of ice."

Gus Junior jumped up. "I'll help."

He insisted on measuring very carefully, jigger by jigger. Hilly would have thrown it in by guess.

"My father's never been to Atlantic City in his life."

"He hasn't?"

"He's funny," he said, smiling, "he'd think nothing of buying a new car, he does it every year, but, boy, try to get him to take a crowd out to a restaurant for dinner! It kills him to pay four-fifty each for steak, when he could buy a big steak for four-fifty and feed four people on it at home. They sure are sold on this town—and on you, Dot-Fran. You should have seen the letters I've been getting! They're crazy about the place here, like they were about California, until they got fed up."

"I like it too, even if I was born here." I pointed at Stan. "That's my brother over there."

"That good-looking guy? Good looks must run in your family!"

We both began to blush, and he picked up the shaker and said, "Come on, let's see if we can sell this."

Mrs. Spindle waved her glass. "Your father is killing, Gus! Or Junior! What shall I call you?"

"Gus Junior," he said, pouring her another martini. He had a way of standing, not saying anything, but still not looking embarrassed.

"He's always been Gus Junior," Mr. Potter said. "Listen, Maizie, this girl here is like an adopted daughter to us. You want to know what I tell people when they ask me how I happened to come way up here to live?"

"Yes, Gus, what do you say?"

"Well, Maizie, I used to say I came up here because it's the only place left in this lousy country where there aren't any sheenies, shysters, or socialists!"

Mrs. Spindle shrieked with laughter, putting her hand over her mouth. I didn't know what he meant, except for socialists, but I laughed with the rest. They called J.P. Graves in Center City a shyster lawyer, but I thought I wouldn't mention it, or Mr. Potter might decide to move.

"But, Maizie, listen, now I say I stayed because on top of that I've got Dot-Fran to sell me aspirin!"

Lucy Balls stopped beside us. I liked Lucy very much, especially before she had too much to drink. She was very pretty, but she never acted a bit vain; in fact, I don't think she cared how she looked, and she was the friendliest person in the world. After she had been drinking a lot, though, you never knew what she might do.

"I love sheenies, shysters, and socialists," she said, smiling at everyone. "Some of my best friends are socialists, Mr. Potter."

Mrs. Spindle spilled her martini, and Gus Junior took out his handkerchief and tried to brush it off her dress.

Lucy meant it as a joke, of course, but Mr. Potter didn't smile; he looked cross.

"That's your funeral."

"Whereas some of the stupidest people I know are Gentiles," Lucy said, not appearing to notice, still smiling. "That's why I've simply got to have another bourbon, Mr. Potter. Come on, Dotty. You will excuse us?"

She pulled me away. "Is the Potted son and heir nice? He looks nice in a dazed way, but, angel, not nice enough to deserve you. I can tell that at a glance. Don't let Mama sell you a bill of goods, and be miserable for the rest of your life. *Where* does Hilly find all these well-fed, beaming, horrid nonentities? For God's sake, let's find the whiskey."

Lucy was a fashion model in New York before she married Jules. He was teaching at Columbia University then, and writing about painting and art. Hilly had piles of magazines with articles he had written on the bookshelves downstairs, but none of them were magazines I had ever heard of. "Prestige, but no pay," she said, when she showed them to me. "Full of obscure, critical observations about obscure critical topics written by aspiring young profs for others of their profession to argue about with their friends who are also all professors. To tell the truth, darling, they *argue* about them, but I seriously doubt if even *they* actually read them. Criticism isn't for the creative, love. It dries the core like alum on the tongue."

As soon as they were married, Lucy began to worry about not having had enough education, so she began going to school again. After three years at Columbia, they moved out west to the University of Iowa, and she kept on taking courses.

Jules said that she ought to be giving his lectures because she knew more about modern art, and damn near everything else, than he did, but another time, sitting on Hilly's terrace eating chili con carne and drinking hard cider, he said, "My wife is the nonmatriculated stone around my neck. No wonder I'll never be president. Of Iowa State!"

I found the bottle of bourbon on the table, and Lucy poured it herself, and took a big swallow.

"No one will ever take your place," she said, kissing my cheek. "Now let's go jump out the window!"

Mrs. Pearl was talking behind us. "When I got my first glimpse of this darling town, my dear, I wanted to get out of the car and kiss the *ground*. I *did*, you know, when we stepped off the plane from Europe. At LaGuardia Airport, I *kissed* the good old USA. If you have traveled in Europe, you will *know* what I mean! But *this* angelic town, so real, so quaint, so *vir*gin."

Lucy nudged me, and took another big swallow of her drink.

"Darling, I simply *adore* every stone, every funny little house, don't *you*? It's too picturesque, and perfect, and my dear, there were the two most *deli*cious urchins in the Post Office this morning with their darling, grimy faces."

Lucy squeezed my arm. "Am I hearing voices like Jeanne d'Arc? Only different! I don't believe my ears . . ."

"Shhh. She'll hear you."

Professor Chubb was headed our way.

". . . and my dear, word came to the store, that darling drugstore, you know . . . it was *help*lessly dramatic, straight out of Erskine Caldwell, off we raced like mad people. I accuse Mina Potter of staging it for our benefit!"

Mrs. Potter looked really shocked, and I didn't blame her, though Mrs. Pearl only meant it as a joke.

"Oh Greta, you horrid, horrid girl to say such a thing. Dear, I know you're teasing, of *course* I know. But, Jim, seriously, have you ever driven out that Mill Pond Road? I was dumbfounded. There are tarred-paper *shan*ties, yes, here, in Contentment Cove!"

"They like it that way," Lucy hissed in a stage whisper, pinching my arm.

"Hell, they like to live that way," the man talking to Mrs. Potter said. "That type would live that way if you gave them a palace."

Lucy began to choke and laugh, and they all turned.

"Franny! And dear Mrs. Balls . . ."

"Dot-Fran can tell us—ask Dot-Fran if they are content living that way? Jim says they do . . ."

"I took an entire film, you know . . ."

Everyone was talking, the Pekinese was barking out on the porch, and the phonograph was playing through all the babble. Gus Junior smiled across the room.

It was a lovely party; I never wanted it to end. There was a big dish of cashews on the other end of the table, and all at once I wanted some more than life itself.

But before I could move, Professor Chubb was there.

"Don't run away, my dear. Let's slip downstairs for a few minutes, just the two of us. Come, for a breath of air."

"Please, Mr. Chubb, you're making me spill."

Lucy leaned over my shoulder. "Are you a Chubb? I thought you were a Pearl. It's frightfully confusing. Is Mrs. Chubb your wife, or are you married to Mr. Pearl?"

"Why haven't I met this long and lovely lady before?"

"You have, darling, you've just forgotten."

Lucy leaned her chin on my shoulder, and gave him her radiant, innocent smile, playing up, but I was nervous as to what she might do next, and whenever I saw that bowl of nuts just out of reach, I felt faint.

"Forgotten? Never, Miss Long and Lovely!"

"Balls to you," Lucy said, "Mrs. Jules. I shall put you in my memory book as my very first Chubb."

"Perhaps we can arrange some other firsts, Mrs. Jules!"

He didn't notice when I wiggled out of their way and left. It made me a little cross, though of course that was silly because I didn't really care.

Admiral Peck called, "Whatsa matter, Franny, an empty glass? Here, I can fix that right up, I'm in business. As I was saying, Mr.— er . . . I had a couple of good hunting dogs in Bonn during the war, liberated them from a Kraut family, best damn dogs I ever had. Training, see, that's the whole answer; oh, breed, too, naturally, goes without saying . . . "

Stan and Hilly were together by the phonograph. I didn't want another martini, but I took it, and a big handful of cashews, and went over where they were. When I saw their expressions I wished I hadn't.

"Join us by all means, Franny. We're having a ghastly tête-à-tête. I've just been telling your big brother to remember this is a party, not a court of domestic relations!" She looked up at him with her impatient smile. "Relax, darling, for God's sake. I am not interested in hearing about your wife's problems, presumably being the main one."

Someone called, "Hilly, come over here, we *need* you."

She nodded at them, laughing, then turned and said over her shoulder, "Have another drink, Stanley, and forget your woes."

Watching her walk away, I felt quavery, as though someone had slapped me suddenly with no warning. She said things like that sometimes, without thinking, but it was the way she had laughed.

Stan stared down at his glass, with the muscles beside his mouth twitching. I tried to keep on smiling, so no one would notice, but my face felt as stiff as a board. I really wanted to cry. The phonograph was playing Marlene Dietrich records in German. They made me feel even worse.

Mrs. Potter said, "*Who* is that woman in the hat, Dot-Fran, with that vicious dog? I tried to pat him, you *know* how I love animals, and the nasty thing nearly bit my hand off. Really, those *dia*monds, did you ever see so many on one hand? She should never take a dog like *that* into a social gathering. Who in the world is she?"

"I don't know, Mrs. Potter."

"Oh, I thought you knew everybody, dear. Maizie, do you?"

"Never laid eyes on her. Look, Mina, there's Lucy Balls. Did I tell you what Sam, the hairdresser I go to in Center City, said last week? Well, Sam told me on *good* authority that he heard Lucy Balls takes dope!"

That made me so mad, I said, "That isn't *true*."

Just then, Dido Weaver pulled me around and kissed me, and said, "Hello, Franny, haven't had a chance to greet you all afternoon. You look tired, honey. Big, busy season at the drugstore? Come on and find a bite of something with me, I'm starving."

The first time I met Dido and her husband at Hilly's, I thought they must be very poor, both being painters, because Dido ate so much. She ate all the time they were there, even the raw hamburger in the refrigerator.

But Hilly laughed and shook her head. "No, no, lamb, on the contrary, Dido's loaded with dough. Her eating is compensatory. She can't paint, that's her trouble."

Mrs. Potter followed us over to the table. "So nice to see you, Mrs. Weaver. Are you and your husband having a pleasant summer?"

Dido smiled and nodded and shook hands, but her mouth was full by that time. There were two of her paintings in Spencer's henhouse, which I overheard Hilly tell Jules were of the Ex-Lax Expressionless school, which made them both laugh themselves silly. I didn't understand the joke any better than the paintings. They just looked like a lot of black streaks to me, but they were the biggest paintings I ever saw.

"It must be so satisfying and wonderful to be a painter," Mrs. Potter said. I don't think she really liked the Weavers, but she always tried to talk to everyone. There was never a person who tried harder to be nice than Mrs. Potter.

"It must be such a thrill, with all this beauty surrounding us. Every time my husband and I drive to Bluff Rocks I say, 'Oh, Gus, if I could only paint!'"

Dido chewed very fast so she could answer.

"But I never paint from nature, Mrs. Potter."

Mrs. Spindle giggled, but she looked serious. "You mean you see things to paint just in your *head*?"

"Oh, I'm sure Mrs. Weaver is teeming with ideas the whole time, Maizie. It's such a treat for us meeting people like you, Mrs. Weaver, people who are so artistic and different."

Dido had eaten all the cheese and crackers, so she reached for the pickles.

"My canvases relate only to nothingness, Mrs. Potter," she said, with her quick smile, offering the pickles. "Do have one before I finish them off—I'm famished. They are a complete disassociation from visual content or form. Perpetual existence, it seems to me, can be achieved only by a new entity devoid of stereotyped relatedness."

"Is that *so*?" Mrs. Potter exclaimed, trying to look interested. "Perpetual existence, you say, Mrs. Weaver? Isn't that fascinating, Maizie? You must tell us more sometime, you must explain it all so we can understand, we poor, ordinary, everyday people!"

"In four-letter words, darling!" Lucy murmured behind us.

It was cool by the open doors to the porch. The sun was low and red, and the ocean wasn't glistening anymore; it lay as flat and blue as a plate.

"Franny, how could you sneak away and leave me with that lecherous Mr. Chubb?" Lucy said. "I didn't believe it of you. What's wrong with our handsome Stan over there? Has he lost his last friend? I'd better rip over and see."

It was almost seven-thirty, and people were beginning to leave. The table was a mess of empty plates, and empty bottles, and empty dirty glasses, and cigarettes falling out of ashtrays.

Admiral Peck had his arm around the Pekinese woman and his head under her hat. They were singing German with Marlene Dietrich. He must have had a way with dogs.

I thought of leaving without a word to anyone, and running downstairs to find Ken. It didn't seem as though I could smile another minute, or utter another single word to anyone.

"Darling, what an utterly divine party," Mrs. Van Buran Chubb Pearl cried, grasping my arm. "Your brother is the most heavenly-looking object I ever saw in my life. I'm madly in love with him, *mad*ly!"

I was so tired I wanted to fall down and die. The noise, and too many martinis, and worrying about Stan, and everything that had happened all morning made just too much. But I managed to say, "Don't forget about Alfeus."

"Oh, my dear, Alfeus is my first, my dearest love. I'm plain potty about Alfeus."

No one was talking in a normal voice, everyone was shouting.

"Mina Potter, how is that marvelous swimming pool coming along? Are you going to have a grand opening? *When?*"

"How pleased the natives must be!"

"Pleased? Aren't they on their *knees* in gratitude?"

"Let them eat cake!" Hilly cried, waving the cocktail shaker. "Who needs a drink?"

Dido pointed at Mrs. Van Buran Chubb Pearl and whispered to Lucy, "Is that the one Henry Luced?"

"You mean the one he loused, darling?"

"Well, the townfolk should certainly be . . ."

"Here's a townfolk right here," Hilly said, smiling at me. "Let her speak up for herself. Come on, Franny. No taxation without representation!"

I felt my face get red; I wanted to sink through the floor. "Everyone appreciates it very much."

"Spoken with true New England enthusiasm and impetuosity," Hilly said, patting my shoulder. From her expression I knew she was feeling sorry for what she had said to Stan, but feeling sorry didn't take it back. I hoped she felt as sick as I did. "Let's drink to Potter's Pool. Bottoms up, chums! Here's to our all catching athlete's foot together!"

Mrs. Potter stamped her foot, trying not to laugh. "You're awful, awful, *awful*, all of you. But seriously, it's becoming a big, *big* problem, it's *cost*ing so much more than we'd planned. Gus and I are at our wits' ends."

"Mina!" Mrs. Pearl screamed. "I have simply the most sensational idea, to solve *every*thing. We'll organize a street fair, while I'm here, to raise money. We get the townspeople to pitch in and donate, and we make it a really gala affair! What heavenly *fun!*"

"Hi there!" Gus Junior said. He pointed at the divan. "Isn't that our reserved seat? Let the old folks wear down their arches."

It was such a relief to sit down, after standing all afternoon, and not to have someone gabbling away on both sides that I could have cried.

"She's something, isn't she; Mrs. Pearl, I mean? A real go-getter."

"It's too bad the pool is costing so much more than . . . "

I hardly knew what we were saying, or cared.

"Oh, don't worry about that. Dad will talk the town fathers around to seeing the light. After all, it's for the good of the town."

He was wearing gray gabardine slacks that matched his gray eyes, with a yellow shirt under a gray tweed jacket with tiny red threads.

"What else is there to do around here, Dot-Fran? How about your coming back to the house with us for supper?"

"Oh, I wish I could, honestly, but . . . "

"Why can't you?"

It was as though we had known each other a long time, but without any of the getting used to.

"Why can't you, Dot-Fran?"

The studio was shadowy and cool, with a damp smell of the sea coming through the porch doors. The afternoon was all over. I felt as though it had slipped through my fingers somehow, when I hadn't been looking.

Hilly was standing in the doorway at the head of the stairs talking to a man in shorts. When they turned, I recognized the gypsy painter. He grinned and blew a kiss.

"Here's a painter, Jules, one of *those!*" Hilly called, with her raspy laugh. "Go find yourself a drink, Mr. Humber, you're amongst friends."

From her tone, I knew that she liked him. I didn't like him at all.

"Who's that guy who just came in?"

"I, I don't know, a painter, I guess."

"What is this, anyway, an art colony or something?"

"Oh no, Hilly's the only one. Except her husband when he was here; well, the Weavers are too, but they don't live here."

"The folks never mentioned a lot of artists being around here. I sure never pictured them in an art colony! Boy, Dad never could stand a lot of longhairs . . . "

"He just came today. Today's the first time I ever saw him, in a trailer."

I was tired enough to die, but I wanted to go to his house for supper more than anything in the world. A long time ago, when I was nine years old, I had the measles and couldn't go to Center City to the circus, and I felt exactly the same way, as though there would never, never be another chance. Only then I had a tantrum, and banged my head against the floor.

Tonight I had a miserable old stick-in-the-mud date with Ken. It was going to be the same old Chevy, with the same old lumpy seat, the same old movie theater, and the same old clean smell on his face, shaving lotion, or men's perfume or whatever he always used, the same old jokes, and the same old good-night kiss, like wearing a comfortable old pair of shoes. Damn, damn, damn.

Professor Chubb was watching me again, instead of Lucy. I felt like sticking out my tongue and waggling my hands in my ears to let him see how much I cared, but I must admit it soothed my vanity a little.

A lot of people were leaving, and we had to get up and say goodbye. Mrs. Peck was trying in a nice way to get the Admiral to stop singing, and take her home.

"You come with us, huh?" Gus Junior said in my ear.

"I wish I could, really I do, but I've got a date."

"Oh, like that. Well, it's sure been nice meeting you, Dot-Fran."

Mrs. Potter and Mrs. Van Buran Chubb Pearl and the professor all kissed me.

"If I can slip away, let me pick you up this evening," the professor whispered. "We could go for a drive, my dear, and get better acquainted. I must get to know what's behind that radiant, sad face. Yes! The most radiant faces are the saddest, always!"

"I'm not going to be at home." He surprised me so, it was the only thing I could think of to say.

They all started downstairs, and I looked around for Stan. The Weavers and Jules and Lucy were sitting on the divan and on the floor talking to the gypsy painter. Jules got up and started looking for another bottle of gin, though none of them needed it.

"Hey, Miss Storekeeper, come on over here," the painter called. "I think you've brought me luck!"

Lucy put an album of Noel Coward songs on the phonograph and started to dance, by herself. She could dance like a ballet dancer, but by then she wasn't very steady on her feet. Her skirt kept getting in the way, so she stopped and tucked it up under her belt, showing her wonderful, long legs.

No one paid any attention. They were all used to it, except Humber, and he didn't seem surprised, just kept glancing at her while he went on talking.

I knew Ken was waiting for me somewhere outside, but I couldn't seem to move. It was growing dusky in the studio and the air flowing up over the seawall smelled cold and damp, but there was still a bright glow in the sky. I couldn't leave without seeing Stan. And I hoped he wouldn't come in just then, while Lucy was dancing, especially with her skirt tucked up. He hated anything like that.

Bill Weaver pulled up his trouser legs, and began to imitate her, shaking his hips and whirling around. It didn't seem funny to me, only embarrassing.

Then I saw Stan watching from the doorway, smoking a cigar and looking unhappy, and disgusted, and fed up. Even though he was my brother, I couldn't help thinking how handsome and young and wholesome he looked beside Jules, and Bill Weaver, and old doe-eyed Humber.

Lucy saw him too. "Darling, come dance with me."

He dodged away from her, and put his hands in his pockets. "You're doing all right."

She danced around him, swaying, and waving her arms. "Darling, you look so sad, I can't bear it. There's something you ought to be told: Hilly is my dearest friend, but she's a bitch!"

Jules laughed. "All of her best friends are bitches. That includes you, Dido."

They all thought that was hilarious. Stan just stood with the cigar in his mouth, waiting for her to leave him alone. His face was pale, which meant he had drunk too much, and he looked as though he wanted to slap her.

Hilly came up the stairs behind them, with a loaf of Sara's homemade bread, and ham and cheese on a tray.

"My God, what a tableau! Jules, control your wife! I will not have my male guests molested by drunken women, unless they're willing, that is. Come on, darling, hide behind me, and I'll fix you a sandwich."

"Don't put yourself out," Stan said.

She gave him a quick glance, and shrugged.

"Who wants a sandwich? How about you, Mr. Humber?"

"If the other offer goes with it," he said, going over to the table.

Jules kicked off his shoes, and put his feet up on the divan. "Hilly, my heart, I wouldn't have missed this crazy mixed-up afternoon. What a bunch of insecure, immature, cliché-ridden characters you've got around here. What hath mercantilism wrought! There they are, symbols and products, well dressed, well fed, and damned near as vacuous as you can get."

"Oh God, spare me that old familiar refrain," she said over her shoulder, slicing ham. "They're well-meaning, and reasonably kind. What more could you ask? Except not to see them too often!"

Dido snitched a slice of ham. "I thought Mr. Pearl was a pet. Did he ever open his mouth? The first of every month is obviously his time to howl. Do you suppose she sleeps with him then?"

"Throwing a swine to Pearl!" Lucy sang, spinning around with her panties showing.

"Anyway, she wants to know where he is all the time," I said.

They all roared, and I felt like a fool. Stan took the cigar out of his mouth and said, "I guess we're pretty old-fashioned around here; when we invite someone to a party, it's because we want to see them, not make fun of them."

Humber lifted his eyebrows, and grinned, chewing away on his ham sandwich.

"Don't be absurd!" Hilly snapped. She was really annoyed. "I invite them because I want to see them, Stanley. The Potters, the Pecks, the Pearls of this world furnish me with endless edification. I admire their sterling qualities, and deplore my lack of them. That's why I'll probably die intestate, eh, Jules!"

"No worse than in prostate, honey!"

"Oh, Jesus," Stan said.

The phonograph stopped playing, but no one turned the record off. It kept on spinning round and round.

Hilly laid down her carving knife. "You look revolting with that cigar, my love. God, why do men think mouthing a cigar adds to their masculinity?"

"Maybe you want somebody who'll laugh at a lot of raw talk, somebody to lead around by the nose."

Humber put down his sandwich and got up. "Oh, now wait just a minute, Chummy."

I hoped Stan would go over and hit him. Hard. Stan had played varsity football his last three years at college. But instead he gave a disagreeable laugh that didn't sound like him at all. "Is it any of his business, Hilary? Just for the record?"

"No," she said shortly, "it isn't. Shut up, Humber."

The others sat looking blank, as though they had frozen that way. Lucy still pretended to dance, off by herself on the far side of the room, though there wasn't any music.

"Sure, shut up!" Stan said. "You heard what she said. Come on, sis, it's time we were on our way. It's been quite a party, Hilary, thanks for the invitation."

He ripped off the white jacket and threw it at her. "Here's something that belongs to you."

It lay crumpled on the floor, with a sleeve trailing through someone's spilled drink. I felt too awful to even cry. Hilly looked at it, and then over at him, and I know if the others hadn't been there watching, it would have been different.

"Au'voir, then," she said. Her eyes were dark, and her face looked suddenly old to me, and hard, and breakable all at once. "If that's the way you want it, darling. Come back when you're feeling pleasanter." She tried to smile at me, but I know there were tears in her eyes, I know there were.

Stan pushed me toward the door.

She turned back to the others. "*Now*, sandwich, anybody?"

It was dark outside, and growing chilly. Fireflies were sparking in the field behind Spencer's studio.

Stan began to shiver.

"It was such a pretty jacket."

"Yeah," he said, starting the car, "it was pretty."

"She wouldn't have been like that if they hadn't all been there."

"Maybe not."

The air smelled like rain, and a big cloud was creeping over the bay toward the point. I felt like crawling off into a dark hole, and never coming out. What had happened anyway? Just an hour ago it had all been so much fun.

We turned out of Hilary's lane at the top of the hill, and there sat the old green Chevy, waiting.

"Go on, Stanners, don't stop. He'll follow us home."

"Oh hell, I'm all right. Go on along with him."

He couldn't look at me, but he doubled his fist and began to pound his knee. "Party's over, Doffy. You were the belle of the ball, anyway. Go on with Ken, to the movies, or wherever you're going."

"Dad will be expecting you in for a minute . . ."

He rolled down his window and took a deep breath.

"Sure. Did you think I was in a tearing hurry to get back home? Guess again, Doffy."

I leaned over and he hugged me hard, trying to smile, looking so cold, and miserable, that more than anything else I began to feel mad. How could she do this to him? It was all so wrong, it was all a stupid mistake, because she loved him, I knew she did.

One night, when just the two of us were sitting on her terrace, watching the sunset, she said, almost as though she was cross at herself, "If he wasn't so pure in heart, if he wasn't so goddamn beautiful—oh, Franny, I don't give a damn, it's almost enough just to look at him!" Then she laughed. "Almost, but not quite!"

The hackmatacks looked lacy and green in the headlights, as though they were dripping tassels.

"Remember that old song, Doffy, about being between the devil and the deep blue sea?" He leaned over and pushed open my door. "Which do you suppose Hilary is? The devil, I guess!"

It was lucky Ken and I went to a movie, where I didn't have to say a word for two hours. Afterward, he decided we should go to the Shalimar Hotel cocktail lounge where we could dance. They had a trio: a piano, an electric guitar, and a drum, with a jukebox to fill in while the trio rested.

They were playing "Fascination" when we went in, and the piano player's wife, a blonde, was singing. A few couples were dancing, and some sailors from the Coast Guard Station were drinking beer, and looking around for girls, but the girls all had escorts.

We ordered beer, too. Almost everyone drank beer at the Shalimar. That was the sort of place it was. One of the boys on the dance floor was in dungarees.

Ken said, "Well, how did you like Plus Junior?"

"He's nice."

"Guess he can't be too ambitious. Mr. Potter got him a job in Florida, with some friend of theirs, but he had to come chasing up here instead of sticking to it. That's happened two or three times, I guess. He claims to have sinus trouble, or something."

"Maybe he has."

"Maybe. Sinus trouble is all mental, you know that? I mean, it's nerves that causes it, they say. Oh, well, his family has got plenty of money, why should he work? He didn't even go through college."

The trio began to play again, and we danced.

Then he wanted to hear all about the party. "Stan didn't look very happy. What's the matter, too much elbow-bending?"

"Oh, he's just tired. He's working too hard."

"Don't make me laugh. Reading all those *Wall Street Journals*! That's supposed to be hard work?"

In one way he was teasing, and in another he wasn't, and I wasn't in the mood for any Della remarks just then.

"Did Mrs. Wister have on a dress today?"

I shook my head.

"These crazy artists," he said, sounding more like his mother every minute. "I guess we're lucky, just being normal."

"Oh, for heaven's sake," I said to annoy him, because he certainly was annoying me, "who wants to be normal?"

The music stopped, and the piano player got up, and stretched, and jumped down off the bandstand. His hair was black, and long and curly, and covered with hair oil to make it glisten, and his dinner jacket was bright blue, and came almost to his knees.

Back at our table, Ken took a long gulp of beer and said, "Well, how about it—is Mrs. Wister an alcoholic?"

I don't know how, or why, but there we were, quarrelling. It made me furious to have him smile in that nasty, tight-lipped, smug way.

"Whatever gave you *that* idea?"

"Oh, I've heard plenty of stuff, don't worry. Some pretty sensational things go on down at her place, you can't deny that. If your dad ever got wind . . . And that Jules Balls is another one."

"Another *what*?"

"Well, another Red, for all I know," he said crossly. "He's one of these longhair intellectuals, isn't he? I pick up a lot of information over on the golf course, and let me tell you, those men over there know what they're talking about. They ought to, all right, they own about half of this country. Old Mac Kramer is a friend of President Eisenhower's. I went round with him last week when we were short on caddies."

"Well, wasn't that a *treat*!"

That made him so peeved that he beckoned the waitress to bring our check.

A sailor was picking out tunes on the jukebox, and I was tempted to smile at him and encourage him to ask me to dance, Ken was being so irritating and stupid.

The jukebox started to roar some crazy rock-and-roll song, and we were getting up to go when a round-shouldered man in a light-blue coat sweater came over to the table and said, "Hello, Ken."

He was smoking a pipe, and wore old-fashioned-looking silver-rimmed glasses. I had noticed him in a booth across the room with two women.

Ken stumbled over his chair, and finally managed to say, "Hello, Mr. Kramer."

"Excuse me for busting into your party this way, Ken, but I'm on my way home tomorrow, you know; I won't be seeing you anymore on the old golf links. Dad mentioned my doing something about a job for you at the Montclair High School. A chap in my office has some drag, and I think we could work something out if you're interested. It would give you a chance to widen the old perspective a little, get into New York for some theater, all that. Why don't you think it over, and drop me a line?"

"Thanks, thanks very much, Mr. Kramer," Ken stammered, "but I'm afraid I'm com . . . committed this year already. I cer . . . certainly appreciate it, though."

"Think it over anyway." Mr. Kramer looked at me and smiled. "Sorry to have busted into your party like this."

"Oh, that's all right, we were just leaving. Miss . . . Miss Hathaway, Mr. Kramer. Thanks very much, Mr. Kramer, I sure do appreciate it anyway."

We got into the Chevy without saying a word. If he didn't feel like talking, that was just dandy, because I felt like anything but.

At the Forks, where the Contentment Cove Road branched off, Joe Peterson was waiting to hitch a ride.

Ken knew it would annoy me, so he stopped to pick him up.

"Plenty of room up front with us," he said, waiting for me to move over.

"There's plenty of room in the back, too."

So Joe climbed in the backseat. "Old Ken, old Ken!" he shouted, pounding Ken's shoulder. "Am I glad to see you. I been standing there by the side of that road for a straight hour and a half."

"It would have been a lot quicker to have just walked home!" I couldn't resist saying.

"Yeah, maybe not quite so long as that. I got a sore foot, you know, infection. The doc told Ma I might lose me my whole foot if I didn't take it easy."

Ken said, "You're in hard shape, Joe."

"Gimme a cigarette, Ken. Come on, gimme a smoke. God, I ain't had a cigarette all day."

Joe scrounged cigarettes the same way he did rides. It was some kind of an obsession. He probably had a whole pocketful.

Ken passed him one, and he lighted it and exhaled smoke in my face as though he hadn't taken a deep breath for a week.

"Say, I got a ride with this feller tonight, in a '58 DeSoto, see, and this guy offers me a reefer! Boy, I sure turned that old reefer down. I don't want none of that stuff."

"Who was it?" I said sarcastically.

"How you think I know? Some feller that come along. Oh, yeah, I *seen* him before."

Ken thought this was entertaining; he even grinned at me, forgetting that he was mad. "And he had marijuana cigarettes, Joe?"

"Hell, sure he did. Lots of people smoke them things—where you been, anyway? They bring 'em down from Canada. This guy offered me a drink, too. He was sailing 'long, eighty, ninety the whole time, drinking right out of that bottle."

"Ninety, huh? He was quite a speed demon!"

"Oh, why don't you stop lying, and tell the truth just for five minutes, Joe, just for a change?" I couldn't decide which one of them annoyed me the most.

He looked so injured and unconvincing that it was comic. "I'm telling the God's truth, Dot-Fran. What would I lie for? Hey, Ken, you see in the paper where them old Globetrotters is coming to Center City next month? Am I going to be up there to see them! I wouldn't miss that for nothing!"

He blew out another barrel of smoke, with his chin hanging over the seat. His head swiveled from Ken to the road to the speedometer to me to Ken, back to the road. Just watching him made me dizzy.

It had started to rain by the time Ken turned up the Mill Pond Road.

"Gimme another ciggie, will yuh, Ken? Come on, be a friend, one more coffin nail."

The Petersons' pickup truck was pulled up close to the back door, minus its hood, which was lying in the grass beside a broken tricycle. The twins had been rolling a rusty oil drum around the yard, and had left it upended in the drain at the end of the culvert.

"Here's one more, Joe, but you better change to filters, before you get galloping consumption."

"Yeah, Winston's is my brand."

He went tearing across the yard into the house, with his head down against the rain. Inside, I could see the glow of the TV screen, but there was no other light on. He reached the door just in time. The rain began coming down in sheets.

Turning the Chevy around, Ken said, "That was pretty nice of Mr. Kramer, wasn't it, offering me that job?"

"Yes, it certainly was."

Wherever there was a light along the street, there was the blue flash of a television screen. People sat up a lot later than they ever used to, before *The $64,000 Question* and *Lawrence Welk*.

"His father, Old Mac, knows Eisenhower."

"You told me that before. Well, are you going there to teach? Where is it, anyway?"

"In New Jersey, for Pete's sake, right across from New York City. Don't you know your geography? That's where *he* lives, the son, his name's Everett. He has his office in New York City."

"Well, are you going to?"

He rolled down the window and pointed across the street toward the Contentment Cove High School, almost hidden by the rain. "I'm going to teach right *here*."

"Here at *home?*"

"Sure thing," he said, in a pleased tone. "I've had my name on the list for the last two years, waiting for a vacancy. Jericho's all right, but I'd rather be here."

The rain was beating on the Chevy as though a giant hose had been turned on. We could hardly hear each other above the sound of it. Ordinarily I enjoyed being in a car when it rained like that, straight down, drumming on the roof and the hood, being so near it, and so snug and dry, but I didn't feel in the mood then. I didn't feel like listening to Ken, or kissing him good-night. I felt like falling into my bed, and sleeping a thousand years.

"They pay teachers more in New Jersey," Ken was saying, "but I'd just have to turn around and pay a lot more for living expenses. Here, I can live right at home. Anyway, it's too darned far away; it would cost like the devil to come home very often. I figure it isn't worth it. Old Man Kramer and I talked about it over on the links, and I told him I was already signed up. I don't know, Dotty, it seems foolish paying out a lot of money just for room and board." His mother's true son was speaking.

A car went whooshing by, and gave us a muffled toot.

"That was Uncle Ted," Ken said, peering after it. "Now where's he been? Oh, I know—there was a Masonic wingding up in Center City tonight. Say, I haven't been over to see the pool this week; how's it coming?"

"Oh, I guess it's galloping along at a snail's pace."

If the saying was true that killing time was the hardest work in the world, then Ken's Uncle Ted was the hardest-working man in New England.

"Just what is that crack supposed to mean?"

He had started to put his arm around me.

"Nothing, absolutely nothing. I'll see you tomorrow. Thanks for the movie, and the beer."

"Oh, now, wait just a minute. What about it?"

"You know your own uncle better than I do, for heaven's sake. Did he ever do anything in a hurry?"

Ken glared at me. "Where's the percentage in hurrying? It's for the summer people, isn't it, and they've got the dough. You and I might as well get it, as the next one. You don't mind sticking plenty of markup on what you sell in the drugstore."

"If they can buy things cheaper at the Cut Rate in Center City, don't think they won't. And if we're talking about *me*, figuring out ways to get something for nothing isn't my idea of—"

"Oh, well," he cut in, with Della's smile, "of course you're different from the rest of us. They're pals of *yours*, all the highbrows and the drunks, anybody that owns a Cadillac!"

It was still raining hard when I went to sleep, with the water chattering in the downspout outside my window. The sound of it made me feel even worse.

Father was always up first in the morning, and had breakfast ready when he called me at seven-thirty.

But just after dawn, something woke me. It was beginning to grow light, and I lay there half-awake, wondering if Father had called, or if I had been dreaming. My head ached from the martinis, and my mouth was dry from smoking too much, but there was some other reason why I felt so horrible that gnawed away at me, until I remembered Ken and our silly quarrel, and what he had said.

I heard the sound again, a muffled thump from somewhere downstairs. It sounded as though an animal had been accidentally shut into the back entry, perhaps a stray cat, nosing in after Beulah's dish.

I put on my bathrobe and crept past Dad's door and down the stairs very softly, so as not to wake him. At the foot of the stairs I heard it again, distinctly, under my feet. It was coming from the cellar, not the back entry, and it wasn't a cat. Someone was stumbling around in our cellar.

It was nearly sunrise. The sky was red in the east behind the horse chestnut. The dining room window had been left open, by mistake, through all the rain, and I could smell the wet syringa. If it had been dark of night, I might have been frightened, but it was daylight, and I didn't want Dad to hear and be upset, whoever it was. That was the very worst thing that could happen, for him to be upset.

Perhaps I just wasn't wide awake enough to be frightened. I tiptoed to the cellar door and eased back the bolt very softly, with my other hand on the light switch. Then, at the same moment, I flung open the door and flicked on the light.

Professor Chubb stared up at me from the bottom of the cellar stairs, blinking from the sudden bright light in his eyes. His forehead was bruised, probably from hitting it against the water pipes, and there was blood on his chin. He was on his knees, trying to scramble up. His trousers were muddy, his coat sleeve was torn, and he had lost his tie. He looked as though he had been through a battle. Even with the light on, our cellar isn't very easy to walk around in. His face looked awful, gray and stubbly with whiskers, with a long scratch across one cheek.

"Oh, my God, oh, my God," he shook his head, trying to see.

"What are you *doing?*" I hissed to keep Dad from waking. I stepped down a step, and closed the door. "What are you doing in our cellar?"

He kept trying to get up, wiping his hand across his face like a blind man. "Oh, my God, this is terrible."

"How did you get *in* here? What did you *want?*"

"Terrrible mistake, Miss . . . Miss Dot-Fran. Have to forgive me . . . must . . . have drunk more than I thought."

I couldn't think, or move. His foolish, dirty, scratched face peered up at me like some horrible creature in a nightmare.

Then my brain began to work again. I thought, What would anyone think, seeing him coming up out of our cellar, looking like a tramp? It made me so angry, I began to shake. I wanted to pick up the big jar of dill pickles and heave it at him.

"Please, please," he mumbled, holding up his arm as though he could see what I was thinking. "Oh, God, Dot-Fran, I must have stumbled in here and passed out. I . . . I just came to a few minutes ago. God, God, my head is killing me. Please, please don't . . . "

"Don't *what?*"

"I . . . I only wanted to see you again, seemed to . . . to be frightfully urgent. Oh, God, I feel so battered and sick . . . you . . . you don't know the monstrous time I've had . . . I'm soaked . . . I'm hurt."

"I wouldn't care if you were *dead!*"

"Oh, please, please, try to . . . to understand. I didn't want to disturb anyone, must . . . must have been terribly drunk, thought I'd come in this way, quietly, and . . . and find you . . ."

"Did you think I lived in the *cellar?*"

He managed to lurch to his feet, and stood, weaving and blinking at me with his bloodshot eyes. He looked sick, he looked like living death, but I had as much pity for him as I would have for a fly crawling across my lunch.

Upstairs, the sun was beginning to stream in, and Dad and Beulah were still peacefully asleep, and there I was, halfway down the damp cellar stairs, in my bathrobe, listening to a nasty-minded, drunken man trying to explain why he had crawled into our cellar in the middle of the night. It would certainly give the neighbors plenty to talk about.

I couldn't stop shaking. "I ought to call Jimmy and have you arrested."

"Oh, God," he groaned, "just show me how to get out of here. Dot-Fran, can't you . . . try to be kind . . . misunderstanding all round. Oh, God, I can hardly move." He looked as though he might cry. "Couldn't you . . . possibly . . . dear Dot-Fran . . . couldn't you drive . . . drive me back to the Potters'? I'm in . . . I'm in frightful shape . . ."

"Turn around and go out that door!" I said, hardly able to speak, "or I'll get my father's gun."

He stumbled around, groaning when he took a step.

"Couldn't . . . couldn't you possibly . . . I'll pay you . . ."

"*Get out!*"

It took him an age to climb the outside cellar steps. My hands were trembling so that I could scarcely lock it behind him. There was a sour smell all over the cellar from his vomiting, and crumbled matchbooks scattered over the floor. Creeping back up the cellar stairs, I picked up a penknife, with its blade broken half in two, lying on the top step, and when I leaned down, there were the scratches he had made at the bottom of the door, trying to pry it open.

The house was flooded with sunlight. Outside, the sky was a clean, bright blue; the grass and the leaves of the syringa and lilac bushes had a shining fresh look after the rain.

I crept out through the kitchen like a thief, hugging myself to keep from shaking, and peered out every window, but there was no sign of him. He had gone straight off down the street.

Beulah came kerplunking downstairs, one step at a time, and came out to find me and rub against my legs. Her purr sounded as loud as an express train in the quiet house, and when I didn't pay attention, she jumped up on the windowsill and sat staring at me, with the little black tips of her ears quivering.

I picked her up and hugged her tight against me, dear, warm, inquisitive Beulah, and then I began to cry. I couldn't stop. The tears poured out, and I just stood there by the kitchen window, holding Beulah, and cried until I couldn't cry anymore. And she sat in my arms, waiting for her breakfast, and went right on purring.

The Town

In October, the twilight sky turns white overhead, straining the last, sharp remnants of day through its fierce brightness.

Long bands of reflected color lie along the horizon, mirrored on the serene, lake-like calmness of the sea.

On many of these evenings, the white fishing boats leave their moorings in the Inner Cove to slip quietly across the bay, one following another, a graceful flock of earthbound birds winging single file to a twilight feeding ground, leaving rippling wakes across the vivid surface.

East of the town in an inlet bordered by the long strip of sand beach, they settle over the water like a covey of ghostly visitors, each launching its small skiff, manned at the oars, and with a figure crouching at the long-handled net in the bow, alert for the mass of schooling herring riding in from sea on the flood tide.

The exultant cries over the water, the slap of oars, the quick flash of a torch, the dim, white boats rocking under the brilliant chill sky: this is a part of fall.

The stars come, and the white sky becomes part of the day that has gone. It is night, clear, cool. Headlights swooping along the road beside the beach slow and pause to count the boats, to watch the sudden rush of oars toward a milling school of fish.

The twin stars of the Coast Guard Station shine unblinkingly across the heathland, where the mist rises out of the swampy bogs, and lies in solid gray tiers across the scrub.

But now it is summer, a different season, in the last days of July.

PART II

Hilary

HILARY said:

It was impossible to get back to work the day after that god-awful party. Humber and the Balls stayed until I had to throw them out. It was refreshing to have someone around who spoke our language, or at least who knew Cezanne and Mondrian, though the man was outrageously opinionated. It was also good to have someone around to argue with Jules, besides myself.

My beautiful Stanley was a sight to gladden a woman's heart, even when moping self-righteously in a corner while the rest of us got rapidly, and riotously, drunk, but it must be admitted, as a conversationalist, he left something to be desired.

My poor Apollo, so sweet, so breathtakingly handsome, so shocked at the depravity of my friends. God! I could resist him as little as I could resist the sound of the ocean or the sight of sunset across Marsh Point.

But things were getting rather out of hand when he put on such a fit of temper before my guests. My affairs of the heart always seem to get out of hand, from the first one on.

I was sixteen then, a sophomore at Miss Phelps's Finishing School for Young Ladies, in Evanston. Dido and I were classmates. Dido was helplessly in love with my brother, John, at the time. She has been helplessly in love with someone ever since, I might add.

John was going to Princeton, and in a rare moment of weakness asked us up to a spring house party, agreeing to furnish a fellow house member for me. Homer Glover was the unfortunate's name. Tall, homely, with a wide mouth, a small nose, very bad breath, and bursting with intellectual fervor. I shall never forget him. If I met him tomorrow, dressed as a Chinese coolie, there would be no mistaking that bad breath.

We hated each other from the instant I stepped off the train. At least he was frank. "Look, do you think this is going to work?" he asked, loping along beside me, with all the grace of a baby elephant. "I mean, if we're incompatibles, what's the use?"

"Oh, give it the old college try," I said. "I don't mind taking you at base value."

"Hey, just a minute, what was that you said?"

But I was busy looking over the sorry prospects.

That night I met Alfred. He was Homer's cousin, small, precise, and unbearably Episcopalian. He hated Homer, too. It was our first, and later proved our only, bond. But I fell for Alfred with a bang that could have been heard back in Evanston.

The next day, he took me in to New York on a wickedly clandestine date, and at dinner in an Indian Tea Shop in Greenwich Village, one flight up, delivered the gospel according to the Glovers, and God, in that order. All due respect to the Cabots, and the Lodges.

Holding my hand, while we gulped our way through innumerable curries, he feared that being born west of the Mississippi made me, though attractive in my girlish way, a hapless heathen, well beyond the reach of civilizing eastern influence.

This so impressed my hapless, heathen mind that I nearly swooned at his feet from sheer delight. However, when he suggested a nearby hotel where the swooning would be more comfortable, and more horizontal—"We need to be alone to really talk, Hilary, somewhere quiet where we can get to know one another!" (a subtle way of putting it)—I firmly said no. To tell the truth, I was scared, not unwilling, and we went to a musical comedy instead.

Oh, the pure abandonment of that night! My first New York theater, my first man of the world, or a boy sent on a man's errand! My first fling at being flaming youth. At Miss Phelps's, we barely sputtered. All made more delectably enjoyable by the image of Homer back in Princeton, waiting at the gate, waiting and waiting, grinding his big, white teeth, and chomping his intellectual fervor.

My brother John was furious too. That kind of sneaky thing wasn't done, just simply wasn't done. To a fellow club member, a pal, a great guy, a real brain.

"We were incompatibles!" I said, in self-defense. "He told me so himself."

And Alfred and I were in love.

He wrote daily, sometimes twice. I cherished his picture, every scornful word that had left his lips, every wave of those lovely pink fingernails, every haughty Episcopalian thought.

I cherished the memory of every moment we had shared, and I was a changed woman. So changed, in fact, that Miss Phelps invited Aunt Phoebe for tea to discuss the matter.

Dido listened through the keyhole, but could hear nothing but the crunching of cinnamon toast.

The denouement came in July, when Alfred arrived for a visit, coincident with a heat wave. Popular song writing to the contrary, our love was not designed to withstand one hundred degree heat blasting straight off Lake Michigan. There is no heat in the United States to equal its pure demonic glee.

Our love affair, far from being a case of the lamb lying down with the lion, became more the lion's getting tired of having his tail pulled.

"You weren't ready for me, Hilary," he said hollowly, sweat beading his forehead as we stood waiting for his train.

"But I was in love with you," I said, rebellious to the end.

He managed a wan, patient smile.

"You need growth. You're a wilted flower; no, I mean a stunted flower, needing the sun. Desperately, desperately! But, my God, where to find it here. Come east, Hilary. Innately you're an easterner, someone with a good deal to give, to contribute . . ."

He closed his eyes wearily, and sweat coursed down his cheeks. "Otherwise, you know, I should never have bothered!"

A swirl of smoke enveloped us as his train chugged into track four.

"You snob!" I shrieked, above the hooting engine. "You prude, idiot, ninny . . ."

He stooped for his bag, and saluted me, with a last bittersweet gesture to vanished love. Travelers brushed past, jostling, sticking out their elbows, bumping their valises.

His small, stern face, with those lovely elevated dark eyebrows, was going out of my life, and with it went my youth, or so I sadly imagined.

"Alfred," I sobbed, "kiss me goodbye!"

He took my face between his hands, and we kissed long and passionately. Baggage trucks, porters, and passengers notwithstanding.

"Goodbye, goodbye, my little mistake!" he shouted tenderly from the train step. "When you mature enough, and the wounds have healed, come back east!"

In midmorning, I gave up muddling around the studio, and drove down for the mail. I felt like hell about Stanley. And almost as badly about Dot-Fran.

It was my fault, of course. I had been stupidly cavalier, with the unhelpful influence of several martinis, when all the poor boy wanted was a chance to weep a few tears on my shoulder. The trouble there being that I cannot bear self-pity in any form, even from him. It bores me to extinction. So there we were. But if apologies would restore his hurt feelings, I would apologize handsomely.

Franny was my immediate worry. I would have walked barefoot over flaming coals rather than see her harmed, but unfortunately that wasn't called for. Instead, her feelings were very likely hurt, too. Very likely! Her expression, at the door, with that miserable jacket lying there on the floor between us, haunted me. So on, Hilary, on to the drugstore, bearing your cross of penitence.

At Potter's Folly, there was great activity. The crew was trundling wheelbarrow loads of dirt from one pile to another, at top speed, distributing the wealth, but very little else, while Gus and Mina, and their steamroller friend from New York, Mrs. Van Buran Chubb Pearl, looked on hopefully.

Joe Peterson loped around the edges, but the sight of my car brought him down to the road in a dead heat.

"Gimme a ride, Mrs. Wister?"

"Hop in, Joe."

His shirt was flapping, his sneakers were untied, and his hair looked as though mice had nested there en route to better things.

"When's the christening going to be, folksies?" I called. "Whose prow are we going to break the champagne over?"

"Darling, that was a simply, marvelously divine party. You're such a gracious hostess."

"Yes, perfectly divine, my dear," Mrs. Van Buran Chubb Pearl boomed.

Gus grunted and waved, and went back to trying to figure out what was wrong with the picture: workmen working, sun shining, boss bossing, no unions, no federal government, Negroes, Jews, and very little swimming pool.

Mrs. Van Buran Chubb Pearl came striding over to the car like an Amazonian lion tamer. And cracked her whip. Unfortunately for her, I was no lion!

"Mrs. Wister, we need your help desperately. With our little fair, you know. Isn't it going to be heavenly fun? We're *bubbling* with plans. I haven't felt so *useful* in years."

Joe responded nobly to this onslaught by exuding affability and B.O. in fairly equal amounts, his beady eyes sidling around Mrs. Van Buran Chubb Pearl like a couple of con men casing an Alfred Hitchcock film joint.

"To tell the truth, darling, I'm swamped," I said, "completely and literally swamped with work. But there must be others." Let good old George do it, and if anybody could locate George, she could, or trample him in the attempt.

It took nerve for a woman of her age and displacement to wear plaid knee shorts, but I must admit she carried it off. Her legs were shapely, with quite lovely ankles. They had certainly done yeoman's duty all those years, carrying the rest of her around.

"Oh, my dear, but just a few posters. Think how marvelous to have our posters made by a *famous* artist. We plan to raffle them off afterward. That darling Mr. Humber is making some too. I thought if you'd each make a dozen . . . We are simply planning to *plaster* the countryside!"

I said, "Sorry to be sticky, and all that, but posters for fiestas are hardly my line, Mrs. Van Buran Chubb Pearl. I'm a serious painter, and I truly haven't the time to spare. Sorry."

The atmosphere chilled. "That *dear* Mr. Humber . . ." she began, dripping icicles.

"Then Mr. Humber is your dish of tea," I said sweetly, thrashing through the ice cakes, "and all the luck to both of you. It just happens I'm in rather a critical stage, just now, as far as my painting is concerned, which I don't dare disturb. It's pure hell, you know, any way you look at it! Let me know when the great day comes, I want to be there with bells on. Off for the mail now—so long."

That dear Mr. Humber was making a dent in several quarters. He had outstayed even Jules and Lucy.

Finally, in desperation, thinking it was at least a step in the right direction, I let him persuade me out to the car to see some of his work. It was scarcely the time, the place, nor the moment for its most advantageous viewing, but there it was, Provincetown naturalism, spawned out of Nantucket fish houses, escaping calendar art by a single hair, and ready, willing, and waiting for the delighted summer tourists to hang over their living room sofas, in memory of that wonderful two weeks last August.

"What do you want me to say?" I inquired, "besides the fact that I'm overwhelmed by your productivity."

"Say I can stay with you tonight," he murmured, caressing my shoulder blades.

"My *God*, no!" I said, in horror, pushing him away. "Why should I say such an insane thing?"

"Why not?"

I stared into his heavy, unabashed gray eyes, and began to reevaluate Mr. C. Humber, in which direction it would be hard to state.

"You're my dish of tea, Hilary."

"Well, thanks very much." The directness of his attack disconcerted me. Perhaps I'd been out of touch too long. Contentment Cove didn't often attract this type, and I seemed to have forgotten how to handle them. "Did you bring me out here for paintings, or propositions?"

"Both. Do you like the things or not?"

"I suppose they're the sort that sells . . . " I began tentatively.

"Christ!" he said, dropping my arm. "You, too? Not the tripe about fine artists, and the others that sell. *You* paint to sell, maybe you don't admit it, that's all. Writers write to get published, and hope to God they sell. This goddamn intellectual Art for Art's Sake crowd makes me sick. So I paint to make my living, and you don't have to. OK."

He lit our cigarettes, glowering. He had good hands, muscular and big-boned.

"Leaving out any sheer urge for artistic experimentation?"

"You can stifle art a lot of ways," he said forcefully, "and you're going to stifle it when it no longer communicates. That's what sheer experimentation amounts to, right now. Crap. What's a picture painted for? To be looked at!"

It was ridiculous standing out there in the fog, with his headlights glaring on those hideous canvases, pretending to argue about art. I wanted to laugh. On the other hand, I hadn't felt so invigorated in months. The man was a menace.

"The creative urge isn't necessarily a social impulse," I said, amazed that I bothered. "There's certainly enormous gratification in having one's work seen, read, assimilated, but my dear Humber, to express oneself in any art form doesn't predicate an audience, per se."

"The hell it doesn't."

His chest was as solid and unyielding as a barrel. Tirades were apparently just part of his sex play. I had a sudden laughable vision of myself as fragile, feminine womanhood, helpless before this overwhelming masculinity, and I fended him off again, rather roughly this time.

"Do we have to fight it out now, Humber? Come back tomorrow and shout some more, if you like."

"Let me stay."

"Don't be so ridiculous."

It was a mistake to have smiled, for there was nothing tentative about his kiss, nothing tender, or burdened with adoration. It had been a long time between kisses like that.

"Goddamnit, go home, cave man!" I gasped, and staggered into the house and turned the key.

Joe broke my reverie.

"You got a spare cigarette, Mrs. Wister?"

Knowing Joe of old, I inquired, "What's wrong with those in your pocket? The ones you snitched from your mother this morning!"

"Aw no, Ma smokes Luckies." He dragged out an unopened package of Pall Malls, with a feeble grin. "Gee, I clean must of forgot I had these. Ain't that comical? See, Mrs. Wister, I had some all the time. You want one?"

"Certainly I want one."

He lit it for me, every pointed tooth gleaming.

"You kid me, don'tcha, Mrs. Wister, you kid me alla time!"

"Is your poor old mother feeling better today?"

"Yeah, yeah, them was sure some pretty flowers you brought her. Yeah, she's all right today. It didn't even scorch our house, that old fire didn't."

"Wasn't up to advance billing, eh, Joe?"

Poor old Abbey was a stout heart, if ever there was one, coming to the Cove thirty years ago as a governess for a summer family, and staying to marry Lister Peterson and bear him eight children. When I was away she wrote me the letters of a poet, no less, evocative, poignant, full of heart's overflowing appreciation of her world. Which, God knows, was meager enough.

Joe was a problem beyond her scope, a throwback to some suspect generation. His inner vision was a strange hodgepodge of heroes and villains, Heigh Ho Silver, and the Black Phantom. Joe was a petty thief, and a congenital liar, not unlikable in his ridiculously affable, beady-eyed way.

"You ain't got time for making posters, have you, Mrs. Wister? Gee, they been going after everybody, everybody's supposed to give something. To the drugstore, they told Dot-Fran she could give a lotta ice cream."

"What are you contributing, Joe?"

He burst into a delighted wheeze. "Me? I ain't got nothing to give. Jesus, Mrs. Wister, when you going to buy a new car? I see a beaut yesterday, Mercury, red with a white top."

The sun broke through the thinning fog, and beat on our heads. I wondered if gray-eyed, self-confident Mr. Humber was out painting another masterpiece this morning. And my Adonis! So hurt, so angry, behind his desk at the bank, with every right to be, no doubt, but that was scarcely a pleasant scene to have forced me into, before guests.

He was no child after all, to be unaware, from the start of the foredoomed limitations of an affair like ours, however sweet, however precious it might be to both of us, and it was both. Without question, it was the very awareness of its transitoriness that sharpened the delight in those stolen hours of ours.

Joe was talking without a break, though I was paying very little attention. "You know what Mr. Potter wants the selectmen to do?" he flung out, his hair whipping, as we raced across the causeway above the sand beach.

"No, what?"

"He was talking to Tom, the first selectman, you know, Tom Barkley, about having the town chip in for the swimming pool, and everybody'd pay for it in their taxes, and not know nothing about it!"

"What!" I yelped.

Joe leaned over, grinning idiotically. "I heard 'em. Mr. Potter had Tom all sewed up, he did, but when they went in to see Alfeus, baby! Old Alfeus, he reared back and said, 'Not by a damn sight, gentlemen!' Old Alfeus don't take off his hat to nobody."

Somewhat reassured, I observed, "What a sneak you are, Joe. No one's safe around here."

"Aw, I wouldn't listen in on you, Mrs. Wister, no sir, you couldn't hire me to, no sir."

"All right," I said as we stopped in front of the drugstore. "Here's a quarter. Now keep your hands out of Abbey's bread and butter money for one day, hear?"

"Gee, thanks, sure. You want another one of my ciggies?"

He held out the Pall Malls, and that skinny boy's wrist, the long skinny length of him in his grimy jeans and flapping shirt, dented my hard old heart.

"No," I said, pushing his hand away. "You think I'm a bum, like you?"

Dot-Fran pretended to be very busy behind her soda spigots when I came in. She looked wan, and tired, and heartbreakingly young.

"Darling," I said, going straight to the point, "I behaved like a cad last night. Please lay it to the demon rum. Please forgive me, I'm frightfully sorry."

"All right," she said, unsmiling.

The store was abuzz with pre-mail sociability. It was definitely not the time to pursue the subject, so, feeling frustrated and rather awful, for lack of nothing better to do I went round and buttonholed Alfeus.

"Look here, what's this snigdom I hear about letting the tax-payers in on Potter's Folly?"

He grinned, old imperturbable himself. Our Alfeus was one of the more attractive products of his granite birthright.

"What exactly did you hear?"

"Never mind, but I'm registering a damn strong protest here and now. Don't raise my taxes with any hidden tolls for that bloody swimming pool."

He gave me an amused look. "Nope, you don't need to lose any sleep over that, Hilary."

We exchanged a look of perfect understanding, as Randall drove up with the mail. Unfortunately for my hope of another moment with Dot-Fran, Mina arrived while it was being sorted.

"Darling," she called at once, "I really shouldn't speak to you at all after the horrid way you turned down poor Greta."

"I'm perfectly cold-blooded about my work, Mina," I said, truthfully. "One has to be, you know. How about my chipping in on something else—look, let me give you ten bucks . . . "

"Oh, that's not necessary, my dear, I understand, of course, though it would have been so grand to have had posters by . . . " She beckoned to Dot-Fran.

The poor lamb broke my heart with her pale face and her refusal to look at me.

"Yes, Mrs. Potter?"

"My dear, I thought you should know, Eddie is in the most ap*pall*ing state this morning. Of course, there was no excuse, simply none, for his bothering you at that ridiculous hour, but Dot-Fran, considering the state he was in, well, I *was* somewhat surprised that you couldn't have made allowances and helped him get home to our house. We're all apt to make mistakes, I think we should all be understanding enough to admit that, of course it was all due to *drink*ing too much, and there was no excuse whatsoever for him to go all the way to the village, bothering you . . . but . . . he was out in that dreadful, pouring rain," she explained to me, "wandering around for hours, and when he finally arrived home he was chilled to the bone. He's in bed this instant with heating pads and an electric blanket, and we should certainly feel dreadfully, shouldn't we, if he caught pneumonia, all from a stupid, silly prank?"

Dot-Fran looked so completely miserable, and undone, that I put my arm around her, not having the foggiest notion what the tempest was all about. "It can't be as bad as that, lamb. Cheer up. Eddie's a lecherous old man, drunk or sober, and don't let anyone say you nay, even Mina!"

She twisted away from me, very close to tears, and faced Mina. "It wasn't just a silly prank to *me*, Mrs. Potter."

With that, she turned and walked back to the fountain, her back very straight.

Mina looked shaken. I doubt if Dot-Fran had ever uttered a word of disagreement before. "That wasn't at all like her," she said, with an unsuccessful laugh. "I don't believe she's really herself today. But I certainly hope she realizes how serious it would be if Eddie develops something from all that exposure. Well, 'nuff said! I'm going to go get my mail, sweetie. See you latterly."

There was all the usual chitter-chatter of mail time. Della Hill and Sara King and Miss Constant had their heads together, giving someone the full treatment. Very likely, Hilary Wister.

I nodded to them, and Della gave me her tight, cautious smile, reserved for nonnatives, for whom she did *not* work. She was a remarkably young and pretty woman, for her age, which was damn close to my own.

Della, and her husband and son, fitted nicely into a sociologist's case history: Changing Social Values in Small Town Brought About By Influx of Summer Population, (i.e.) Willingness of natives, inexplicable in view of their independence about many things, to be pressed into quasi-servant category, (a) Corresponding loss of self-respect, and sense of responsibility, moral.

Della was not a believer in the integration of Contentment Cove's social classes. In her book, anyone who could afford summer sojourns away from home, or, like Admiral Peck and the Potters, retirement, belonged to a different breed of cats, and she believed in keeping to her own side of the bed, and making the most of what Providence had so thoughtfully provided. Them! I had to respect her point.

Her attitude was somewhat like that of a nephew of mine when he came back from peacetime service in Germany. Everything back here in the States assumed an aspect of nightmarish, throwing-money-away horror. Haircuts cost a dollar, bourbon was so expensive he and his wife all but gave up drinking. The supreme sacrifice! Though I'll wager Frankie never bought a bottle of bourbon in his life before he went to

Germany. In Frankfurt, or Bonn, or Stuttgart, bourbon was as cheap, and therefore as unexceptional, as muscatel back home.

They maintained an apartment, with maid, on a staff sergeant's salary. They had never had it so good. In fact, they had never had it. The Kraut maid—their affectionate designation, not mine—made Julia a camel's hair coat, and a lace tablecloth, for peanuts, or more likely, cigarettes.

As for Julia, with no meals to get, no housework to do, and capacity for little else, the poor child was forced to take up her time with a round from the hairdresser, to a Kaffee Klatch, to a movie with the girls, to the Post Exchange, and back to the hairdresser. It sounded like a fate worse than death to me, but she expanded like a rose; also like a balloon. All those Kaffee Klatches.

So their return to the States was sheer, anticlimactic misery. Seventy cents for a movie! In Germany, they were free. And food! Who could enjoy their meals at such prices?

In two days they were beginning to talk about ways of getting back to Never-Never Land, and their Kraut maid. Frankie re-enlisted within two weeks of his return to civilian freedom.

The Potters and the Pecks were Della's Germany. She had never had it so good either. All winter she waited for spring, eschewing seventy-cent movies, and seven-dollars-a-bottle bourbon.

Her husband waited too, on a year-round salary paid him by a Chicago corporation lawyer, for mowing lawns and setting dahlia bulbs over a three-month period. His round for the other nine encompassed the daily paper, TV, and naps. I wish I could say he appeared bored, rather than only extraordinarily rested!

Kenneth II was a good-looking, black-haired lad, with his mother's quick, cautious smile, and her ingrained niggardliness, which often passes for thrift.

But who was to blame them for preferring easy to hard work, and the expenditure of small rather than large effort? God knows I sat not in judgment!

Dot-Fran was staring out the window behind the fountain. I felt a strong maternal instinct to take her in my arms and comfort her. "Franny, won't you tell me what this is all about?"

She faced around reluctantly. "I'd rather not talk about it."

"Darling, you're making me feel very badly . . ." There was the damned, impersonal, inhuman bulk of the soda fountain between us, and the buzzing storeful of people. She was out of reach in some private misery, in a way that suddenly frightened me. "Fran, my dear, *don't* shut me out like this."

Her face flushed, and she said quickly, "He crawled into our cellar last night, stinking drunk, he clawed at the door like a cat trying to unfasten it and get upstairs where I was. It . . . it makes me sick even to think about. And Mrs. Potter says I should have driven him home! I don't care who he was, or *where* he was visiting, I wouldn't have taken him an inch if he'd been *dying* right there in front of me."

"In your *cellar?*" I repeated incredulously.

What a ludicrous, unbelievable picture: Eddie, the bald, well-born, one-time English teacher, who had dredged up his mother's name in one of my encyclopedias to impress me (unfortunately I was too foggy at the time to grasp what her call to immortality consisted of) ; Eddie, crawling into the Hathaway cellar in the dead of night on his circuitous, drunken, ineffectual route to Franny's bed.

I was repelled, and outraged, I could cheerfully and without a twinge have shot the man dead, but I couldn't repress a snort of laughter.

"You think it's funny!"

"Oh, my God, Franny, *no*, darling. He deserves to be shot, he's a stupid, ridiculous fool. Dear child, I didn't mean to hurt your feelings . . ."

"Any more than you meant to hurt Stan's yesterday?"

Joe was sidling closer; Della Hill was watching us with obvious relish.

I indicated our receptive audience, and said, "Be angry with me, darling, if you like, I deserve it, very likely, but I'm devoted to you, at least know *that*."

"You could laugh at *any*thing!" she said bitterly, turning away.

Feeling frustrated, monstrous, and incredulous that I had dug myself into such a hole with my faithful acolyte, I left it there and went over for the mail.

There were two letters of immediate concern, one from Stanley, one from my estranged husband. I took them out to the car, still very much disturbed, still pondering over what I could possibly do to restore Franny to me. Her unhappiness and animosity played as much hell with my peace of mind as though she were my own child, flesh of my unruly flesh.

I opened Spencer's letter first. He wrote,

> Via the grapevine, I have been apprised of your affair with a handsome native. Not that I give a damn, my dear, but you might at least satisfy my curiosity: Who is it? I while away the time here deciding between one of the Kings, and the Postmaster, par excellence. Better come down for a visit before it reaches the recriminating stage. You have never been able to terminate anything gracefully.

Dear, venomous Spencer. If he could only see the lithograph I was doing of him. Close-set eyes, preoccupied expression, thinning hair. Its title, *Hindsight!*

But then, the Weavers had seen a new oil, unmistakably me, in his studio, bearing a strong resemblance to an English pug.

> The hotel next door is full of deadly people in two-tone shoes,

he wrote,

> who come staring along the fence. You could properly stare them down, if you were here, the ones, at least, that you didn't ask in! Bill and Dido paid a visit last week. Dido ate most of a gigantic steak, leaving damn little for the rest of us, and a large bag of fresh mushrooms, which I was planning to send you. C'est la guerre! She was quite amusing about their last visit at your house . . .

He finished off,

Phone me up when you get this, old girl. I miss the familiar rasp of your voice.

Reasonably faithfully,
Spence

I lit a cigarette before I opened Stanley's filled with a strong urge to delay, to simply sit there with it in my hands (my name in his urgent, rather nice scrawl, the bank's dignified return address in the left-hand corner, with the cut of their clock tower above it), to put off the confrontation as long as possible.

And I was right. If it had only been an angry note, accusing me of bad manners, faithlessness, anything. Or asking my pardon for his own display of boorishness.

No. He wrote, asking me to marry him.

To *marry* him.

My Apollo, so young, so unrealistic, so unaware. He had come to me like the visitation of a myth, a divinely beautiful male being. But one can't marry a myth, nor live it beyond its fantasy. And we were beyond it now. With a vengeance. In one hideous leap, we had outdistanced all fantasy, and were smack in the middle of a mundane, unpleasant marital mess. Whose fault? It made very little difference now.

Steps passed along the pavement, screen doors banged.

I sat there in front of the drugstore, with my hands on the wheel, unable to move, an inert, stunned, frozen mass. I would have cursed anyone who paused, anyone who spoke.

At last my battered sensibilities reasserted themselves. I tore a sheet out of my sketchpad, and wrote his answer quickly, as though the pencil seared my fingers. Perhaps it did.

My dear, my dear, my dear—I am forty-three, you are still in your twenties. I'm cantankerous, and tired, and impossible to live with. I would surely make you miserable in a week, and murderous in a month. A fate I may deserve, but they would jail you for it.

Forgive me, darling, marriage isn't for us. I thought we both realized that from the start. We have a few memories no one else shares, remember those, and forget the rest.

This is goodbye, darling, finis, the end. It has to be. I don't believe in wakes, or resurrections, or needless pain for anyone concerned.

> e milli bacci,
> H

There was a stamped envelope in the glove compartment. I popped it into the outside mail chute, before I could change my mind, and drove on home, howling quietly and tenaciously the entire way.

My mother would have been cheered at that unmistakable sign of feminine weakness, my lack of which she was constantly deploring.

For the final straw to that morning of all mornings, Chauncey Humber's car sat in the driveway back of the house, and he was waiting for me in a chair on the terrace, looking very much at home.

"Where in the hell have you been all morning?" he inquired politely, by way of greeting.

"I've been for the mail."

"Get any?"

"That is certainly none of your business."

"Oh, are we in a mood this morning?"

"Perhaps I am. At any rate, I'm afraid I'm not very good company."

"No need to apologize," he said airily. "If the food's good, I'll stay anyway."

The noon sun was growing hot, burning through the last high remnants of fog. A bee droned in the honeysuckle.

The intrusion of this one importunate voice shattered the
Point's peaceful quiet as effectively as five o'clock commuters
ever shattered a moment of relative inactivity at Grand Central.

"Look, if you don't mind . . . another time I'll . . . "

"Obviously you're not working," he said reasonably, with a sud-
den ingratiating smile, "or I wouldn't dream of disturbing you.
What's the problem anyway? Don't tell me there's Trouble in
Paradise?"

"I have no intention of telling you anything. And why aren't
you at work?"

"Because I wanted to come here—to see you, Hilary." His
heavy, gray eyes were on me like an enveloping tight garment.

In spite of myself, very *much* in spite of myself, I felt my hostil-
ity lessening. When one is forty-three, God knows, proofs that
one's attraction for the opposite sex is still potent are received
gladly from any source.

"And I paint to make a living!" The touch of sarcasm seemed
to go naturally with his sexual advances.

It irked me nonetheless. "Look, Humber," I said, "let's have no
mistake about this: My work is more important to me than anyone, or anything."

He sat up. "What makes you think mine isn't goddamn important to me?"

"Because you bastardize it."

He grinned unpleasantly.

"Here you are," I said, feeling driven to elaborate, "as free as air,
by your own admission, free to go wherever you choose, whenever you choose. You've been smart enough to avoid the usual
entanglements; you're not tied, as I am, to a house, to the stupid
conventionalities of weeding gardens, giving cocktail parties,
answering mail. What excuse have you got then, for turning out
the things you do? Do they satisfy you, gratify you?"

"Sure, when they sell! I've sold more paintings this summer
than you've sold in the last five years."

"And what exactly would that prove, my dear?"

"I'll tell you what it proves!" He snatched my sketchbook, and leafed through it contemptuously. "I'll tell you one thing that it proves: I don't paint vicariously from a sketch I made ten years ago. I don't feed on a lot of ideas about art, or on arty ideas, I go ahead and damn well paint pictures, and sell them. Sure, we're living in a commercial age. All right! Art is commercial, it's buying and selling."

"You're so dead wrong."

"Oh Christ, let's go for a swim," he said, in sudden utter good humor. "I didn't come here to argue with you, Hilary."

He jumped up, ripping off his shirt. "Come on, honey, before lunch."

His brown chest was matted with silken, golden hair.

Unwillingly, I said, "At last, a man with hair on his chest."

"Do we have to bother with suits?"

His complete audacity, after the stresses of the morning, was at least revivifying.

"What a damn fool you are!" I said, amused.

"You wouldn't shock me, you know, Hilary!"

"No, I suppose I wouldn't. Run along and leave me in peace, will you? I'm tired, truly, I'm completely done in."

He put aggressive hands on my shoulders.

"Oh, go away," I said, feeling the hard, muscled trunk of his body, "for God's sake, will you please stop?"

Instead, before I could protest, he pulled me down, his mouth hot and urgent against my breast.

"I said *stop it*. God*damn* you."

Immediately he drew back, surveying me languidly through his heavy lashes, in complete self-possession. "Whatever you say, Hilary. We can just *sit* here!"

I got up, uncertain whether to slap him, or to laugh, and also, disquietingly enough, not finding myself wholly unresponsive.

"I'm going," I said, "if you won't."

He looked at me with something like suspicious amusement. "Running away?"

"I have to go to Center City," I said, to my own utter amazement. "No, I'm not running away, don't flatter yourself so, Humber. You're welcome to whatever's in the refrigerator, as long as you seem to have expected lunch."

Why was I going to Center City? Leaving the Point on a hot, midsummer day to drive fifty, tedious, uncomfortable miles? Why? Conscience? It was a little late for that.

But perhaps better late than never. I had the sudden urgent necessity to see Stanley—my letter wouldn't reach him until tomorrow—to *see* him and to make this ending between us as painless, as unembittering, but as final as possible, which was quite impossible, of course. But, above all, I wanted no tattled tales of my entertaining another man to wound him more than he already would be wounded. This breaking off of our affair had nothing to do with anyone else, he needed to know that, and I needed him to know it.

It was ending because it must, because it had fallen of its own weight, because it was no longer a relatively harmless, though intense, dalliance. I had never meant to threaten the foundations of his life. No, I had never meant to. But had I ever considered that I might *not*? My hell sparkled with laggard good intentions, too little, too late, and too damned inconvenient to be intended at the crucial time.

Spencer's nasty reminder, "You've never been able to terminate anything gracefully," stuck in my throat like a bone. And fifty miles of familiar, unrolling asphalt, concrete, sprawling villages, forests of beech and birch, sunny hills and valleys gave me plenty of time to consider the royal mess I had made of things generally.

As usual, in summer, Center City was fiendishly hot, jammed down between its hills, and crowded with tourist traffic.

The dim lobby of the Center City House whirred with fans. I waited for him in the empty cocktail lounge. It was three-thirty.

When he slid into the chair opposite, I had the old, instant pleasure at the sight of him, the bronze cap of hair, those incredibly blue Hathaway eyes, the well-molded features.

"A bad day, darling?" I asked automatically, and stupidly. "It's always so damned hot in this town."

"Yes, it's always hot," he agreed noncommittally.

"I'm sorry we quarreled yesterday, my dear."

"What do you want, a martini?"

"Yes, double."

"I'll have a beer," he said to the waiter.

The man withdrew. His radio above the bar at the back of the room was softly spatting out a sportscast.

"Did you get my letter, Hilary?"

"That's why I came."

"I want to marry you," he said, with an effort, sweat standing on his forehead. "I'll do anything you say, *any*thing. We could go away somewhere . . . "

We were silent while the bartender left our drinks, and slid a fresh bowl of salted peanuts between us.

"My dear, can't you see how impossible any talk of marriage is?"

It was harder to say than to write, harder even than I had envisioned, facing his straight, tortured gaze.

"No, it's not impossible."

"Darling, please try to be sensible. It was unwise of us, *mad*, from the first night on. We *knew* that. But let's have no regrets, darling, no regrets . . . " I heard my voice trilling on, in numb amazement, "It was a time I shall always cherish, a lovely, lovely interlude. But Stanley, my *dear*, in the very nature of things, it can't count beside your home, your family, your job, all the things that make your life."

"You make my life now." He was very pale.

"No," I said cruelly, and gulped down the rest of my martini, wishing that I was drunk, drunk, staggering, blind drunk. "I'm not really a part of it, Stanley, nor are you a part of mine. We're not children, we know what the score is. For God's sake, let's not torture ourselves. Can't we do this without histrionics? Everything ends, my dear, and this was never supposed to be the romance of the century."

"It would be easier to take a knife and cut my heart out."

"Please, Stanley . . . "

"I'm in hell, Hilary. If you won't marry me, I hope to God I have the sense to kill myself."

His slumped shoulders, and desperate, white face frightened me. I reached for his hand, praying for reason, and the right words.

"No, Stanley. You're young, you're extremely attractive, you have a wife and two children. Your whole life is ahead of you."

"Not without you."

"Darling, must you spoil all the fun we've had? That's what you're doing, you know?"

The bartender was hunched on one knee, listening to his ball game, watching us from the corner of his eye; the slow-motion fan whirred overhead, the shaded blue lights glowed on each table, as though there could never be another sun. An occasional burst of normality came from the lobby, voices, steps, laughter.

"It wasn't just something to pass the time—with me!" he said bitterly.

"This sort of thing is damnably hard, Stanley, for me as well as for you. Please don't make it more so."

His face seemed suddenly that of a stranger, alien-eyed, anguished. I felt a shattering, desperate need to get out of there, away from those ghastly blue lights and his white face.

"You'll have my letter in the morning. It's not at all the end of the world, darling, but you must see now why we can't let it go any further. God knows it's bad enough as it is. Promise me not to do anything absurd . . . promise me, Stanley."

"No," he muttered through twisted lips, "nothing absurd, Hilary."

I don't remember going out through the lobby, past the leather armchairs behind the potted ferns, past the newsstand and the airlines counter, the bored bellboys, and the prissy room clerk, out, and behind the wheel of my car. I may have covered it on a dead run.

At least it was over. Perhaps not gracefully, but surely with some saving grace. God knows how it had gotten so out of hand, when it started as the most innocent of byplays, intended neither to hurt nor harm.

And what adult hasn't resorted to byplay, now and again? But it was no use trying to rationalize an agreeable, let alone a happy, ending. I felt horribly depressed, emotionally disemboweled in a frightful way. Spencer, I'm sure, would have said it served me jolly well right.

I drove back slowly. The top was down, and the slightly cooler air of late afternoon, rushing past the windshield, felt good.

As the road left the outskirts of the city, and ascended through the thickly wooded stretches of beech forest, with the near slopes of the surrounding hills already shadowed, and blue metallic glimpses of the lake visible through the trees, I thought how different it had all been when Spence and I first drove through this stretch of country, and discovered Contentment Cove.

How different the Cove itself had seemed. There were no Potters, Spindles, or visiting Chubbs and Pearls then. Carver and Hazel Peck came for a few weeks each summer, but they were as unattuned to the year-round life of the place as the tight elite of islanders.

The ghastly thought suddenly occurred to me that Spencer and I had been the harbingers of change; we ourselves had been the first to come.

But in those early days, whole weeks would pass without our stirring from the Point, weeks of painting, reading, listening to music, watching the miracle of daylight and dark from our front steps.

Abbey's cleaning mornings were the break in our isolation, and we looked forward to them with the avidity of detective story fans. Her vivid accounts of village happenings never paled, though we knew the participants only by name, and were quite satisfied to hear of their exploits from an uninvolved distance.

Spencer began taking a day off several times a month to go fishing with the King boys, getting up at an ungodly hour in the morning, and not returning to the house until dark, wind-burned and ravenous and dirty, and filled with well-being. He came home those nights invariably pleased with life, with the Kings, himself, the lot of a fisherman, the sketches he made, even with his waiting wife.

We felt enormously lucky not to be stuck in an airless, New York apartment, or leading a half-ass life in some arty suburb. I even grew reconciled to a yearly visit from Spencer's parents.

Gradually "the couple out on the Point" grew into the scheme of things. Alfeus began to hint at the responsibilities of taxpayers, especially those who required an extra three miles of snow removal. We even went to an occasional supper in the vestry, for the benefit of a new organ (for the church!) or a new carpet, or a new electric potato peeler for the new school. Though I must say the latter cause struck me as verging on the decadent. I was even trapped into one Woman's Club meeting.

In those long-gone days, we took walks along the shore, and discovered sandy spots to swim from in the hot sun of midday, lying naked on the warm rocks afterward to dry. We discovered a lovely horseshoe beach of round, polished stones, swampy patches of speckled cranberries. We knew every rocky headland.

When friends made the trek to see us, they stayed the week-end, a week, sometimes a month. We painted, argued, lay about in the sun, fished off the rocks, and hardly ever, in those glorious days of yesteryear, got drunk. Or needed to.

Jules wrote his critiques, Lucy tanned her beautiful shape and read Ruth Benedict's *Patterns of Culture*, Spence and I sketched, and painted.

We walked miles, over the rock-strewn pastures, to favorite spots along the shore for picnics. We were young, and vigorous, and productive, and lighthearted.

No one bothered us. Abbey cooked and cleaned, and the village life, through her eyes, fascinated and amused us. We were of the Cove, and yet apart from it: a perfect relationship.

But like all perfect relationships, it was doomed.

Came the revolution. Came the Retired, colonizing as they came. It was Mediocrity, with a fixed and regular income, on the march! Raising their standards high: pineapple and marshmallow salads on every table, and a pastel flush in every home.

They raised the Post Office to third class, they raised the value of real estate, and they raised hell generally with our slow, seductive, self-sufficient, innocently beautiful Cove. Perhaps it wasn't strictly the rape of innocence, but it was more fatal.

I remembered Dot-Fran as a little girl of twelve, in the good old days, bright-haired, and shy as a gazelle, flitting in and out of the drugstore, with her flushed, radiant, clear-eyed smile. Stanley, I saw only rarely, on school vacations, dazzlingly blond and school boyish in his white sweaters with the big college numerals. And I saw him at his mother's funeral, to which Spencer had insisted it was our duty to go.

At seventeen, after her first year away from home, as a student at the state university, Dot-Fran made a big gain in poise. She gained something else at college—a dark-haired, quick-talking lad from Saugus, Massachusetts, an engineering student, who chased her home that summer, and stayed on with a job at the fish wharf.

I saw Lyle at least once a week, when I stopped by for fresh fish. He was an extremely likable chap, open-faced, friendly, and articulate. Stripped to the waist, in his skintight dungarees, he very soon became the indispensable man on the wharf, but he always had time for a chat, and a cigarette, after weighing out my haddock. Therein lay part of his considerable charm.

I learned from our chats that he was a freshwater fisherman, a canasta expert, a Democrat, and a Sigma Chi. I favored him highly over Ken Hill, and it was apparent that Dot-Fran did too.

She never mentioned the accident to me, even when we became close friends. At the time it happened, Spence and I heard a number of versions from Abbey, each more gruesome than the last. The truth I finally had from Stanley, as simple as it was hideously tragic.

The day before Thanksgiving holidays, in Dot-Fran's second year at school, Lyle and a fraternity brother picked her and the other boy's date up for an afternoon of hunting. Hunting was usually a happy euphemism for secluded walks in the woods around the north end of the lake.

But that sunny November afternoon, the boys came equipped with shotguns.

Lyle and Dot-Fran piled into the backseat of the car, with the guns under their feet.

The boys knew a particular site, an old logging camp, that turned out to be at the end of a long, miserably rutted woods road, some fifteen miles off campus. They reached it at last, jolted and bumped into high, good humor.

Lyle jumped out first, helped Dot-Fran alight, and then reached back along the floor to pull out the guns.

There was a sudden explosion. He doubled over, without making a sound, his stricken eyes going to Dot-Fran.

"Hospital, hospital, quick!" he gasped.

Back they jolted over that rutted nightmare of a road.

He lived for two days, three nights.

"She had never met his family before," Stanley said. "Dad drove her down to Saugus for the funeral. They got there about six, on a Saturday night, all the stores were lighted, the streets were full of people like any Saturday.

"All at once, she said to Dad, 'I can't go any further.'

"He said, 'You can't go any further, Doffy?'

"She just sat there, shivering, and shaking her head.

"So Dad stopped at a filling station, and called Lyle's parents to explain to them, and they turned around and drove back home that same night. Poor kid, she just couldn't take anymore."

Small wonder.

That was the winter of the great snow in Contentment Cove, the winter that our road went unplowed for ten days.

Spence and I snowshoed to the village, dragging an old moose sled that the barn had provided to haul back our supplies. Our reception at the Post Office when we finally arrived was memorable. Alfeus supplied not only our mail, but two bottles of whiskey, Mrs. King insisted on our coming in for a hot lunch before starting the long trek home, and Mr. Hathaway presented us with a freshly baked apple pie, boxed for traveling.

As we mushed clumsily along home, draped to the teeth in scarves, boots, and parkas, we were greeted from nearly every doorway, across mounds of shoveled paths, and drifted driveways. It was like the camaraderie of survivors of an earthquake, an armistice, an act of God to be shared without social constraint. It remains one of the warmest, happiest memories of my life.

Curiosity drove me to call on Mina and Gus soon after they moved into their renovated house, taking Dot-Fran along for window dressing.

If suburbia was on the prowl, I wanted to size up their forces. They turned out to be formidable. The old Harvey Place boasted a newly asphalted drive, as black, smooth, and impervious as a super highway—to the front door, to the back door, to the barn, probably to Heaven.

Mina opened the door to us, all smiles and hospitable confusion.

"Hello there," I said, breaking the ice with my customary clatter, "we're paying you a formal call. Wherever did you find all that asphalt—under the highway commissioner's bed?"

"Why, Mrs. Wister, my husband was in the contracting business, you know, until he retired. But what a treat and an honor, come in, do. And Dot-Fran, how nice, my dear. We're in a perfect mess, which you'll just have to overlook. Why, if there's anything my husband could help you out on in the building line I know he'd be more than glad . . . he gets a wholesale price, of course."

"That's very kind."

Dot-Fran's wide-eyed admiration as she surveyed the chintzy chairs, wall-to-wall carpeting, the outsize venetian blinds at the outsize picture windows (I admit it looked a comfortable, bright, pleasant, though wholly undistinguished room) goaded me. "But all that asphalt. I can see you really hated to stop." Which was, I also admit, snide, uncalled-for, and completely unnecessary.

Mina was a sport. "Wait till you meet my husband, my dear," she said, with such a hospitable smile, that I squirmed with shame, "if you're interested in that sort of thing. And you will

meet him, you will, because we're here to stay, you know! Oh
yes, we think of ourselves as Contentment Covites now!"

I stopped squirming and felt better. "Sounds like a religious
sect, Mrs. Potter! You're not starting one, are you?"

"Of course you're teasing!" she said, with good grace. "Oh, I
know you artists, and writers! Oh yes, I've been told all about
you, you see, and what a famous painter you are! I just hope we'll
be invited to that studio one of these days, but my dears, sit
down, do, you just have to take us as we are, all the mess and
confusion. We're selling our Texas home, and our furniture hasn't
all arrived here yet. Heaven knows what we'll do with all of it."

Dot-Fran wasn't uttering a word, so it seemed up to me to
spur our good hostess on. "Putting all your eggs in one basket,
Mrs. Potter?"

"Yes, my dear, exactly! We've sold out completely down there to
make this our permanent home. It was a modern, lovely house,
with all the conveniences, but still we didn't want to be saddled
with two places to look after. Last winter, of course, we took a
Caribbean cruise, but the weather! If one could only depend on
the weather, what a difference it would make. Gus, my husband, is
threatening to buy a cabin cruiser now that we no longer have
the Texas house to think of. He says we could live on *it* winters,
but I must say I think I'm beyond the age to go hopping around
on a boat. I do value my comfort, and I'm ready to admit it. After
all, what else do we have in life? But speaking of the asphalt, I
must tell you that in Texas, we had the entire lawn asphalted.
Painted green, of course. Oh, it was such a relief, none of that
constant fuss of watering, and cutting and trimming."

Dot-Fran took a deep breath, and found her voice. "You probably couldn't tell the difference, at a distance."

God bless her innocent, receptive, straightforward heart. My
love for her reached a peak at that moment.

Mina was much pleased. "My dear, you're quite right. But Gus
went to enormous trouble getting the right shade. He's a perfectionist, you know. Nothing would do but *exactly* the right paint.
He drove miles before he found it."

I couldn't resist; in fact, I didn't try. "The asphalt's always greener in the other fellow's yard, eh, Mrs. Potter! Now do show us around."

Poor old Jake and Ma Harvey. How their eyes would have bugged, and their tongues wagged. They would have loved it. The west wall of the living room had gone into a gargantuan picture window, whose glare was endurable only on dark, rainy days; the parlor bedroom had been knotty-pined; the kitchen gleamed with shiny, big electrical appliances, the only possible omission being an electric chair. Or perhaps there was one.

But it remained for Dot-Fran to spy the pièce de résistance. "Oh," she cried joyfully, "look at the fireplace. It's so *big*. It used to be brick, didn't it?"

It was big. It was utterly, monstrously ugly.

Mina sighed happily. "We *are* proud of our new fireplace. The old brick chimney just fell down into the cellar. It was a frightful mess. Someone suggested using it again, building it up again, but, my dear, Gus would never hear of it. He's a perfectionist, as I told you. He insists on the best. Secondhand bricks would never do for him. So! You see what we *did*! These stones are from our very own beach. Every one! Gus picked most of them out himself, slipping and sliding over those slippery rocks until I was wild. It has a Heatilator, of course, the largest they make."

She went tripping happily out to the kitchen for martinis, which I welcomed as rain on parched ground.

Dot-Fran looked at me, pleasantly bemused.

"Look, darling," I said, taking her arm, "here begins and endeth the first lesson. This monstrous specimen of human endeavor should be known as the rock-eat-rock type of architecture!"

Mina's martinis were second to none, but drinking them that day seemed to spell the end of a chapter. Or better, the beginning of one.

The Potters, and their counterparts, came, saw, and devoured.

The colloquialisms, the village tales of the last one hundred and fifty years, were consumed and regurgitated. The folkways of

Contentious Cove were pounced on as though folk had never before existed. The kind they hopefully envisioned never had.

The Cove's present aborigines they saw as strong, simple, honest to a fault, trustworthy to a man, slightly retarded, and childishly shy; in short, the willing, hardworking salt of the earth.

This was during the honeymoon. When they got out of bed, and started getting acquainted, there followed an agonizing reappraisal, a lifting of the scales. A spade began to assume the disappointing aspects of a spade. Paradise was still a stagger or two away, it seemed.

For instance: It was a dear, perfectly exquisite place, but local prices were so *much* higher than Center City's chain stores. One wanted to encourage local initiative, but, my dear, one simply couldn't *afford* to pay ninety-eight cents for sirloin, when in Center City one could buy it for ninety-five.

Oh, one remained devoted to the land of one's adoption, but one came to admit there were flaws. Decided inconveniences. Television reception, in a fringe area, was notably bad, not nearly as satisfactory as it had been within a few miles of powerful transmitters, but surely something could be done? A mountain or two shaved off, Boston moved a little closer?

And the Center City station had dropped Dave Garroway's program, that was beyond comprehension. As well as the fact that there were weeks when *The Saturday Evening Post* didn't arrive until Wednesday. Wednesday! It must certainly be due to carelessness, or neglect of their duties on *some*one's part, and one looked forward so to getting the *Post*.

Then, of course, taxes. One had been led to believe that in this section of the country, real estate taxes were low. It just simply turned out to be untrue. One heard the *rumor* that if the town's business affairs could be straightened out . . . but naturally one had to tread very carefully in saying anything to that effect. They were *very* clannish. That nice Mr. Putright who retired last year, a CPA, offered to audit the town books simply as a public service, to bring their bookkeeping methods up to date. My dear, he couldn't make head nor tail of it, and I do hear that he wasn't given much help or encouragement. He finally had to simply bow out, and let the town officers go on keeping their accounts the same way they always had.

So it went.

Contentious Cove's Retireds retired only at bedtime. They ran for town office, for the Republican Town Committee, for top banana in the Holy Order of Masons, for their mail. They ran gift shops, painting classes, hobby evenings, hospital auxiliaries. They ran the rest of the population ragged.

They formed Committees to Investigate the Possibilities of Luring Heavy Industry to Our Township, when presumably they themselves had come because there was none. Fortunately, the survey conducted by the Committee dredged up only one male between the ages of eighteen and sixty who was willing to work.

The Retireds joined farm extension groups, and learned how to prepare clam chowder for nine hundred people, something every well-dressed housewife should know. They bolstered the air watchers for Civilian Defense, until not a single subversive seagull passed unreported.

In short, well-intentioned, warmhearted, idle, and ill-equipped for leisure, they had the incessant urge to re-create in their own image, destroying with sure, middle-class efficiency what had primarily attracted them, destroying in the name of love, and bearing gifts.

Actually, Spencer was much more disturbed about the whole thing than I was. He couldn't stand bores.

"How's the Howard Johnson set?" he would inquire when I came back from the village. "Quick, give me the latest bulletin on what's pastel in plumbing!"

Gloomy, gloomy was the day when Ned Spindle joined the Kings' fishing party.

That night he said morosely, "I know how many business trips he has made to Chicago, I know how many shares of American Tel and Tel he has, and furthermore, I know exactly how many gallons of fuel oil his furnace burns per minute—or maybe it's per week."

"You got along beautifully, then, darling!"

"Oh hell, there's lots more. Spindle on education: too damn much of it; Spindle on art: I leave all that kind of stuff to the women, maybe they get something out of it."

"Knowing one's limitations is a sign of maturity, dear love!"

"Hilary, for God's sake! But the frightening thing is . . . "

"I know! The King boys think he's a whale of a good chap. And why shouldn't they?"

"My God, why *should* they? Except that he has a substantial bankroll, and his wife wears a beaver coat. That's the sole reason, the whole criterion. He could be a dirty crook, a defiler of women, a snob, which he certainly is in his stupid way, a bastard, which he doesn't miss by much, but as long as he's well-heeled, he's a great guy. He's got money! If he's got money, he's got to be smart; if he's smart, ergo, he's someone to admire."

"It's an old story, darling," I said, yawning. "And if it will cheer you, my beaver coat is newer than hers!"

By the time I had reached the Forks, the air was much cooler, with the promise of a damp breeze off the ocean. The morning fog, burned off by the hot midday sun, was creeping back over the bay, obscuring the islands and the horizon. By evening, it would shroud the Point.

Far from being cheered by fifty miles of reminiscence, and the social enigmas of the Cove, I felt more thoroughly ill-spirited than for a long time. Like an old horse nearing home stable, I hurried toward the blessed solitariness of the Point, a cup of tea, and a Seconal. Perhaps after a night's sleep I could face the morrow.

It was past six when I drove through the Cove, deserted save for a half a dozen cars in front of Hamburger Heaven, their occupants feasting on ground steak and french fries, lobster rolls, homemade pies. The thought of food sickened me.

I whipped across the sandbar, past Potter's Folly, and up the hill, thanking God that I hadn't met anyone who required nodding, smiling, even waving to. Almost home, and the thought of sanctuary was never more urgent.

But the gods were reserving their revenge. Like a shiny, chromium-plated chariot of doom, the Potters' convertible came nosing up out of my lane, Gus Junior at the wheel, his father and mother crammed in beside him.

God. God. God. They stopped. I stopped.

"Darling, we'd given you up!" Mina cried, as I tottered back to greet them.

"Luck," I croaked. "Come on back and have a drink. I'm just in from Center City. What a hellhole that town is."

"I don't think we'd better, dear. It's late. But there *is* someone waiting!"

"Who?" I demanded flatly.

"Darl, can't you guess? He's such a dear, so attractive, and masculine, and *so* brimming with talent. We've had the nicest chat, haven't we, Gus?"

Humber—again. When I felt incapable of the effort required to swat a fly.

To make things doubly dandy, Mina was a ferocious gossip.

"And we think, we just think we may have him do a painting of our house while he's here. For our Christmas gift to each other!"

Gus Junior hung over the wheel, whipping his eyelashes. He was gotten up in yellow linen slacks, and reminded me irresistibly of a doll minus its stuffing.

Unable to respond either to the news of Humber's awaiting me, or to his immortalizing the Harvey Place, I took a desperate grip on my reeling senses and the door handle, and inquired, "Where are your guests? Haven't shipped them off?"

"Mercy, no! We wouldn't dream of letting them go. Dear Eddie is still in bed, so Greta and George stayed by him while we took a minute to run over here. By tomorrow he's promised me he'll be himself again. We want you to come have a drink with us then, and of course bring anyone along that you like, just *any*one!"

Just anyone with gray eyes, and handsome calves, answering to the name of C. Humber. Subtlety was one of Mina's strong points.

"Now promise! We won't stir until you say you'll come."

"You know me, and parties," I said weakly. "Wild horses and all that." I hadn't enough life left to manufacture an excuse.

A clammy breeze came creeping up the hill from the sea.

"Good girl, good girl!" Gus boomed, with suspicious heartiness. I didn't like the glint in his eye. "If you need any help keeping that feller down there under control, call on your Uncle Gus! You never know how these artist fellers will behave."

"Why, how touching, Gus," I said, too sharply, but unable to cover up. "I don't anticipate any trouble, and I shall send him packing at any rate. It's been a long, hot drive and I don't feel my social best!"

"Now that's a word I can do without."

"Cigarette?" Gus Junior asked, learning across his parents.

I had a sudden flash of insight that behind that uncreased Miami Beach shirt, and those soulful dark eyes, was hiding a scared, incapacitated, inarticulate boy trying desperately to hold up his end of the stick. It made me not one whit happier to have discovered him. But as long as there were cigarettes to offer, doors to open, goodbyes, hellos, polite kisses on elders' cheeks, he would be able to cover up his abysmal secret, and get along.

"No thanks, doll. What word, Gus?"

"*Social.*" Gus grunted. "That's all you hear, social this, social that."

I wanted to quietly tear my hair out, or to die quickly and numbly there on the stark bareness of my gravel lane. This was the price I paid for emerging from my cloister, for drinking their liquor.

"Dear Gus! Unfortunately, you're a social being along with the rest of us."

"No, by God, I'm not. Let's get this straight right now. I like to be alone, by myself, don't I, Mina? Yes sir, all I want is to be left alone. Leave me out of this socialistic stuff."

"My dear, it's true," Mina said, looking alarmed. "Gus has never been socially inclined."

"All you artists may be Reds," he said, warming to his subject, and looking quite handsome, with his eyes flashing and his cheeks flushed against that mane of pure white hair, "but not yours truly. And I can be perfectly happy not to see a soul day in and out, working out in my shop, and fiddling around. No sir, I got no use for socialism in any form."

"Gosh, that's pretty funny," Gus Junior said, making a gallant effort, "anybody taking Dad for a socialist."

Or taking him.

I watched the fish tails disappear, controlling a mild case of hysterics.

The whole, hideous, hot, farcical day no longer seemed to touch me. I felt on some high, fog-shrouded plateau, drained, purged, gutted, exhausted, and above all, completely alone.

To drive the moral home, it suddenly came to me that I had owed my poor old mother a letter for weeks. The truth was, I had never brought myself to tell her of the separation from Spencer. The old girl was very keen on him.

Standing there, slowly congealing in the clammy embrace of fog, I wondered why my generation had been so impelled to hate their mothers. For we had, one and all, lamentably, incontestably, and intensely hated them.

Lucy's was too protective, Dido's was an aggressive old horror, my poor old thing was a weird, absurd, unbearable fount of sentiment. She cried at parades, funerals, weddings, movies, reunions, separations, anniversaries, birthdays, old family silver, babies, old men, the flag, the president, the king, and God. Not necessarily in the order of their precedence. She also often laughed—through her tears.

Tomorrow I would write her a long, daughterly tome, with xxxxx's at the bottom. What were a few xxxxx's off my typewriter when it gave the old girl a boost.

To my horror, I began to cry, in that cold, foggy blur of sundown, while a squirrel rattled sarcastically from a nearby tree. Gloom, or was it only twilight, seemed to creep over the lane like a vast cobweb. The patch of yellow mustard springing out of the sparse gravel at my feet was the only color left in the gray, dripping world—that, and the aluminum mailbox with S. WISTER painted on it in big, block letters.

Finally I tottered back to the car, and fell into the chill, leather seat. My dampened spirits were promptly joined by a dampened posterior. It might as well have been raining for the last half hour. Shivering and miserable, I put the top up, and coasted down the narrow, rocky lane to the house.

The first sight to greet me was an untethered trailer parked beside the barn, its door open. Humber's. This explained the gleam in Gus Potter's eye. It also explained why they hadn't come back for a drink.

He came sauntering out of the front door of my house, looking perfectly at home.

"Are you out of your mind?" I demanded furiously. "What do you *mean,* bringing that thing here?"

He strolled across the terrace, holding a half-eaten pear, his gray eyes imperturbable.

"Have we got to play games, like teenagers, Hilary?"

"Did you possibly think I would allow such a thing?" I screamed.

"You women are all alike," he said, wearily biting into the pear. "I thought there was a slight possibility that you might be different. But the more sophisticated, the same difference. OK, honey, let's analyze the situation. What did you go to Center City for, the ride?"

"It's none of your damned business."

He shrugged, losing a trace of his equanimity. "All right. But, for God's sake, you went up to give Hathaway his heave-ho. It was very decent of you, too, considering it's a hell of a long ride."

"TAKE YOUR HANDS OFF ME."

He spun the pear into the grass. "Anything you say. Let me fix you a bite to eat, and then why not go right to bed? You look fagged. I'll clean up the dishes, and then you won't hear a peep out of me."

"Take yourself and that damned trailer out of my yard. RIGHT NOW."

"Oh my God, Hilary, tonight? Aren't you being a little bit unreasonable? What are you concerned about, dear, your good name? After having your wide-open fling with a married man, and scion of the local druggist to boot! Come on, at least be reasonable. You're worn out, you've put in a hell of a day; tomorrow if you say the word, I'll move."

"You'll move tonight."

"All right, all right, calm down."

"You can either move that thing, or I'll call the sheriff to do it for you."

He lifted his eyebrows, stuck his hands in his trouser pockets, and stared at me. "Well, well, so we've had a complete change of heart!"

"Did I give you any earthly reason to presume that you were welcome to move down here, bag and baggage?"

"Well," he said affably, rocking back on his heels, "as long as I'm here, why don't we let things ride."

"Because I will not have it!" I shouted. "Can't you understand plain English? Take your damned trailer, and get *out!*"

His face lost some of its arrogance. In fact, he looked like a brash boy who has been slapped.

"All right, I will. But I figured you as an adult woman living an adult life."

"I am an adult woman living in a small, provincially minded community," I said, getting a grip on myself. "That apparently hadn't occurred to you. I do not exist in a vacuum; perhaps you do. I don't deny living my life as I see fit, but that includes a certain amount of responsibility, which you don't seem to recognize."

"Oh sure," he sneered, "the opposite of pomp and circumstance is slop and happenchance!"

Perhaps because I was so near utter exhaustion, and because the whole thing suddenly seemed hardly worth all the noise, I laughed.

Then, mistakenly trying to alleviate an intolerable situation, I said, "There's another kind of responsibility that apparently doesn't concern you either. Painting a prettied-up picture of the Potters' house isn't a job for someone seriously concerned with painting."

Now he was the one to be enraged. Thrusting his face close, he said venomously, "You're pretty damn patronizing, aren't you? Let me tell you something you don't seem to realize: You and that buck who was here yesterday are sterile, *sterile*. Mouthing a lot of arty hogwash about ideas and motivations and visual elusiveness. What the hell is visual elusiveness? Now you see it, now you don't? Let's go back to the Potters. They're the people who make money, they spend money, they raise children, they build houses, and they buy paintings! They're middle-class tradesmen, you say. What's wrong with that? Sure, they probably don't know what visual elusiveness is. Or what Cezanne was trying to get at. Who does? Sure, I could paint differently if I wanted to. What the hell, I'm earning a living, I'm giving the public what it wants. What are you giving it, Hilary? Go ahead, think hard! You gave it plenty to talk about when you latched on to Hathaway, didn't you? And now you've washed it up because you got damn well tired of him; you got a sudden acute attack of responsibility to the community. Bull! When you left here you were ripe to come back and sleep with me tonight. All right, you've changed your mind. But don't give me this other crap."

"Get the hell out of here," I said. "I had no intention of sleeping with you. Just go, that's all."

But there was no stopping the bitter bile that spewed out of him.

"I've met a lot of women like you, Hilary. You're the type who loves to kid themselves. Telling me how great and wonderful it is to be free and unhampered, to be pounding around the country in a trailer, without an inch to call my own. My God! Listen to me just one minute, I want to straighten you out, Mrs. Wister!" His face was twisted with fury. In the grip of his private demons, he looked a madman.

"You don't envy me, Hilary, or anybody else. You don't envy my being free to come and go. You've got just exactly what you want, you know that? A fancy setup! Your flower gardens to weed, and your goddamn cocktail parties to go to, your goddamn fancy studio decked out with a lot of paraphernalia you don't need and probably never use, where you and your friends can sit and get drunk and talk about art.

"You're the type that's always playing around—playing around with the idea of how nice it would be to ram around the country in a trailer—only you make damn sure you won't have to first! My God! Playing around with one of the natives too, as long as *you* score the game, and call the moves, and can keep everything nice and sophisticated, if that's what you want to call it. Do you know what I think, Hilary? I think you're a goddamn liar!"

This was retribution, with a vengeance, this livid, agonized face spitting hate.

It was impossible not to see the hysteria underneath, fired by rejection and criticism. He was a man driven to excesses of compensation—for what? Sometime lack of love, of caresses, of a conventional home, of a child's normal ability to cope?

"Humber," I said, with no anger left, only an intense desire to be forever rid of him, "when I said I envied you, that I envied your not being saddled with a home and its responsibilities, your being free to come and go as you pleased, and where you pleased, I couldn't have meant it more."

He turned, his face calmer, and stared at the house. I stared at it too, as though mesmerized: its good old New England lines softening in the twilight, the terrace that Spence and I had built brick by brick, the heavy-hanging trellis of Concord grapes. Without a word, he turned slowly and stared at the barn, stained red, with the cock vane high on the peak, then across the shaggy field of hay at Spencer's studio up the path amongst the tall spruces.

Spence and I both loved that tangled, golden, unkempt field. We never allowed it to be cut.

Humber had recovered himself. He smiled, rubbing his forehead. "God, what a catfight!"

I thought briefly that he must be cold in his khaki shorts, with the damp, foggy chill sweeping in off the Atlantic.

"You'd really like to be rid of it, Hilary?" he inquired pleasantly. "You feel it's a burden, having a house like that?" His heavy shoulders bulked against the fading sky; his eyes were obscured.

With enormous relief that the battle was over, I said, "I envy you your freedom, Chauncey."

He took an easy, lithe stride to the edge of the field and leaned down. A rosy blossom of flame grew under his hand, leaped up, spread, and began to race through the grass like a thirsty fiend.

"That should do it!" he said over his shoulder with a grin.

"YOU FOOL, FOOL. PUT IT OUT!" I screamed.

The barn was illumined. The Point was abruptly torn from its dark pool of twilight into a nightmarish, flickering light.

I raced into the house for the Indian pump which Spencer always kept filled beside the pantry door.

"You *are* a liar, then?" he said, as I came staggering down the steps toward him. "You don't want to be rid of it, after all!"

"Take the pump, Humber, put it out, yes, *any*thing. My God, *quick*!"

He wrenched it out of my hands, and swung it to his shoulders. With a quick look at my face, he turned and ran heavily after the crackling, voracious, spreading pillars of flame.

He was adept, and moved rapidly, pumping with all the strength of his powerful arms, but it was one man against a raging monster.

Panic unhanded me, and I stood there like a stunned idiot. His sharp barks brought me to my senses.

"A pail of water, quick. Wet a broom. GODDAMN IT, get your garden hose, and soak the barn."

I stumbled across the blackened stubble, between rings of wicked fire, feverishly refilling the empty pump while he flailed savagely with the broom, hauling the garden hose to its scant length to send a feeble spray against the shining barn.

Gasping, choking, weak-kneed, singed, and terrified, abjectly, wholly in the grip of terror.

"HERE! HERE WITH YOUR BROOM. MORE WATER—WATER!"

Minutes, hours, an eternity later, a car came speeding down the lane, spewing loose rocks from its tires.

Carver Peck jumped out, wasting no time on greetings, and hoisted an Indian pump to his shoulders. I wanted to fall on his neck, and die of gratitude.

"Saw it across the bay," he yelled, and was off, waving at Humber. "Got to get in front. I'll take this side."

Carver might be given to drink, to occasional pomposity, certainly to raucously bad jokes, but there wasn't a man in the world I would have welcomed more at that moment.

I was suddenly blind, from the smoke, from hysteria, perhaps from tears.

Another car jolted onto the lawn, and another, filled with men. Alfeus was there, calmly handing out pumps, and instructions. "Fill up with the hose, boys. Fan out."

He gave me a reassuring smile. "You had to pick my wife's birthday to celebrate on. It's a hell of a note!"

The night became a jumbled nightmare—voices, glare, pounding feet, slamming doors, openmouthed spectators trooping across the terrace (Plus and Minus peering from their Cadillac, with the Pearls, and Gus Junior), Joe racing by with a slopping pail in each hand.

Carver had assumed command, as by some natural force. His round, red face, his bulky, hoarse-voiced figure was everywhere. "Ted, get a bucket brigade to the shore. Joe, out there to Humber with that water, boy, on the double."

He snapped at me hastily, "Keep it up, keep it up, old girl."

Ted Hill, Angel, Ken, Junior, the Kings, all sweating, grinning, efficient, formed a chain to the seawall. How I loved them, *loved* them, every one. I had no idea where all the pails came from, only thanked God they were there. No one of them could have worked harder, or more willingly, if it had been their own hearthside threatened.

Dot-Fran appeared beside me. Her face was rosy in the glare of firelight. I suppose mine was the same.

"Oh, this is awful, Hilly. How did it ever start?"

"Oh God!" I hugged her hard. Her body felt frail in its slenderness, but with its own tensile strength. "Hold me up a minute, darling, will you?"

"This is awful," she repeated, her arm supporting me firmly.

But there was no time to stand there, savoring the sweetness of our reunion. Even my futile broom-wielding was something. She picked up another, and we worked rapidly side by side toward the barn where Mrs. King, majestic and big-bosomed, protected a strip along the foundation, moving with amazing speed. God bless her.

Abruptly, the gentle touch of wind from the water lifted, and veered.

"THE STUDIO, BOYS. WATCH THE STUDIO!"

But we were powerless against that sudden freakish air current. A spruce tree ignited with a roar, cascading sparks shot into the air. Spencer's studio was directly in the wind's path. It was doomed, though the men fought fiercely to save it.

I evaded the Potters, grouped with their guests on the edge of the terrace, and crept into the shadow of the grapevine, wordless, and sick, grimy, drenched with sweat, and exhausted to the point of collapse.

The studio put on a good show. It burned fiercely and quickly. First the windows belched smoke, with breaking glass tinkling delicately; a thread of flame ran along the edge of the roof, then with steady, inexorable, white haste the sturdy walls turned paper-thin; for a moment it stood like a rosy, breathing ghost against the night, then it became a smouldering, smoking heap of debris.

The flames leaped from spruce to spruce surrounding it, like a ghastly series of giant torches. The sound of their burning will never leave me. Spencer would forgive the trees less than the building.

Hysterically I found myself promising, *I'll build you another studio, Spence, with better light, more space . . .*

Build him another? You'll build him another? The heartless vis-à-vis in my brain mocked. Oh, by all means. Go to your cast-off Apollo for a bank loan to rebuild your estranged husband's studio!

It was after midnight when the last spark was out, save for the glowing bed of coals that had been the studio's foundation.

The crowd drifted away, leaving a littered yard and trampled flower beds. What did it matter? The house, the Point itself was safe. I grew hoarse at my inadequate attempts to say thank-you.

Carver was the last to leave, as he had been the first to come. "Rum go, losing the studio," he mumbled, mopping his tired face. "Wish we could have saved it for you, Hilly."

I threw both arms around him. "Oh God, Carver, I can't possibly thank you."

"Hey!" he grunted. "Just helping out a neighbor, least a feller can do."

He jerked a thumb at Humber, slowly crossing the lawn toward us. "Stout feller. Worked like a madman. Glad we had him on our side."

The lights of his car disappeared up the lane. The quiet descent of darkness was unreal. There were scattered lights inside the house, but on the lawn the chill, early-morning darkness was soft and enveloping.

The great, desolate patch of field was clearly defined, with its acrid, choking smell overlaying the salty sea air. Beyond the barn, the barren skeletons of the spruces stood tall and forlorn against the eastern sky.

Humber dropped the tank to the ground with a grunt. His face was grotesque with dirt, and weariness.

"Sit down before you fall down. Here's a cigarette."

We sat for a while in silence. The long rote of the tide sucked in and out; birds, awakened by false light, called from the woods, and a single, sustained note answered from somewhere in the grapevines.

"I'll never forgive myself for this, Hilary. I must have gone crazy."

"Thank God we finally got it out, that's all."

We sat close together, too tired for words or recrimination, too tired to move.

"You're a damn game woman." His voice shook.

"Thanks, Humber," I said. "You're pretty game yourself, when the chips are down."

"I don't suppose . . . we couldn't go on from here, Hilary?"

"No, it's a dead end street, Chauncey."

"And we're sure at the end of it," he said, with a wan laugh. "I wouldn't blame you if you turned me in, you know."

"Don't be an utter damn fool." I touched his cheek. There was no equivocation between us.

He sat inert, his head bowed. When he stirred, he reached for my hand, and pressed his forehead against it for a long moment, then he rose with a groan.

"I'll go hook up the trailer, and get the hell out. Could . . . could I drop you a line now and then, Hilary?"

"Write to me, Humber, of course, write to me. But don't go until morning—I guess it is morning. Don't go until you've had some sleep."

We stood there facing each other, two blackened, sweaty apparitions. It was one of those rare moments when two people, barriers down, feel utterly, painfully close to one another.

"Where will you go?"

"Oh, God, west, I guess. Arizona, or Mexico."

I put my arms around him, and we embraced wordlessly, in a strange, mutual resignation.

I turned to go in. "Surely let me hear from you . . . "

"I'll write, Hilary."

In the morning, when I woke at last, stiff and aching in every joint, the car, trailer, and Chauncey Humber were gone.

But I was too tired for sleep when we parted. Warm milk and Nembutals had no effect.

I wandered about the studio, unlighted except from the hall, watching the sky over the dark ocean, standing outside in the cold morning until I was thoroughly chilled, then restlessly closing the doors to wander about the room again.

It wasn't a matter of reliving the day's and evening's events; I had no stomach for that, nor enough composure to bring order to anything, least of all my thoughts.

But perhaps some such process was at work, making some sort of subliminal evaluation. How instinctual is a human being in times of stress, how motivated by the subsurface of his mind?

At three-thirty, I hobbled downstairs to the telephone, and dialed the long distance operator. As she dialed the number, the faraway, insistent rings breaking the quiet of a sleeping house stirred me with a strange, dazed disbelief.

Then Spencer's sleepy, irritated voice. "Hello? Hello?"

"Spence."

"Hilary! What in the hell's the matter? Are you all right?"

"Spence, I want you to come back."

There was silence. The wires hummed, an insect drummed against the window screen. For a horrid moment, a sour phlegm of fear rose in my throat, and I felt that I should vomit.

"Are you tight, Hilary?"

"No, no, I'm not tight. Come back, Spencer, please come back. Take me away somewhere. Oh God, I need a change."

He laughed, and yawned. "Did you get my letter today?"

An enormous, overpowering wave of relief swept over me. I sank back against the chair, and felt the clammy touch of the telephone against my cheek as unbearably sweet. A slow, delicious, slumbrous lassitude invaded my aching fibers.

"Of course I got it. Don't be so damned evasive, darling. See here, if you've got someone on the string, I'll kill the bitch."

"It's the middle of the night, for God's sake. I was sound asleep."

"It's three-thirty in the morning, you ass. When will you come?"

He laughed again, sounding remarkably good-humored considering the hour. "It'll take me a day or two to get straightened out here, Puss, get my duds packed and the house in order. What do you mean, take you somewhere? What's the matter with the Cove?"

"I'm sick of it. It's not the same anymore."

"What is?" he said, through another yawn. I could see him dangling one slipper, legs crossed, eyebrows raised, clutching his robe over his knees against the damn cold.

"Well, I'm damned glad about this, you know. It's about time you got some sense."

"Day after tomorrow, Spence?"

"We'll see. I'll ring you."

"All right, darling, I'm going to bed—I'm dead. But don't dawdle around there all week."

"Hell, no," he said. "Take a pill now, Puss, so you can go to sleep."

The Town

Each fall, when the leaves turn on the maples and elms and beeches, seems more beautiful than the last. Even sunless days have their own dulled radiance.

The summer places are closed, and the town takes off its girdle and feels comfortable again, and has a baked bean supper to raise money for a new cemetery gate.

The Woman's Society for Christian Service bakes the beans, and makes the salads, and sets the long tables in the community hall, and not one of the two hundred and thirty-four people who attend have had a cocktail beforehand. There are lemon, chocolate, apple, and mince pies, the mince made with venison mincemeat, angel food and sponge cakes, and one chocolate cake with coconut icing.

The high school boys play pool in the Masonic anteroom while they wait for the second table. By eight-thirty, the dishes are washed, and the hall is dark.

On sunny days, as warm as September but with a sharper definiteness of daylight, there are storm windows to wash, and reputty, gardens to be stripped of frostbitten pea vines, and the wilted stalks of corn. There are apples to gather, unless they are left to drop soundlessly into the thick grass, a toll for deer and porcupine.

On Halloween, the Woman's Club gives a children's party. But the drugstore, the Post Office, and Harvey's Grocery have their windows soaped all the same, and the blue and white telephone booth at the corner of Hamburger Heaven is tipped over on its side.

In Jericho, a gang of boys ride through town spattering houses with red paint.

The next day, hurricane warnings go up for the entire Eastern Seaboard.

In the Post Office, at the counter in Hamburger Heaven, in a neighbor's kitchen sharing a midmorning cup of coffee, everyone speaks of one topic with growing interest: the coming storm.

It comes creeping slowly out of the Caribbean, up along the coast of Florida. Twenty-four hours pass. In North Carolina, millions of dollars are lost in crops, resort hotels are destroyed, fishing boats lost.

Everyone in Contentment Cove is listening to the menacing radio newscasts, watching the television pictures of windblown destruction a thousand miles away.

"I hope it wears out before it gets way up here!"

Hatteras. Atlantic City.

A slow, relentless monster is striding up the coast.

It reaches New York City, flooding streets, disrupting schedules. Ninety-mile gales howl off the coast, raising thunderous seas.

Due to hit Boston by nine tonight.

Center City at eleven-thirty.

Storm warnings, ladies and gentlemen, are up all over New England, fishing craft, ships at sea. Board exposed windows, secure aerials, stay indoors, and off the roads.

As long as daylight lasts, cars wind along the shore road to Bluff Rocks where surf is beginning to fly. Lobstermen are busy putting extra anchors to their boats. Two deep-sea draggers, out of Gloucester, tie up at the wharf to wait out the storm.

Excitement grows! The stores sell out of milk, bread, canned dog food, flashlight batteries.

Mile by inexorable mile, as the day darkens, the storm creeps closer. The wind increases, rain begins to fall. The Inner Harbor turns slate gray, hostile, and the slim, white boats turn taut faces south.

Contentment Cove is ready, still following the reports, glad not to be a lonely farmhouse atop a hill, but to have neighbors with whom to share the latest bulletin, from whom to borrow a ladder to secure an upper window.

By nine, the rain and wind have settled into a howling storm.

A tree is down, blocking the road, near the Coast Guard Station.

No one tries to sleep. Who could sleep, with the roar of the wind, the thunderous rote of the sea, the rattle of loose shutters, the lash of rain?

From opposite sides of the Inner Harbor, headlights pierce the driving rain, spotlighting the tossing boats, and a lone human shape desperately at work on a lobster storage car. A whole season's work goes if the car blows adrift.

Men, women, children are abroad, along the seething harbor, huddling in the pelting rain, running about on heavy-booted feet, waving erratic lights.

At the sandbar, the flooding tide sweeps the macadam road, retreats, sweeps, retreats, leaving a wake of debris, pebbles, seaweed, sand.

A car hesitates on the town side, catching the rampaging tide in the beam of its lights, waits, waits, and then darts suddenly forward and across on the sea's retreat, gunning its motor, pebbles and sticks crunching wildly. Dr. Hammard is on emergency call, with one of the Kings driving his new Dodge.

By ten, the electricity fails; the telephone lines are dead by eleven. So, at last, undressing by flashlight, and by feel, the Cove gives over the night to wind and rain.

During the dark, wild hours of morning, the tide turns. The storm has passed the peak of its ferocity.

Very gradually the wind abates, though furious gusts continue after daylight. The sky clears, the rain ceases.

In bright morning sunlight, with the last tattered clouds scudding overhead, the damages are assessed. Two skiffs have been lost, the Kings' big birch is down, several lobster boats damaged. The float at the Island Yacht Club has been smashed, and shingles blown from many of the cottages. Streets and highways for miles are littered with limbs and leaves.

This year's big blow is over.

PART III

Mina

MINA said:

It was one of those days when nothing could go right. From the very beginning to the end. I imagine we all have experienced such as that, but I hope and pray that that one will be the last of its kind that I shall be called upon to undergo.

To start with, Eddie Chubb displayed no intention of getting up, making the third day in a row. It wasn't the meal trays or the constant running up and down stairs for some or other member of the household that I minded, for I did not. As long as a person is a guest in my house I want and expect him to be made as comfortable as possible. If I had considered him to be a sick man, Dr. Hammard would have been called immediately. But as it turned out, fortunately for all concerned, all he had was a chill, and in my opinion, after two days in bed he was as well able to get up as the rest of us.

When a person is at home under his own roof, what he does is his own affair, but I always supposed that when you were visiting under someone else's, you endeavored to make as little trouble and upset as possible. I guess that just shows how outdated and old-fashioned my ideas are!

But I say again that it was not the extra work that I minded in the slightest; it was the fact that I could not rely on his word. I myself am a person who believes in doing as they say they will do.

The night before, with his own lips, Eddie assured me that he would get up the next morning, as good as new. Otherwise, I should never have invited guests in for cocktails.

"Has Baldy taken root in there?" Gus asked while he was shaving. Our master bedroom has its own connecting bath. "Are we going to have him for the rest of the summer?"

"Kindly remember the fact that he is an invited guest under your roof, Gus Potter," I said. "That is no way for you to speak. But what I do *not* understand is his telling me one thing last night, which I depended upon, naturally, and went ahead with plans which I would not have made otherwise, and now he shows no inclination to be a man of his word."

"What would he want to get up for when he has two women waiting on him hand and foot? If you were both thirty years younger now!"

"Don't shout, Gus. The walls have ears."

"You know as well as I do, Mina, that he's staying in bed because he hasn't got the nerve to show his face after that lousy stunt he pulled down at Dotty's."

It is useless to pretend that it doesn't wear me out to entertain, as much as I always look forward to it. My nerves had been completely on edge since Eddie woke us at six-thirty in the morning trying to let himself in, when we had all supposed him upstairs peacefully sleeping.

It was hard to understand how such a totally uncalled-for occurrence ever took place. His appearance that morning when he arrived home was shocking beyond words. It seemed that he had awakened very early, before daylight, and had decided to go out for a long walk. In the drenching rain! Everyone to his own taste, I'm sure.

He walked clear into the village, a distance of one and seven-tenths miles, and if he had only let it go at that, all would have been well, outside of a good wetting, but having got there, he went on to the Hathaway house. He admitted himself that it was a strange thing for him to do.

Of course the real reason behind it was the way he drank all evening long, one highball after another. When Gus or I didn't hurry to refill his glass—we scarcely ever have anything ourselves after dinner, and don't think it at all necessary, especially after so many cocktails—he simply got up and helped himself. Which we of course didn't mind; (we like our guests to make themselves at home), but I did feel like reminding him that it wasn't water he was pouring out so freely.

As for his reception from Dot-Fran, it was no less than he deserved, having the door slammed in his face. Appearing there at four or five in the morning to wake her out of a sound sleep, with her father in his condition too, with a bad heart, and himself resembling a tramp in the bargain, which he certainly did.

However, the fact that he *was* a guest of ours, and was soaked to the skin, and battered and bruised from having fallen down and heaven knows what else, might have been expected to help her stretch a point in his behalf, knowing from all past experience what a dear, understanding child she was.

But if we can be said to have learned anything in life, it is that many times things do not turn out as one would normally wish and expect.

What hurt me most, by far, was Dot-Fran's own hostile attitude toward me when I tried to discuss it with her. She was almost sullen, before Hilary, and answered me very shortly, which was a side of her nature completely unknown. The second time, fortunately, I found her alone.

"My dear," I said, "you had no need to be so short with me yesterday morning. I want you to know that Gus and I are every bit as shocked by Eddie's strange behavior as you are. I do hope dear Mr. Hathaway wasn't startled or upset . . ."

"He doesn't know anything about it." Her face was flushed.

"Oh, I'm so glad he wasn't disturbed, Dot-Fran. That is *such* a relief. So we can relax again, can't we? Eddie is going to be perfectly all right. He was simply chilled, that was all."

She looked straight at me, in such a peculiar way, that I added—if only I hadn't—"We *are* glad, in spite of everything, that it was only a chill, aren't we?"

"It doesn't matter to me, Mrs. Potter."

"Oh, come now, my dear . . ."

"I WISH I HAD CALLED THE POLICE!" she said.

Those were her very words. I WISH I HAD CALLED THE POLICE. I couldn't believe my ears. I simply had to turn and leave her without another word. The world might as well have been tumbling around my feet as to hear such a statement from our own beloved Dot-Fran.

Couldn't you imagine the headline in the weekly paper? "A Guest of the Potters Arrested for Molesting a Young Girl," or "Drunk and Disorderly Guest of the Gus Potters Arrested for Disturbing Peace."

What a ludicrous, horrid position we should have been placed in. It made me positively sick, so sick and disturbed that I couldn't bring myself to repeat it to Gus.

But I began to wonder, for the very first time, if Eddie would ever have done such a strange thing without *some* provocation. After all, he was an educated professor, and his family was of the best.

I really blamed Hilary in some respects, I must say I did, for the way she exposed Dotty to all her own set, so much older and all of them very sophisticated, to put a *good* face on it (sometimes I wonder if that kind of behavior *was* what is generally regarded as being sophisticated, and if so I'm glad Gus and I were never educated enough or drinky enough to become so), whereas Dot-Fran herself was a simple village girl.

Well, at any rate, 'nuff said. I was as sick at heart as I could be, and I really felt it my duty to go attempt to make things right with Mr. Hathaway, though when I should have an opportunity, with a houseful of guests, was in the lap of the gods.

When Eddie Chubb arrived back at our house that morning, you could have wrung water out of every article of clothing he wore. He had managed to fall into a ditch, or so he said, and tear his trousers, and his face was as gray and pasty as death.

I may add that after this experience, I don't have to rely on anyone else's opinion to inform me about learned professors, and what they are capable of! Live and learn, Mina!

"The fact remains, Gus," I said, "that little as I condone the man, and I may say it is all I can do to keep from expressing my entire feelings along that line to Greta Van Buran Chubb Pearl, the fact remains, whether *you* like it or not, that he may have had *some* slight encouragement."

"A bellyful of our liquor was all the encouragement he needed."

"Don't be coarse, Gus; you can never bear to face up to reality, when you don't agree with it. That happens to be one of your great troubles."

"Just let me ask you this, Mina—what would a good-looking girl like her want with that bald, old goat? She was probably just polite. I never see her when she wasn't. So he got drunk, and got some fancy ideas, and went sneaking off down there to see her. God knows where else he went! One thing's for sure, he looked like hell when he came dragging back here with his tail in the mud!"

Greta came out to the kitchen where I was getting breakfast, already dressed and made up like a fashion plate. The sun was pouring in, and I had thrown all the doors open, it was such a lovely, warm, heavenly morning.

Having already heard her in Eddie's room, I said, "And how is Eddie this beautiful morning? Isn't he planning to come down for breakfast? As he promised? It's nearly ready."

"Darling, he's too awful! I hate him, I do, truly. But the man claims he's still a perfect mass of bruises, from that dreadful fall into that frightful ditch. Isn't it terribly *dange*rous to leave places like that for innocent people to endanger their lives? He says all he asks for in this life is some of your good coffee, and buttered toast. Really, he's beyond words, Mina. Stamping around in the rain trying to wake up pretty girls! But the poor dear *is* perfectly sunk, he's so ashamed, and he *knows* he's being this perfect bore about staying in bed . . . "

"My dear, not at all, if he *feels* that badly. I'm just so afraid his whole visit will be spoiled, and it's such a perfect day. Do run out and pick us some posies for the breakfast table. All will be ready in ten minutes."

While she was outside, I took the opportunity of having a word with Mr. Eddie Chubb myself. He looked surprised when I came tiptoeing in with his coffee, and there was certainly no need of tiptoeing. He was sitting up in bed, wide awake and bright as you please, reading Gus's last issue of *True Magazine*. And I had carefully put the *National Geographic* on his bed table, thinking it was the only reading matter we possessed deep enough for a professor.

"Why, Mina! This is sweet of my hostess. I expected the ex-Mrs. Chubb."

"You lazy boy, lying there in bed, being waited on. Look at the lovely sunshine. I declare I ought to pull those covers right off!"

"Mina, my sweet, if you only knew how baffled and disgruntled I feel. This has been the most severe traumatic experience!"

He looked awful, with great pouches under his eyes, but if he felt well enough to joke like that, it made me all the more certain that he was well enough to get up.

"Eddie, I'm sure I don't know what you're talking about. As far as I myself am concerned, it's past and forgotten. What you need now is to get up and have a nice long sunbath down on the shore. Don't forget about the little party of friends we have invited in for this afternoon!"

"Oh my God!"

I went over and adjusted his window shades, determined to hold my tongue. After all, he was my guest and not at all well.

"Mina, darling, has . . . er . . . has Miss Hathaway mentioned anything to you?"

"Yes, we've discussed it, Eddie," I said. "As a matter of fact, I mentioned it to her. We were all badly frightened here at the house, you know, which was hardly to be wondered at, considering the state you were in. Now wouldn't it have been nice if you had come down with double pneumonia! Yes, Dot-Fran was still very wrought-up. She was rather rude to me, in fact."

"Brrrr," he said, shivering, "she's got a cold eye for such a beauty. Rude, eh? She gave me a rebuff I'll never get over, Mina. No fool like an old fool!"

"I simply said that considering the way it was raining that morning—"

"That wasn't rain, the sky was falling! Is . . . er . . . she coming this afternoon?"

I shook my finger at him. "What a silly boy you are! Give me credit for more savoir faire than *that*, for goodness' sake! No, this will be the older crowd, the Pecks, of course, the Spindles, Mrs. Wister and her friend . . . "

"It was a ghastly traumatic experience," he said again, smoothing the cover over his knee. "At *my* age. I could cry, Mina, I really could. How shall I ever be able to apologize? To you, and to her?"

"Why, just say you're sorry if that's the way you feel," I said, handing him his coffee. "I'm sure that's what I myself would do. And I'm sure it would be accepted in the spirit it was intended. I guess we're all of us human once in a while; if we weren't this would be a different old world, wouldn't it!"

He laughed heartily, which made me doubly certain he was perfectly able to get up. "Ah, Mina, sweet, 'To err is human, to forgive, divine.' "

"All you need is to get up out of that horrid bed."

"It's a very comfortable bed in a very gracious house."

He could express himself so well, in such a graceful way, that it made his other failings seem all the more out of character, and peculiar in one of his background and education. His wanting to apologize made me feel a good deal friendlier toward him.

At the door, I said, "Don't bother to get dressed, just come down in your robe. Greta's outside already. Upsy-daisy, now!"

But he didn't upsy-daisy one inch. He stuck to that bed as though he was planted.

So, of course, Greta took him up a tray, with a single rose on it that she had just picked. I expected Gus to make one of his typical, crude remarks when he saw that rose, but he only said, "The Professor's got himself a bed of roses, Greta—what's he want with that one!"

After Eddie was taken his tray, the rest of us finally assembled at the kitchen table for breakfast. I really thoroughly enjoyed serving breakfast in my kitchen. There was a lovely view of the water, and my red-checked tablecloth and napkins, only twenty-nine, ninety-five, from Hammacher Schlemmer, looked just like a setting in *House and Garden.*

"Where'd you leave that last *True*, Dad?" Gus Junior asked his father, as soon as we were all seated. "I spent an hour hunting for it last night."

"Don't ask me. You seen it, Mina?"

Greta said, "Darling, if it has wild beasts and naked men on the cover, I'm afraid I took it in to Eddie. How perfectly ghastly when you wanted it so much, child? I'll run right up for it after breakfast."

"Don't worry about it, he'll live," Gus said. "How'd you sleep, Pearl?"

"Pearl sleeps like a baby, don't you, lover?"

George Pearl was one of the quietest men I have ever known, bar none. That is not to say that he wasn't friendly and pleasant, when spoken to, but his natural inclination seemed to be to take the backseat. He seemed happy to doze in the sun most of the time with a cigar in his mouth.

He was perfectly killing one night, though, after we had all had several martinis. He came stumbling out to the kitchen, while I was doing my addled best to get our dinner on the table—martinis *do* go to my head—and, of all things, fumbled around trying to get hold of my hand.

"George! For heaven's sake!" I said. "You'd better clean your glasses, they're all steamed up from these carrots. What in the world would Greta think if she caught you out here behaving in this manner!"

"God bless you, dear, terribly in love with my wife," he mumbled, falling off my kitchen stool, "marvelous woman, marvelous."

I tried to steer him toward the door, but he held on to me for dear life. He actually had tears in his eyes. It may have been steam.

"You go on in and sit down, George," I said, "that's a good boy. My goodness, we can't stand here in a loving embrace!"

"Great treat," he muttered, wiping his eyes, "can't begin to tell you, great treat to be here in your lovely little home, can't thank you and Gus enough . . . "

I presume that he meant it, because after they returned to New York he sent me a set of a dozen matched zippers in assorted sizes. I've never seen a set like it in any store anywhere.

Halfway through breakfast, we were interrupted by a long distance telephone call.

"It's the Center City Guarantee Trust, Gus," I called, laying down the receiver, "for you. Now what do you suppose they can be calling about?"

It was time for Della. She was always prompt, one reason that I was so happy with her. There was a strenuous day ahead; not only was there the house to clean and tidy up, but canapes to prepare for the afternoon cocktails, and another meal yet before that time. It was my plan to get everyone out of the house so that Della and I could have it all to ourselves, and make the work fly.

"Greta, dear, what are your plans for this morning?"

"Darling, I'm going out and settle myself in a quiet spot and just work away like a little beaver on every little, tiniest detail for the gala. I intend it to be a perfectly *howl*ing success. Oh, Mina, dear, it's such fun, such *fun*, planning this lark for these dear people. I want them to enjoy every minute of it. It will be something so new to their dear, old country ideas."

The thought of that fair, or gala, whatever it was going to be, hanging over my head, made me want to lie down and die, though I thought she was a grand, wonderful, darling sport to suggest it. But there had been so much going on the last several days. Greta possessed such an abundance of energy, really more than seemed quite normal.

"Greta, let me give you just a wee little hint of warning. Don't expect too much, dear, you know, from the villagers. Sometimes they're like children. You have to coax and tease, and even then . . ."

"Haw, haw!" George Pearl said.

With my nerves so frayed, that *haw, haw* of his, and the smell of his imported cigars made me want to scream. It didn't matter what the conversation happened to be touching on, or whether a remark was intended to be humorous or not, if George suddenly roused himself and felt it was time for him to contribute, he blew out a poisonous cloud of smoke and said, "Haw, haw."

"Darling, I *adore* the villagers, they're such angels, all of them," Greta said, raising her eyebrows in a way I did *not* like.

"Why, of course, naturally, I do *too,* but dear, you must remember that the standards are different here. Now where can Della be? She's *never* been late before."

Gus Junior pushed back his chair and stretched, and said, "Guess I'll run down for the mail. Excuse me, Mrs. Pearl, Mother."

"It isn't time yet, Gus Junior," I said, nipping that in the bud. "Wait and drive me down later, dear, like an angel."

I wanted a chance to find out how my son felt about what had happened. Men are so unpredictable, one never can foresee what reaction they will have. Gus and I were at swords' points, it seemed, simply because I tried to be objective.

I was every bit as attached to Dot-Fran Hathaway as he was, but that didn't mean that I couldn't try to be fair.

He was shouting into the telephone in the way he always did, as though everyone else was as deaf as he was getting to be. Right at that moment, I felt every bit of my age of sixty-six. I just wished I could leave them all right there in the kitchen, and go find a quiet corner where I could sit down by myself, and let the rest of the world go on about its business.

Della was late, the very morning when I needed her most; Gus was annoyed about some stupid mistake the bank had made; and Greta sat there facing me with that superior, snobbish smile, as though in three days she could tell me all about the town I had lived in for three years. But I realized that I mustn't allow myself to start finding fault with Greta, when I myself had invited her to come, and had planned and looked forward to her visit with such pleasure. It would lead to nothing but that old nervous indigestion of mine.

Gus Junior got up, looking sulky, and went into the living room and turned on the TV. But to go down to the village at that hour would have meant his hanging over the soda fountain for the entire morning.

The final straw was Eddie Chubb lying up there in my guest room bed. I did hope and pray he would muster enough strength to get up by afternoon. In the meantime Della and I would have to clean around him, and hope he would be able to entertain himself.

Gus slammed down the telephone and came stamping back to the table.

"Holy cripes, what do you know about this! Lascomb up there at the Guarantee Trust called to tell me something was wrong with my bank balance for the swimming pool account. The lousy guy wanted me to drive up there and straighten it out for them. You hear *that* one, Mina! That's one for the book. The bank gets screwed up and expects their customers to come dig them out of the hole! I said to him, 'You mean you expect me to drive to Center City on a morning like this, Tom, just because you got a lousy teller up there that can't add and subtract?' I said, 'I got a houseguest here, and we're going trout fishing, and you better come down here and go with us, and clean out your cobwebs!' That's a hot one, hey, Mina! Tom Lascomb won't hear the last of this in a hurry."

"Haw, haw, don't need to give me a thought," George Pearl said, blinking. "Business comes first, understand that very well."

Gus held out his cup for more coffee. I was glad he could see it in its humorous light. "Not anymore, George, old boy, I'm retired! Hell, you're my guest. You don't think I'm sucker enough to drive up there on account of a lousy mistake the bank's made? Look, I can tell them jokers to a penny where my accounts stand, but let 'em worry it out for themselves, that's *their* headache. I tell you, George, I didn't stay in the contracting business for thirty-odd years by overdrawing my bank balance. Let 'em worry it out, I'm no sucker. That pool account has got a three-thousand-dollar balance as of this minute, but I'm damned if Ted Hill's going to get his hands on it. That lad doesn't realize that I can tell the time of day in this construction game. And old Tom saying, 'It appears there's some discrepancy here, Gus; we wondered if you would have the kindness to help us clear it up.' 'A day like this?' I said to him. 'What's the matter with your adding machines!' I put old Tom up a tree!"

Greta and George appeared to find it very amusing. She was having her fourth cup of coffee, which meant that I was unable to get the dishes cleaned and into the dishwasher, without rudely getting up and leaving her. That was one of my faults, wanting to get whatever was to be done, *done*. If Della had only been on time, her arrival would have stirred us all up.

Greta never came down for breakfast without putting all her makeup on. I couldn't help a catty thought as to how she would look without all that mascara and eye shadow. I'm afraid I'm still old-fashioned enough to believe that when women try to compete right beside men in the business world, it robs them of some of their precious femininity.

"Isn't this priceless, Pearl?" she said, jabbing him with her fishing pole of a cigarette holder. "Whatever would *you* do, lover, if the Chase National called you before breakfast?"

"Haw, haw," George said, true to form. "Haw, haw, good joke, ducky."

"Darling," she said to Gus, "I simply adore the thought, don't you!"

As though Gus didn't know the Chase National as well as she did. Gus had a disposition that couldn't be pushed too far.

"No, can't say that I do, Greta."

I said soothingly, "I'm sure even a bank as large and famous as the Chase has been known to make errors. Everyone makes mistakes, no matter who they are. But it's so ridiculous that they should bother Gus about it, when he is so careful about his accounts."

"Come on, Pearl, I said we were going fishing, and damned if we won't!"

"Bring in some nice trout, and Della can fix them for lunch," I said, trying to sound bright and cheerful. I really couldn't understand the bank's making a mistake like that, and going to the length of calling us about it. It seemed a strange way to conduct their business. Anyone knowing Gus knew him to be the last man in the world ever to overdraw an account. He was too successful a businessman for that, running a big contracting business which he had sold for over one million and a half dollars. And now that he was retired, he was every bit as meticulous about his financial affairs, if not more so.

It seemed inconsiderate of Mr. Lascomb to expect him to give up an entire day to going to Center City, when the difficulty must have been caused by their own carelessness.

"Dear, wouldn't you like to go too?" I called to Gus Junior, who was sprawled on the sofa watching television. "Fishing, I mean?"

"And be eaten up by flies? No thanks."

Gus Junior had always been the possessor of a very sensitive skin.

But before the fishermen could get started, the Peterson boy, Joe, called at the front door, asking for a job at the swimming pool.

I was surprised at his tall, grown-up appearance standing there in the hall, as he didn't hesitate to step right in. Joe did not have a very savory reputation, and I was sorry to see that his eyes were just as shifty as ever.

Of course, there were circumstances one had to take into account. He came of a large family, and very likely there were times when there was precious little in the cupboard to eat, let alone furnish children with toys and attractive clothes.

For that reason Gus was an advocate of birth control. Mr. Peterson was certainly one of those men who just shouldn't be allowed to rear children like rabbits, with no possible chance of adequately providing for them, but that was usually the kind with large families.

As Hilary once said, though it certainly was no joking matter, "You can see how they spend their long winter evenings!"

Hilary was sincerely devoted to Joe's mother, and I must say Hilary was a very warmhearted friend when she saw fit to be. It is my belief that she helped the Petersons considerably financially.

But had I been as Hilary was, a lone woman living alone on that lonesome Point, I should have been apprehensive about Joe.

The way she made jokes, and gave him money, as I have often seen her do, keeping him at no distance whatever, which seemed unwise, especially considering who she was.

But Hilary was never one to concern herself with worries such as would occur to the rest of us everyday people.

I made a mental note to look over Gus Junior's clothes and see what I could take over to poor Mrs. Peterson. It's my belief in life that we should do all in our power to help those less fortunate than we are.

Gus was just coming downstairs in his new Abercrombie and Fitch waders, for which he had paid seventy-nine dollars and ninety-eight cents, made of pure Brazilian rubber, so much better than any of the cheaper imitations.

"Go see Ted Hill, boy, not me. Hill's the contractor on the job."

"I seen Ted. He said he wasn't hiring no more men."

I suppose every town, even Contentment Cove, has its bad boy. It made me uneasy, though naturally I concealed it, to watch him standing there shuffling his dirty feet over my carpet, and his eyes darting around over everything like a hummingbird. However, I consoled myself by thinking that probably the poor boy had never been inside a house such as ours before. It was only natural for him to be curious.

"Well, I'm sorry, son," Gus said, "you didn't make it around there soon enough. That's the way the cookie crumbles."

"Yeah, guess I was too late." He was watching the TV screen with his odd one-sided grin. "Old Dave Garroway. He's got a pretty good program."

He was a strange-looking boy, so tall and gangly, and yet with that sly twist to his face.

"OK, son," Gus said, with a smile, "that's the story. Better luck next time."

"Yeah, better luck next time. Say, Mr. Potter, you got a cigarette?"

"Hell no," Gus said. "I don't smoke the lousy things. Gus Junior, give the kid a cigarette, and he'll be on his way."

Greta and George were peeking through the dining-room door, but I didn't feel it necessary to perform introductions, so I said, "I'm sure you'll be able to find work elsewhere in town, Joe, if you just keep trying. We have to say goodbye now. It's a very busy morning for us."

When he had finally gone, I shooed them back into the kitchen. Greta had such violent enthusiasms, one never knew what peculiar thing might appeal to her next. I was beginning to have the dreadful suspicion that a lot of it was just plain attention-getting. But who was I to sit in judgment. She was a somewhat different person than I had previously supposed, from our acquaintance on the South American cruise. I could fully understand her success in her business career. I'm afraid she was a dominating and aggressive woman.

At last, as I was getting my breath from Joe's visit, Della arrived. Kenneth, her son, came in with her, carrying the basket of yeast rolls, and loaves, which she baked for us twice weekly.

"Well, Della, my dear, it's unusual for you to be late like this. I was afraid something had happened."

I observed Kenneth's ears turn red, as he set down the basket. It was reassuring for a young man of his age to retain a sense of duty and obligation, all too rare in our day and age. Kenneth had always made a good impression. He was quiet, and polite, as well as being an attractive boy.

"Oh, Kenny's dog had one of her fits," Della remarked in a rather offhand manner. "We had to see her through it before he would leave. I didn't think you'd mind a few minutes, especially where this was supposed to be the Admiral's day. I never get there before nine, they wouldn't be up."

I couldn't help the tiniest feeling of exasperation.

"Well, there's no need to waste time over whys and wherefores now that you're here. This is going to be a busy day—I just hope between us we can manage everything. There's cleaning and lunch, and then guests coming in for cocktails . . ."

"Oh, you got guests coming for cocktails?" she said, looking blank. I had begun to recognize that look, as fond as I was of Della. If she didn't feel like doing what you wished her to do, she simply pretended not to understand. "I thought you wanted me just the morning."

"Oh, my dear, no, I most certainly need you for the entire day. There are three houseguests here in the house, besides my son— surely you realize how much extra work . . . "

Gus interrupted us, hurrying in from the Caddie, which he left running in the driveway. I had thought that he and old skinny knees (why do some men insist on wearing shorts!) were safely out of the house and on their way.

"Mina, where's my cap?" he demanded.

"Why, in the car, dear, where you always keep it."

Gus owned a bright plaid cap, which he had bought in Scotland. He always wore it when driving the Caddie with the top down. I often said that he was as attached to that cap as he was to his wife! He kept it under the dashboard on a hook, which had been installed there for just that purpose, and consequently his cap was never taken out of the car.

"By God, it's gone, Mina! Now WHERE'S MY CAP?"

Kenneth and his mother exchanged glances. When they noted that I had observed them, Della giggled. "That boy did look comical, Mr. Potter . . ."

It was far from a laughing matter to us. Gus doted on that cap, and though I doubt if Della realized its value, being unaccustomed to imported goods, it was an expensive cap of the best Scottish wool, which we all know to be the very best there is.

Gus immediately grasped what had happened. "Did you meet Joe? Did that lousy kid have my cap on? He went right by the Caddie when he left. Hey, Della? Did that lousy kid steal my Scotch cap?"

She had her blank expression again. "My goodness, Mr. Potter, I'm sure I don't know one thing about it, only we did see Joe . . ."

"WAS HE WEARING MY CAP?"

She giggled. "If he wasn't a sight, Mr. Potter, sauntering along with that rainbow of yours on his head!"

"Where?" Gus snapped.

Another crisis. When I was so far from feeling myself to begin with, this seemed more than I could face.

Della's attitude seemed so strange, and unlike her, in view of the fact that an outright theft had been committed. It showed me that no matter how well you think yourself established in the village's good graces, let one of their own be accused, and you see that they're still *very* clannish.

"Where did you meet that lousy kid?"

Greta's theatrical, deep laugh came floating down from Eddie's room. I said a prayer that she would only stay there until we got this matter settled.

"He was headed back to town, Mr. Potter," Kenneth said, with a noncommittal stare exactly like his mother's. They might as well have been two wooden Indians.

I was very proud of Gus. He controlled his temper, deciding to make light of the whole sorry incident.

"Well, damned if I can spend the morning chasing him up, when I promised Pearl out there that I'd take him fishing," he said, giving Kenneth a friendly slap on the shoulder. "Tell you what, Ken, if you go get my cap back from that lousy kid, there's a couple of dollars easy money in it for you. It will have to be cleaned, and that's a damned nuisance right now when I wear it most, but we'll let the whole thing pass this time. Tell him to hand it over to you, and I won't make any trouble. But you can tell him that he had damn well better keep his dirty hands off my property hereafter, or he won't be so lucky."

I wanted to cry with relief. It was just the sort of small occurrence that can cause so much trouble. The important thing, really, was to get the cap back.

"Gee, Mr. Potter, I'd like to help you out, but I'm on my way to work over at the golf course, and I'm late now."

"Hell, it won't take you five minutes to catch up with him. You know where his hideouts are. Tell him that he's damn lucky I don't clap him up before the judge."

When Della had started with the vacuum cleaner, I stepped outside for a moment.

Greta was established in a lawn chair down by the water, wearing the big Mexican straw hat that she had bought in the gift shop over at the Inn.

It was a gorgeous, perfect, cloudless Contentment Cove day. How heavenly it would have been to stretch out on the chaise, and not feel a care in the world. But for me that was out of the question.

As the years went by, and how fast they went by, entertaining guests, and all that it entailed, such as the cocktail party that afternoon to prepare for, represented more and more effort.

Della's casualness about arriving so late was upsetting. I depended on being able to depend on Della. Using an animal as an excuse plainly showed that she knew where my soft spots were.

It was one of my disappointments that we didn't have a dog, or a cat, but Gus was against it, and I did agree with him that a pet would tie us down. So I tried to be content with taking our steak bones to Mike, the Kings' big boxer, and an occasional special tidbit to Simple Simon at the drugstore.

I did weaken once, and bring home a darling little green-eyed, orange puffball from the Coloniers, but it turned out badly. The dear little thing wasn't housebroken, and it ran about the house like a little tiger, sharpening its claws on the furniture, and nearly ruining every curtain in the house.

Gus and I are just alike in that we are perfectly silly about our house, having to have it always in apple-pie order, or we are miserable. The last straw came when Mittens, which I named him for his adorable double paws, upset a box of Gus's best Havanas from his bureau onto the floor, and Gus trampled over most of them before he discovered what had happened.

When I took Mittens back, Mrs. Colonier was sitting on the doorstep, with all his beautiful, fluffy-haired brothers and sisters tumbling over her lap, and in and out of the ramshackle barn, that looked as though it would topple if you blew at it.

"You bring the liddle one bek? She bozzer you?"

Mrs. Colonier was a striking woman, in her dark European way, with those flashing white teeth, and big brown eyes.

"My dear, I discovered she wasn't housebroken."

"Housebroke? Hell, she live all time in barn. Ah, look at liddle pansy face, Mama's got her bek now! The kids, they cry all day they find she is gone."

"If only I didn't make such a pet of whatever I have—but I can't seem to take them as casually as you do, Mrs. Colonier."

She laughed, and shooed them all off the step, and got up, looking at me in that dark, smiling, foreign way, that always disconcerts me because I wonder what in the world they can be thinking.

"Yeah? Well, like I say to Angel, you got somezing love, you got grief too. In dis house, plenty love, and plenty mess, too, hey! Plenty grief, like I say. All in lifetime, Miz Potter!"

Driving away, I couldn't help thinking what courage the woman had, living there in little more than a shack, with very few of the modern conveniences, rearing five small children. I suppose, though, viewed from her European standards, where poverty is an everyday thing, it might look altogether different to her, and at any rate, she must thank God she is here, rather than there, where she can at least have the advantages of the democratic way of life.

"The electricity's gone off," Della announced, opening the kitchen door. "My, it's nice out. Too nice for anyone to stay cooped up inside a house, a morning like this."

The day of all days when the electricity chose to fail.

"That may be all very well, dear, for those who can ... "

"That painter didn't stay around long, did he?" she said, lighting a cigarette.

Ordinarily, I enjoyed my chats with Della, hearing the village tidbits, but at that particular time my mind was too taken up.

"What painter, Della? To whom are you referring?"

"The one with the trailer. That was at Mrs. Wister's helping fight the fire. They say he left early this morning. Wasn't it a living miracle they ever saved that house and barn?"

"Yes, it certainly was. That was a *frightful* scare. You say Mr. Humber has gone? Left town, you mean?"

"He left early this morning, and he told somebody he was headed to Mexico."

"I can't believe it, Della. He told us only last night that he would paint a picture of this house."

I was so looking forward to having a painting of the house to hang over the mantel above the fireplace, one showing all the lilac, and the chestnut tree in bloom. Of course they had gone by, long since, but Mr. Humber had said he could use his imagination to that extent. It was the one Christmas present I had my heart set on.

"Only last night . . ."

"Maybe he figured it was getting too hot around here!" Della said, with a sly look.

I was scarcely in the mood to puzzle out obscure insinuations, so I said, "Well, dear, come in when you've finished your cigarette; we can at least get the canapes made," and I myself went in to call the Center City Power and Light Company.

The girl who answered the telephone rattled off an excuse about blasting, and road construction. "Power will only be interrupted for a short period, madam."

"Don't you think that it shows a lack of consideration for your customers, many of whom are stockholders, like myself," I said, trying not to sound impatient, or unreasonable. "I have never known this kind of thing to happen in any of the cities where I have resided."

"You are living in a rural area now, madam, not a city."

"Naturally I'm aware of where I am presently living."

There was no use arguing with a poor office girl, and taking out my spite on her, so I hung up, making a mental note to write the Center City Power and Light exactly what I thought of them.

On the spur of the moment, being already seated at the telephone, I decided to call Hilly.

"You can start mixing the cheese spread for the canapes," I said to Della, "until the powers that be decide to give us the advantages afforded by electricity again, for which I might say we pay as much here, if not more, than anywhere else in the country, and in return receive service such as this!"

I had had so little chance to talk to Hilly at the fire. We had all been terribly upset and concerned for her, and the exhausted way she looked. But when I managed to hold onto her long enough to ask her to come back with us for the night, she only shook her head and was off again.

"Hilly, you poor darling, I hardly expected you to be alive this morning. My dear, we felt so helpless. Isn't there anything you need? Isn't there some way we can help, even a teenie weenie *bit*?"

She surprised me by sounding just like herself.

"All's well that ends well, Mina!"

"But, my dear, we should so like . . ."

"Spence's studio was the only casualty. Thank God there was nothing in it. But it looks a wasteland hereabouts, and smells worse. I think I'll do a disappearing act, and let nature heal its wounds."

"You mean go away? Oh, Hilly, you *can't*, you mustn't, we should feel utterly lost without you."

"Oh, you'll bear up, dearie," she said, with her little bark of a laugh. "See you this afternoon. Five?"

"Try to make it four-thirty, dear. You know how Gus is about his meals. If he doesn't eat as usual, he's a bear! And Hilly, do bring your friend along!"

"Right you are," she said, and hung up.

That certainly didn't sound as though anyone had left town for Mexico. I had long since learned not to rely on hearsay. Probably he had only been moving his trailer to another location, and I was considerably relieved at *that*!

Artists may be different from the rest of us, and perhaps for that reason they have to be given the benefit of the doubt, in many cases, but grant all that, there were still times when I thought Hilary Wister, famous artist or not, deserved a good, sound spanking.

Judging by appearances, the Stanley Hathaway episode was over, which could only be a blessing for all concerned. I considered it one of the biggest mistakes of Hilly's life, but she was too headstrong a person to be guided by friendly advice, in any form.

Gus Junior had overhead them quarrelling at the party. A woman of Hilly's talents, and perception, should have realized from the beginning that Stanley, besides being a good deal younger, was not of her world, or upbringing, and as for him, I had very little patience with such as he, a married man and a father.

At eleven-thirty, Gus Junior drove me down for the mail.

On the way, I said, "Dear, perhaps I hadn't told you this before, but that nice Kenneth Hill, Della's son, who came in with her this morning, has been a beau of Dot-Fran's for some time."

"Yeah, I know. She had a date with him the other night, after Mrs. Wister's party." He still sounded sulky.

"Well, my dear, I just wanted you to be aware."

"I'm *aware*, Ma. What was Eddie up to yesterday morning, any-way?"

"I'm sure I'd like to know myself, Gus Junior. Though I can tell you he's very sorry and anxious to apologize."

"To her?"

"Yes, to Dot-Fran. He's very much upset, I'm glad to say. Of course, in my opinion, he hardly knew what he was doing all evening."

Gus Junior gave a short laugh. "He was stoned, all right. But a guy like him, to go to her house like that . . . maybe she isn't as innocent as she appears."

"Gus Junior!"

"All I'm saying is why would he . . ."

"Gus Junior, you know how your father and I have felt about Dot-Fran Hathaway. You know from my letters how deeply attached we've been. Oh, dear, really, I don't understand how such a thing happened, I just can't bring myself to understand how it ever came about."

"Don't get so wrought-up, Mother."

"How can I help being wrought-up!" I said, dabbing at my eyes. "Your father and I practically made her one of the family. Gus Junior, she was rude, really rude, yesterday, as well as defiant, and antagonistic. It was such a shock to have her speak to me in such a way, *that* is what really bothers me so, to have her change before my very eyes, and exhibit this foreign side . . . Surely *I'm* not to blame."

"You brought him here!"

Fortunately we had reached the drugstore, and I could get out of the car. If we had exchanged more words, I'm afraid both of us might have said things to later regret.

Of course it was true that I had invited Eddie to our home in Contentment Cove, and one could say otherwise the whole nasty occurrence never would have taken place, but it was unnerving, to say the least, to have my own son throw such a thing in my face, in that sullen tone, when only a moment before he had been the one to speak unfairly about her.

I failed to understand the young people of the present day and age, even when they were my flesh and blood. Both my husband and my son seemed ready to disagree and take the opposite view with every word I uttered concerning this miserable affair. But it was Dot-Fran's threatening me, which it amounted to, with the police, that I could not forget, nor forgive.

Though I've never been a fanciful person, it suddenly seemed that morning that some wheel in the natural harmony of life had slipped a cog, making everything in God's beautiful, logical universe a little out of whack, especially us lowly human beings.

Gus Junior had gone diving straight into the drugstore like a homing pigeon, so, striving to put on a cheerful face—I don't believe in advertising your troubles on a billboard—I went into the Post Office.

It was my day of all days, and no mistake. The only person in the Post Office, beside Alfeus, who was naturally behind the window, was Miss Ella Constant, the one person in Contentment Cove with whom I was not on cordial terms.

I had nothing in the world against Miss Constant; in fact, I should have been eager to meet her halfway, and be friends, but she plainly showed what her attitude was toward me. It wasn't worth my time and effort to cuddle up to an iceberg, and get nothing but chilblains.

"Good morning, Alfeus!" I called. "I just hope you have oodles and oodles of letters for me this lovely day. And of course I'll take Mr. and Mrs. Pearl's and Professor Chubb's mail also. I presume you would have included them in our box, however. Oh, I wonder if that package from Hale's arrived this morning? I do hope so, a *large* package? Good morning, Miss Constant. We always have so much mail. I tell Alfeus we must be his star patrons!' "

"Good morning, Mrs. Potter." Miss Constant gave what I'll be generous enough to call a smile, and moved away from the window to give me room.

"Isn't this one of our typical, *perfect* Contentment Cove days, Miss Constant? I just don't believe anywhere else in the world can boast of July days such as this, do you?"

"As far as I know, Mrs. Potter, we've got no more corner on good weather here than on anything else!" she said, fiddling with her pocketbook.

I fully expected some such response, so at least I wasn't taken by surprise. I suppose the poor little soul, in her low-heeled shoes and denim skirt, had missed so much in life, never having married, neither she nor her brother, that such sour comments were only natural.

We had attempted to buy property from the Constants in the beginning, when we first made our big discovery of the Cove.

Gus even went to see them, though the real estate man advised him that it would do no good, and it didn't.

But I was just as glad that Miss Constant didn't demand my attention, for I was curious to look over and see what Gus Junior was doing.

He sat down at the end of the soda fountain nearest the Post Office, and even if I happened to be his mother, I must say anyone would have agreed that he looked very attractive in his chocolate brown slacks suit of matching shirt and trousers, with a bright plaid belt to set it off. Florida is way ahead of New England in men's clothing styles.

He was talking to Dot-Fran with no sign of the sulky look he had shown his mother. She wore a faded blue shirt, no doubt belonging to her father or brother, and dungarees. I realize that dungarees are the accepted article with all the girls, and fortunately Dot-Fran possessed a slim, attractive figure, but in a public place such as the drugstore and Post Office, frequented by all the visitors and summer people, it did seem that something more feminine would have been more suitable.

But she was a very pretty girl, in whatever she wore, with that lovely wavy blonde hair, and her blue, blue eyes. Looking at her I wanted so much to be able to forget her last remark to me. It showed how little respect or consideration she held us in, contrary to our fondly held belief along that line.

As though the day held not enough to cope with, I began to feel a twinge of my old nervous indigestion pains.

"The joint was jumping around our house yesterday," I overheard Gus Junior say with an embarrassed grin. "Mother kept me busy all day chauffeuring her around."

She looked at him with that straight, dear look of hers, through those long lashes, not saying a word. Of course she was hurt and angry, and frightened of what might have happened—she was only a girl, barely in her twenties—but, oh dear, that bold, hateful way she had spat at me about the police.

"I certainly wanted to get over here, Dot-Fran. Quite a place you got here!"

"It's all right, I guess. Can I get you anything?"

"Sure, I'll have a Coke."

When she came back, and plunked it down before him, he glanced around to be sure he wasn't being overheard. Two town boys were eating ice cream at the street end of the counter.

In the Post Office, beside me, Miss Constant was showing Alfeus her swollen ankle. He came out into the lobby to inspect it, leaving me there at my box, not knowing whether I had collected all the mail or not. Alfeus was sometimes very casual, so that I made it a point each day to ask if there were additional packages or other mail that couldn't be included in our lock box.

However, that was one time when I had no wish to hurry him, as I was very much interested in what was taking place across the way, or the wire, as the case happened to be. I was quite near Gus Junior, though hidden from his view by a pile of cartons.

"Look," he said to Dot-Fran, looking very much embarrassed, "I want to tell you, I don't know what the score is around here, but I never met that guy until day before yesterday. I hope you don't blame me for any of this?"

I pretended to be looking at my San Antonio newspaper.

"Why should I?"

"Well, don't, that's all," he said, trying to wheedle her into a smile. "A drunken bum is all he is; maybe he *claims* he's a professor!"

A very pretty way to talk about his mother's guests.

Just then Miss Constant spoke to me. At the same time I noticed Hilary's car driving up outside. In my confusion I dropped all my letters, and the *Center City Times*, as well as part of the *San Antonio Observer*.

Alfeus came rushing over, like a gentleman, to pick things up for me.

"I asked how your swimming pool was coming along?" Miss Constant repeated. As though she didn't know perfectly well how disappointingly slow things were going on the pool. Everyone in Contentment Cove knew.

"Why, rather more slowly than we had hoped, Miss Constant."

Alfeus handed me back my mail. Across the pile of cartons, I saw Gus Junior lean over the fountain to hold his cigarette lighter for Dot-Fran. They were laughing! As though nothing ever in the world had ever happened. One minute a serious discussion, the next all is forgotten.

"Well, I dare say there's no rush," Miss Constant said, with her smug, little smile. "We always have the Atlantic Ocean to fall back on, don't we!"

I held firmly to the thought that I was *not* going to lose my temper, though my head might be buzzing from Gus Junior's wholly uncalled-for manner of speaking, from Miss Constant's jibes, and from nervous indigestion. I was determined not to become annoyed and say something I should later deeply regret. Everyone has their own reasons for being so sour and unpleasant; I tried my best to remember that.

"Rome wasn't built in a day, was it, dear Miss Constant!" I replied. "Oh, here's a letter from England, Alfeus, did you notice that stamp? Why, Miss Constant, I expect with all of us it's much the same: There's not progress to be made without overcoming various obstacles, and that pertains here as well as anywhere. Of course, in my opinion, the future of Contentment Cove lies ahead, don't you agree? There's no need for this town to sit back and bemoan its lack of progress. Think what we have to offer the public, this beautiful, unsurpassed scenery, absolutely unspoiled. Lots of lovely, desirable people would be thrilled to come here, if they only knew, and bring revenue to the town. What a boon it would be for business prospects, if only that ocean frontage of yours was available, Miss Constant! But I expect you'll be prevailed upon to sell one of these days, won't you? Much as one hates to see change, there's no standing in the way of changing times, is there!"

Miss Constant stared at me, and went limping back over to the Post Office window. "I am reminded of an old saying, Mrs. Potter," she said. " 'The more things change, the more they remain the same.' I don't know whether that's reassuring or not!"

Having no idea what that was meant to imply, I made no answer, but at least we had spoken together, which was surely a step in the right direction.

"Goodbye, Alfeus," I called. "I've *such* a busy day ahead. Goodbye, Miss Constant."

As I hurried down the steps outside, I heard her say, "Well, now that the *rush* is over, I'll take my mail, Alfeus, if you please. I notice this is handout day!"

I very nearly lost my footing. Handout Day. Naturally I knew exactly what she meant. That sour little woman had stood there, and watched me take our social security checks out with the rest of our mail.

Not that I was ashamed of it; she was perfectly welcome to examine all of my mail if she chose. But, my dear, why should she bear me such ill will and unfriendliness. I had never done her a moment's harm in word or deed.

As long as Gus and I had been forced to pay the outrageous taxes we had paid to the United States government, we felt a perfect right in receiving back what was due us, as millions of others did. When you observed the way millions of people accepted government handouts, for their due, which wasn't our belief and never had been, we felt no hesitancy in taking what was ours by law.

Gus said they had started taxing brains in this country in 1932, and I guess a lot of people agreed with him. People like us, who worked for what we had, were taxed into the ground to support every lazy, shiftless Tom, Dick, and Harry, who preferred not to lift a hand.

And Eisenhower, much as I hated to admit it, being a Republican, though not his brand, was not changing things one iota. Far from it. He was calling for more, more, more, more of a trend to socialism with every day that we drew breath.

But why, *why* should Miss Constant want to cut me like that? It did cut me deeply. Though I don't wear my feelings on my sleeve, I can be very easily hurt by such as that—not so much by the remark itself as the unkind intent behind it.

Alfeus laughed.

"Yep, handout day! When are you and Harry going to put your rap on Uncle Sam? Maybe with social security, you could afford to build us another swimming pool!"

My feet were rooted to that step. I couldn't move.

"What I don't believe in, I don't subscribe to, Alfeus," she said. "You know that perfectly well! I didn't believe in handouts when Roosevelt started it, and I don't any more now that it's a Republican handing it out, just because they don't *dare* to have the courage of their convictions. There's one thing I may say, thank God, though I haven't much company with me nowadays, *I* don't keep my principles in my pocketbook!"

She might better have slapped my face. My hands trembled so I could scarcely hold onto my mail. And *Alfeus* too!

We had been so happy, felt so sure that we were liked and welcomed, and respected in Contentment Cove. And now, with my own ears, to hear Alfeus himself make such a remark behind my back. Alfeus, whom we had regarded as a friend, and trusted neighbor, ridiculing our gift to the community, a gift costing us thousands and thousands of dollars; Miss Constant, having the supreme gall to imply that we had less principles than she did.

But I couldn't stand there, like a graven image. Somehow I managed to get on down those dreadful, few steps, and into the drugstore, repeating over and over, Don't you dare to cry, don't you *dare* to show that anything is wrong, Mina Potter.

"Hello, hello everybody!" I cried, hoping my voice didn't sound as quavery as I felt.

Hilly, wearing slacks rather than her usual shorts, was leaning on the fountain, talking to Gus Junior.

Perhaps with the aid of several aspirin I could get through the next hour.

"How can any of you bear staying under cover this glorious day? Oh, Hilly, darling! You look tired, my dear, and no wonder. What an ordeal you went through. Dotty, would you give me a glass of water, please. Gus Junior, are you ready to drive me home?"

He gave a deep sigh, as though he was constantly called upon to interrupt the most important moments of life to wait upon his mother. "Any*time*, Mother."

My dearest wish at that moment would have transported me miles away to the heart of Africa, with no one but friendly, smiling, savage tigers and lions for company.

"Come along with Abbey and me," Hilly said. "We'll gladly drop you off."

Yes, there was poor Abbey Peterson, the mother of the boy who had stolen Gus's cap not two hours before, looking at the rack of anniversary cards. Hilly always seemed to be driving her about.

"Thank you, Hilly dear, but it's nearly lunchtime. Gus Junior will just have to postpone his conversation for another occasion."

Such a response from my own son was the last straw on poor old camel Mina's back. When a grown man of twenty-five years old looked for his entire support from his father and mother, one might expect some small regard and concern for their feelings in return. Not that we begrudged maintaining him; naturally, the money would all be his one day. Nonetheless, it was a great worry to us that he had never up to that time found any worthwhile interest or work, and that he hadn't found himself some nice girl to marry and settle down with.

Gus Junior had not wished to attend college, as he was not the studious type, and, as he said, it did seem foolish to waste four years of his life on something he had no interest in.

Neither his father nor I had gone to college ourselves, so we could scarcely insist against his will, and inclination. In fact, Gus felt that there was entirely too much stress laid on a college education, under the modern, socialistic, educational theories. He had very strong opinions against the whole present-day system. He did not approve of the federal government's stepping in as it had, and the way all of us, willy-nilly, were taxed into the ground to put a lot of harebrained theories into effect, which only turned out to mean children were receiving *less* education rather than more, and not preparing them in any way, shape, or manner for the real battle of life.

In Palo Alto, California, Gus Junior's main interest being in cars, his father and I bought him an interest in a used car lot. But he proved to have too nervous a disposition for selling. In fact, he developed a severe body rash, and had to remain in bed for several weeks, in great discomfort, which was definitely attributed by the doctor to that cause. In California, everything goes at such a hectic pace. I had no idea of the methods those salesmen used to high-pressure people into buying their products. That kind of salesmanship would never succeed with such as myself, and I certainly didn't blame my son for not wanting to compete with it.

One of Gus Junior's high school teachers suggested the armed forces as a career for him, and I would not have been averse to it. However, to qualify for officers' training required a college degree. In any case he was never enthusiastic about the army, and reached the point of resenting any mention of it, so the subject was dropped from then on. Subsequently, we have discovered that his nervous allergies would have disqualified him.

I think Gus Junior spent the happiest years of his life in San Antonio, Texas, after our move there. He became acquainted with a chum, whose father owned a boat charter business in Galveston, on the Gulf, and Gus Junior enjoyed going out on the boats with Tony more than anything he had ever done, helping with the fishing, and talking with the various customers with whom they were in close confines all day. His father and I were pleased, as at least it was a healthy, outdoor occupation. Perhaps if we had stayed in Texas, he could have started a charter fleet of his own.

But as it turned out, Gus and I became fed up, and moved to New England. Gus Junior didn't wish to stay on there alone, so far away, so his father was fortunate in finding him a job with an Ohio friend, who had transported his business to Tampa, Florida. Byron owned an Oldsmobile Agency, and Gus Junior seemed very content with him at first. Byron sent him, with four or five other boys, up to Detroit or Chicago by plane to drive back convoys of used cars which he bought at auction.

As Gus Junior enjoyed being on the go, and loved driving, it seemed ideal for him, but as luck would have it, his kidneys would not stand the punishment. He wasn't one bit happy just staying in the showroom in Tampa, so Gus finally wrote him to throw up the job, and come north to spend the summer at the Cove with us, which would enable him to get a good long rest, and we could then decide what the future held.

Dot-Fran gave me a glass of water, and then went down to the far end of the counter to pet Simple Simon, who was curled in his usual spot on top of the cigarettes and cigars.

I wondered if she and Hilary were less friendly than usual, on account of the break-off with Stanley. The Cove families were very clannish, as I had previously noted.

"Well, see you latterly," I said to Hilary, and rose to go, having downed my aspirin and glass of water. When there directly across the street I saw Joe!

With Gus's imported, pink plaid cap from Scotland stuck on the back of his head. He was sauntering along staring across at the drugstore as though positively daring me to see him, and then he saw our car. He snatched the cap off his head, and ran past the hardware store into the alley, out of sight.

I didn't know *what* to do! I was tempted to say nothing, go out, get into the car, and drive along home. There was a limit to the amount of unpleasantness I could stand in one day.

But there was Gus's favorite cap almost within my grasp. He would never forgive me for having made no attempt to retrieve it, and how could I ever explain? Furthermore, the boy shouldn't be allowed to get away with such a bare-faced theft, grinning that imbecilic grin over his shoulder.

Dot-Fran had seen him too. I knew by the quick way she glanced at me over the counter, and instantly turned away. Of course she recognized Gus's cap very well, she had seen him wear it a thousand times. It was obvious that the sight of it on Joe struck her as very humorous, quite apart from its having been stolen.

Distraught and upset as I was, I could appreciate the humorous aspect, but I could *not* stand there and allow Gus and myself to become laughingstocks. It was somewhat a matter of our self-respect.

"*Quick!*" I cried across to Alfeus. "Stop the Peterson boy. Across the street there."

A doubt flashed through my mind as to whether young Kenneth Hill had made any effort at all toward going after Joe.

Everyone whirled and stared at me.

Naturally there wasn't a moment to lose. I hurried to the door. "He went behind the hardware store. Over there. Oh, be *quick,* somebody!"

Alfeus met me at the top step, he on the outside, myself on the in.

"What's Joe done now? What's this all about, Mina?" He had a maddening, calm smile.

"He went behind the hardware store, Alfeus. He has my husband's cap."

"I guess she saw that kid with Dad's cap."

"Go after who, Mrs. Potter?"

Everyone was interrupting, asking questions. Alfeus seemed determined not to understand. He stood there blocking the door, with that uncomprehending grin, while in the meantime Joe could have run halfway to Center City.

It was infuriating. I was ready to die with frustration, and the cramps in my stomach, and the fact that absolutely everything in the world seemed to be against me that morning.

"Dot-Fran! You saw him! Didn't you see that boy wearing Gus's imported Scotch cap?"

She giggled, hanging her head like a silly schoolgirl.

"Is she talking about my Joe?"

"For God's sake, Mina."

I tried to answer them calmly.

"Joe took an expensive cap out of my husband's car this morning."

Alfeus wasn't smiling as calmly now. Unpleasantness of any kind was not to his liking, nor any more to mine. I would have given five years of my life to have been spared this ordeal.

All I could see before my eyes was Abbey Peterson's dumpy little figure, with her hair stringing out of its net, the sort worn by the sardine packers, and her angry face glaring at me.

"You say my Joe stole something?"

"Yes, he certainly did, Mrs. Peterson. A very expensive imported cap."

"He told me he was going to ask for work."

Gus Junior had joined me. "He did, and when he left he snitched Dad's cap out of the Caddie."

"For God's sake, how do you know?" Hilary said impatiently. "Gus may have lost it."

"Gus isn't the sort who loses things," I said, though it was not at all her affair. "And furthermore I just saw him, over there across the street. Dot-Fran saw him too, though she seems to have lost her tone. He was wearing it. Then he saw our car here and ran—like any thief!"

In the light of hindsight, I deeply regret using that explicit word to Mrs. Peterson's face, but I was goaded beyond my patience.

She stared at me like a demented woman. Before I could escape she pushed Gus Junior aside and clutched my arm. I fully expected to have her fingerprints for life.

"You're calling my son Joe a thief? Because you have plenty of money you think it's all right to stand here calling my boy names, and not care how it makes a mother feel?"

"I do care, I assure you, Mrs. Peterson, but also I care that my husband has lost a valuable article of clothing, of which he is very fond."

"A cap!" she screamed at Alfeus. "She says my boy stole a cap."

"Now Abbey, don't get excited."

She was more than excited, she was hysterical. Her eyes blazed. "Right here two days ago, my house was on fire. You happen to remember *that*, Mrs. Potter? Pouf! Pouf! That was all the concern it was to you, to go running to see, that was your big concern, like it was a newsreel. Now it's a different story! You don't stop to hesitate to accuse my boy when you think he takes a *cap*. That's more important to you than our maybe losing everything we own. That's your kind, the big *I am*! *Ain't* it! You give my husband a job so you think you can treat his family like dirt."

"Alfeus, let me by."

He moved then, at long last. I think he was fully as shocked as I was. He stepped quickly inside and took her firmly by the shoulder. "Abbey, for Christ's sake, pipe down. Do you want this all over town?"

"I'll get Gus's cap back," Hilary said, "don't worry about it, Mina, it's as good as in your hand. Come on, Abbey, I'll drive you home before you have a heart attack."

Alfeus muttered, "Go ahead, you've got the right idea. Get her out of here."

Every word uttered had been overheard by everyone in the store and Post Office. There were half a dozen people gaping from the Post Office lobby, and Mrs. King with several other women were congregated outside, waiting to see the body brought out.

Though my knees would barely hold me up, I managed to make my way to the car and clamber in.

Alfeus hurried after us, clearly very much upset.

"Don't worry about the cap, we'll have it back in jig time. I'm sorry Abbey lost her head like that."

"So am I, Alfeus. Let's say no more."

"She's had a rough time of it—that kid is enough to drive most people out of their mind. God, Mina, I wouldn't have had this happen for the world."

"Nor would I, Alfeus. It has distressed me more than I can say. Now please drive me home, Gus Junior."

If only I could have had a few minutes alone to collect myself. But it was not to be. At home there were guests to think about.

Gus Junior looked over at me. "Wait till Dad hears about this. He'll send that guy packing so fast . . ."

"Don't mention a word before Greta . . ."

"Gosh, no, she's nosy enough as it is."

At least there was one cheering sight as we turned up the drive. Eddie was sitting out on the lawn in the glider, dressed in his nice brown lightweight Brooks Brothers suit.

I could hear the rumble of the vacuum cleaner from the house.

If only I could have dismissed the rest of the morning as one can a bad dream. But it lay in the pit of my stomach like a hard stone, around which I must draw every breath.

One feels respected, looked up to, happy, in the little niche they make for themselves, and suddenly, pouf, not at all; you find instead you are the butt of malicious, gossiping tongues; those whom you have most trusted and liked snicker behind your back, and betray traits you never remotely suspected.

But there was no use in standing around moaning. Human nature is human nature, good and bad. Life goes on its way, regardless, and we can make the most of it, come what may.

Eddie was baggy-eyed and pale, but at least he had finally gotten out of bed.

"Darling!" I cried, trying desperately to be gay, "Eddie! I'm so *glad* to see you out here. This lovely sun is just what you need, now, isn't it? We shall all have a martini before lunch to celebrate your return to the fold! Gus Junior, can't you go fetch the gin and fixin's?"

I had never needed a martini so much in my entire lifetime.

"Dearest Mina, you're always the thoughtful hostess."

He got up with a groan, and came over to put his arm around me. "I'm going to be a nuisance to the last! There's a two-thirty train out of Center City. I'm very anxious to take it, Mina!"

"Eddie, you don't love us anymore?"

"My dear, I'm a complete and utter wreck. I've got to get home to my doctor."

"But we're having cocktail guests this afternoon. Who would drive you? Oh, you can't leave today, Eddie, you simply *can't*."

"Darling, I must. It's life or death, believe me. That goddamn infernal machine roaring all morning has completely finished me."

"Oh dear, what a shame, but we *do* have to keep reasonably clean."

"How about it, kid?" he said to Gus Junior. "Drive me into town, will you? My bag's right there in the hall. We haven't much time to spare."

"Before lunch?"

"I'm afraid so."

"Where is Greta?" I demanded.

Guests for cocktails, no matter. Lunch, no matter, let my son make a four-hour unnecessary drive on an empty stomach, which would certainly make him late back for the party. Thank you very much! From a houseguest I scarcely knew, and whose company I had had every expectation of enjoying.

"Greta's having a mad," he said airily. "She's gone off some-where—but she's a ghastly driver anyway. Look, I hate being a bore, but I really must make that train."

"It does seem . . ."

"Yes, it certainly does," he said, giving my shoulder a squeeze. His breath was dreadful; it convinced me that the man was really sick. "Be a Boy Scout," he said to Gus Junior. "Fetch my bag, and we're off!"

Gus Junior looked at me, and shrugged. "I could get a ham-burger somewhere, I guess. Let me have a little cash, Mother."

"Tell Gus many, many thanks," Eddie said, kissing me on both cheeks. "Can't tell you how very much I've enjoyed it. And do try to convince my ex that I love her passionately!"

I sank down on the glider, and watched them roar off down the driveway. Everything was quiet; the vacuum cleaner had stopped. No doubt Della had interrupted her cleaning to watch proceedings.

There were white sails on the bay, like gulls wheeling over the bright, blue water, yachts from the Island Yacht Club. It was hot in the direct sunlight. Around the corner of the house, where the breeze touched, it would be cool. Two light-green butterflies flew up out of the snapdragons and fluttered off toward the water.

I remembered that I hadn't even read my mail.

As soon as they had left the drive for the main road, Eddie made it plain to Gus Junior that he wanted to stop off at the drugstore. It would only delay them a minute, he said, and he couldn't bear to leave town without stopping.

It was exactly twelve noon when they stopped out front. He was so wobbly that Gus Junior got out with him.

Being lunchtime, there was no one else there at the moment. Dot-Fran was perched behind the fountain reading the daily newspaper.

Gus Junior repeated the whole scene to me afterward, word for word. He himself felt very nervous at what might take place between them.

But they had barely entered the store when Alfeus appeared. Gus Junior is positive that he did not come in behind them, from the street, which could only mean that he had some concealed way of opening the wire partition, of which very few persons were aware.

Dot-Fran just sat there, looking very much surprised, still holding her newspaper. She seemed as surprised at Alfeus's sudden appearance as she did to see them.

Alfeus nodded to them, and sat down at the end of the fountain. The atmosphere was very tense.

Just at that moment, Simple Simon clawed at the screen door behind Gus Junior, making him jump. He is highly excitable, especially at such a time, like myself.

"Let the boy in," Alfeus said. "It's his dinnertime."

Gus Junior stepped back and opened the door for him. That somewhat broke the tension.

Eddie leaned over the fountain, and said, "Miss Dot-Fran, I'm leaving; I'm being driven to the train, but I had to stop, if only for this brief minute, to plead your forgiveness for my behavior the other night."

She looked straight at him without answering.

It was something of a surprise to Gus Junior to see that her expression could be so bitter and unyielding. At least Eddie was making an apology, like a gentleman should.

"My dear, surely you can . . . can say one kind word in farewell, to ease my conscience, to let me go in peace—one word?"

"No! Just go."

He tried to reach her hand. "At least a hand clasp. Is that too much to give? My dear, you're being very cruel to an old, sick man."

Simple Simon jumped up on the fountain beside him, arching his back, and purring, as though it was all an enjoyable occasion.

Gus Junior observed to me later that Eddie's face was a pure study, wanting to push the cat out of his way, but feeling obliged to pet it instead.

"At least your cat is friendly!"

She reached over and lifted Simple Simon off the fountain, away from him.

"Now go on and leave," she said, still holding him in her arms. "I don't want your apology. You're the only person in my life who has ever acted like that. Do you think after *that* you can walk in here and say you're sorry and I'll shake *hands* with you?" Her voice was shaking.

"I can only say how sorry I am . . . at least, anger is most becoming, my dear . . ."

Alfeus interrupted him, turning around.

"Allez vite, Mr. Chubb!"

"I beg your pardon?"

Gus Junior was as completely at sea as Eddie.

"Your time is up," Alfeus said very quietly, lighting a cigarette. "Miss Hathaway has asked you to leave."

Eddie's face turned red. He hadn't anticipated anything such as this, and whatever else I may think of Eddie, I must say I'm sure his intention in stopping to apologize was sincere.

"Ah, I see, we have a self-appointed guardian! It doesn't seem quite necessary, though, does it? Am I doing harm in any way to Miss Hathaway by wishing a brief word of farewell?"

"We don't take offense around here very easy, Mr. Chubb. We stand quite a lot before we get up on our hind legs, so judging by the fact that Miss Hathaway's asked you to leave, she must have good reason to . . ." He got up. "So if I were you, I'd leave. Right now."

If I needed any more convincing as far as Alfeus was concerned, there it was. That he would speak in such a manner to a friend and houseguest of ours, before our own son.

Gus Junior was uncertain what to do, so he opened the door and said, "Come on, Eddie, or you'll miss your train."

Our lunch was delayed because Greta simply didn't come, and didn't come, and no one knew where to look for her.

When she finally appeared, Gus was ready to fly. His biggest peeve was having to wait meals. I had not had any chance to speak with Gus privately, as both George Pearl and Della were about the house. At least I had the good sense not to let Della get the slightest hint of my state of mind. So we had martinis and waited.

When I spotted Greta's floppy hat at the end of the driveway, I hurried down to meet her. One thing one may say for Greta— she didn't pretend to be other than she was. Being late for lunch was least on her mind, and she didn't pretend otherwise.

"Darling," she said, clutching my arm, "I am so furious I really don't trust myself to speak. Just don't mention his name! I shall never, *never* forgive him. Wretched man!"

Between our late lunch, and clearing up the kitchen afterward, as Della was busy elsewhere, I had barely time to get changed and bathed before cocktail time. In one way it may have been just as well that it was rush, rush, rush that afternoon, leaving no time to brood over my thoughts, as I was in no condition for doing so. I could even begin to understand why some poor souls become alcoholics.

Hilary was the last of the guests to arrive, as was almost always the case. But this time, to our amazement, she brought Jules Balls and his dreadful wife along with her.

"Jules and Lucy came down this afternoon to celebrate with me," she said, waving her hand to show all the turquoise rings.

"Celebrate what? It's a surprise, darling, but you'll know soon enough! I'll give you a clue, though—I'm not pregnant!"

"But where's Chauncey?"

"Humber? He's gone, thank God. Gone with the wind!"

"Why didn't you tell me?" I cried. "I didn't believe it when Della said so this morning. He had promised to paint our house."

"No, he's gone. Darling, you'll never know how lucky you are! What's up with you, Gus! You look like a thunderhead. Thought this was supposed to be a party!"

Trust Hilly to come right out with a remark like that, when she was perfectly aware that Gus didn't get along well with the Balls, especially Mrs. Balls. It was hard for Gus to hide his feelings.

"Well, it's a damn good thing he's gone," he growled. "There's getting to be too many of you lousy artists around here!"

"Too many lousy artists, or too many of you louses?" Hilly shot back, at which everyone roared, naturally. There were very few who could get the better of her.

"No, as a matter of fact, Gus," she said, "it turned out that Humber and I were practically related. Brother and sister under the skin! Small world and all that bloody rot, wouldn't you say!"

I shepherded everyone out to the lawn chairs. I often said that our lawn was the choicest spot in Contentment Cove, on afternoons when not too chilly, which it most certainly wasn't on that occasion.

Della came out and passed around the plates of lobster and crabmeat sandwiches, and the cheese dip and crackers, and we used the tea cart as a portable bar.

Greta talked to the Balls, who, thank goodness, were being most affable, and polite, on their best behavior. I think it's quite true that most people will react in that way if given half a chance. I could even see why some thought him a distinguished-looking man, with that gray hair and young face. He could be very charming, and astute when he so desired, as when we discussed the foreign aid program, and he agreed with me that Eisenhower had proved a great disappointment to his party, in turning around and embracing all of "That Man's" programs.

Carver Peck, being a pushover for an attractive woman, managed to get himself sat down beside Lucy Balls. They seemed to find plenty to laugh and talk about, but, heaven knows, Carver was never in his life at a loss for words.

Hazel Peck was a marvel the way she never seemed to mind how he carried on, or with whom. She treated it all as a joke, as part of his party manners, which I suppose, in reality, was all it was, but a good many wives would have divorced him.

I heard Maizie Spindle telling George her story, which I had been forced to listen to at least twenty-eight times, of taking Mrs. King some wonderful expensive imported cheese when they were clearing out the refrigerator one fall, and dear Mrs. King's saying, "Oh, this is just lovely, I've been wanting to make a welch rarbit!"

Hilly said to Gus, "I don't quite know what to make of it; Dotty called just as we were leaving to ask if I'd seen anything of Stanley. The child sounded worried. Oh well, he's probably damn well absconded with the bank's funds. What else is a bank for!"

"I've got a bone to pick with you, Hilly," Gus said, bumbling down on the grass beside her. I wondered how he thought he was ever going to get up, with all those martinis under his belt.

She rumpled his hair. "All right, Gus. Grrrrr. Who gets the first bite?"

"Gus," I said, "Maizie needs another drink."

"Get her one then," he shouted, grinning. "Don't try to distract my attention. I got to thrash this brain question out with Hilly. Now look here, tell me this, how come all you arty intellectuals look down your nose at anybody that can make money? Like Lawrence Welk? And Liberace? The other night I took particular notice that you didn't have any of their records. You've got a lot of other lousy names no one ever heard of, or gives a damn about, but no Lawrence Welk and his Champagne Music. What's the reason a man's got to be starving before you'll admit he's got a good orchestra?"

"Darling, grant me just one lone thing! The privilege of my own taste. Thank God there's no law yet in this country compelling me to buy Lawrence Welk records!"

"No law? Of course there's no law. But it's damn good music. You know how many million people watch his TV show? That's my point, damn it. If anyone's popular, you lousy intellectuals won't give them a decent break. What's the matter with Liberace? Anything the matter with the way he can tickle those old piano keys? You bet there isn't! But you sit there with that snobby look on your face . . ."

"Look, angel, you go ahead and *listen* to Liberace. I'll take Rubinstein. And why can't we both be happy?"

"Because it's a fake, that's why, a lousy fake. You and the rest of the snobs listening to opera and all that lousy crap. Tell me *who* you think you're fooling? Hell, nobody enjoys hearing a bunch of fat women yowling at the top of their lungs."

"If you'd break down and go sometime, darling, you'd be surprised how thin and beautiful some of those yowling women are!"

"Give him hell!" Carver Peck called. "What does he know about culcha? He's nothing but a boss carpenter with a winning streak!"

I sometimes felt that Carver's attempts at humor were less than so.

"Hell, if I want to see a beautiful woman, I can go look at Marilyn Monroe."

"That figures!" she said, holding out her glass to Ned Spindle. "Quick, Ned, save my life! I need another drink."

"So what do you mean, it figures? When a girl can make the money that girl's made, she's got it, and don't you forget it!"

"Got what? Falsies! All right, Gus, my love, let's look at it your way. Instead of Garbo, take Marilyn Monroe and Jayne Mansfield. Instead of the New York Philharmonic, give the great American public Lawrence Welk and Liberace. It's a lovely prospect! Instead of the Royal Danish Ballet, we can watch Elvis wave his pelvis. Substitute the drama of *This Is Your Life* for the Old Vic's *Romeo and Juliet*. And oh yes! for the politically curious, there's *Time* and the *New York Daily Mirror*, in clear, concise four-letter words. For intellectual stimulation, hallelujah! the *Reader's Digest* condensed versions. For spiritual uplift, Norman Vincent Peale out of Mary Baker Eddy. Oh yes, Gus, we've got everything at our fingertips, in terms a ten-year-old could readily understand. A backward ten-year-old. And to top off the rosy picture, we're governed by a confused general, and General Motors. It's a great new world, Gus, all yours! Take it, darling, enjoy it, *fight* for it!"

Hilly was sometimes like that after a drink or two, talking so fast and confusing you so that you ended up with no idea what she really meant, if she did herself. And I couldn't see that she had answered Gus's question. He could not bear any hint of snobbery of any variety. It was one of his fixations. Though, of course, he knew very well that as far as Hilly was concerned, she was not one bit high-hat.

She got up. "Jesus, what an oration. Where's my glass?"

Ned handed it to her, and pointed above our heads. Across the blue of the sky there were numbers of the white trails that jet planes make. It made me dizzy to look up at them, but it gave one an awed feeling just the same, at the thought of the faraway majestic heavens being marked by man in that beautiful fashion.

I looked around for Greta. It was unusual for her not to be in the center of things. But instead she was walking across the lawn behind us. I observed that her face looked flushed, but owing to what had happened previously, I attributed it to Eddie and too many martinis. It seemed to me that she might be dramatizing herself the tiniest bit.

I was telling Hilly of my letter that morning from San Antonio, with an account of a dear friend's passing. A lovely woman, just in the prime of life. Everyone supposed her trouble to be cancer, though the family never said so in so many words.

My friend wrote that she had never in her life seen anyone look so beautiful when laid out in their bier. Cyrus, her husband, had the hairdresser to whom she always went in Dallas come to prepare her hair, and she was wearing a lovely dress she had just purchased from Neiman Marcus, of midnight blue shot with gold thread. Also she was wearing her emeralds, and her diamond pendant, as well as the fabulous diamond ring which her husband had presented to her on their last wedding anniversary, at which party Gus and I were present as invited guests. She always wore it fourth finger, left hand, from that time on, along with her wedding ring.

It was a moving letter. I presume that Cyrus had wished her to rest in death with all the things she had loved most in life.

Reading, and thinking, of the San Antonio friends made me feel a wee bit homesick. There were many desirable things about living in a city like San Antonio, including our host of friends and acquaintances. It gave me a twinge of regret to think how hasty we had been in disposing of our lovely home there.

"Say, what's wrong with Mrs. Pearl? A droppie too many?" Maizie giggled. "I guess she's trying to walk it off. Us country girls can hold our liquor, hey, Mina! But don't you imagine that even in *Texas*, he had that jewelry removed before she was put in the ground?"

We were interrupted by Carver Peck and Hilly running hastily past us.

"My God, I tell you she's choking!" I heard Hilly cry.

I turned in time to see Carver seize Greta and push her to her knees. It was an alarming sight to see one of her air and dignity treated so unceremoniously. Before I could stir, he bent over and struck her between the shoulder blades. It made me wince.

I suppose it seemed necessary. In any case, whether or not, now that it's all over, there's no way of knowing.

Before any of us could recover from the shock, he helped her up, and between them he and Hilly walked her into the house.

George and I hurried to follow. He was still clutching his glass, looking panic-stricken, poor man.

"She's all right now," Carver called from the door. "Another minute or two and it might have been all up, chum!"

George groaned, and took off his glasses. Without them he looked so pathetic that my heart went out to him. There were big white rings around his eyes where the glasses had prevented tanning, so that he looked for all the world like a skinny, middle-aged panda.

"You're sure she's all right?"

"Right as rain. Hey! Be careful, everybody!" Carver bellowed, "Mina's trying to choke us with those lobster sandwiches of hers!"

"My, did you need to be quite so *rough?*" someone called.

"That woman was choking," Carver snapped. "And you were all sitting here like sticky wickets letting it happen."

"Well, my goodness," Maizie giggled, "but we hardly know her!"

"Mix everyone another cocktail, Gus, quick!"

It was while I was inside that they decided to walk over the hill to the swimming pool. It was only a short walk through our spruce grove.

Greta looked shaken and white, but she seemed to be all right. "I'll just stay here on the divan for a few minutes," she said. "Darling, I've never had such an appalling experience. Go on back to the party, lover, for God's sake, and stop wringing your hands over me. Your sweetie pie is all *right.*"

George gave me a sickly smile, still minus his glasses—I hope he hadn't mislaid them—and went wandering out, clutching his glass.

"Better stay right there, Mrs. Pearl, and take it easy for the rest of the day," Hilly said.

At that instant the telephone rang, and I went into Gus's study to answer it. The eventuality furthest from my mind was another call from Mr. Lascomb at the bank, but it turned out to be none other.

"My husband is very busy just now, Mr. Lascomb," I said. "Just give me your message, whatever it may happen to be. We are in the midst of entertaining at cocktails, and one of our guests has just been taken ill, so you can readily see how very inconvenient . . . "

It was a bad connection. I could scarcely hear, but I did grasp something to the effect that it was confidential and urgent!

"I am very well acquainted with all of my husband's business affairs, Mr. Lascomb." I tried not to sound impatient, though wondering at the same time what was going on outside, and if anyone was helping Gus provide our guests with another drink, which I knew they sorely needed, judging from myself after witnessing such an experience. "So please just go on and tell me what you are calling about, and I will inform my husband, you may rely upon it. If it's still something to do with the pool account, which is entirely separate from our personal checking accounts, I can assure you that Gus says it is *not* overdrawn in the slightest. He is too much the businessman, first, last, and always, for that!"

The wire squealed, and buzzed, making him sound like a bad stutterer, which knowing Mr. Lascomb as I did, was not the case, but I finally heard the name of Stanley Hathaway.

"Yes, yes? What about him?" I shouted.

It seemed that the bank, as nearly as I could gather, had been unable to locate him all during the day, and thought he might be in Contentment Cove.

I was more confused than ever. It sounded like unpleasant complications to the Hilary affair, both for herself, and for his family. He had no doubt come here on her account, but I didn't feel called upon to relay that information to Mr. Lascomb.

"Why in the world are you telling me all this?" I demanded. "As I've told you repeatedly, I have guests who this very minute are wondering what has become of their hostess."

More stutters and squeals and buzzes, and all I could ascertain was the fact that it was his dear wish that we wash our hands of guests and cocktail party, and whatever else we might be concerned with, and hurry immediately all the way to Center City, with our checkbooks under our arms!

By this time it seemed that Mr. Lascomb might be playing us a bad joke, but I couldn't summon up enough strength to really care.

"Oh, Mr. Lascomb, it just is not in any way possible. My dear man, what you can't seem to realize is that we are in the process of entertaining people from *New York* as houseguests, and are this minute trying to conduct a cocktail party in their honor. I'm afraid you'll just have to get along as best you can. My husband can assure you that his accounts are in order. I'll have him call you tomorrow. I'm sure that in time you will be able to straighten everything out all right. We know Stanley, of course; in fact, we attended a cocktail party only a day or two ago at which he was present also. If I see him, I'll tell him you called. Goodbye, Mr. Lascomb."

Hilly came out of the downstairs powder room as I hung up the receiver.

"Did I hear Stanley's name? What is going on around here, Mina? I'm completely in the dark."

"My dear, no more so than I. I can only tell you that a man at the bank has taken the trouble to call us twice today, and this time for some unknown reason he informed me that Stanley has not been at the bank, and might be here at Contentment Cove. He wanted us to come trundling up to Center City, mind you, with all of our personal records, because *they* have made some stupid foul-up in our account. I could only tell him again that it was out of the question because of our guests."

Hilly stared at me strangely. Her eyes were hard and shiny, as though she might burst into tears.

"Well, dear, it's none of our business. If you don't mind my saying so, you would do well to avoid seeing him. Come, what we need is another drink."

"No! I've got to go, Mina," she said, with that peculiar expression. "Oh, God, *God*! What a beastly mess."

It was then, following her out of the house, that I discovered the rest of our guests meandering up over the hill toward the swimming pool. Lucy's scarlet skirt and Maizie's pleated blue nylon dress were just disappearing amongst the trees, the grove which we cherished so at the top of the slope.

Hilly shouted, but it was too far for her voice to carry.

"Jump in my car, Mina, we'll drive round."

"Hilly dear, I don't understand why you feel you must rush off."

"Oh God! You will soon enough."

With that she dashed into her car like a person possessed, and pulled me in with her. I'm not as agile about scrambling around as I was when fifteen, sad to say.

We went careening down the drive on two wheels, and out onto the main road. I was never more frightened in my life. Fortunately the ride to the pool took only a few minutes.

In the light of after events, it is plain to see that Hilary guessed the entire situation from the moment of my receiving that telephone call. She was sure that Stanley Hathaway was headed for her house, and she could think only of getting there first, to try and bring him to his senses. But she did not see fit to divulge her thoughts to me at the time, and I can only thank her for being spared, if only for a few hours.

Prior to our arrival at the swimming pool, our cocktail guests came hurrying down the path, which heaven knows wasn't meant for narrow skirts and high heels, but that only added to the hilarity. On three or four martinis most of us seem to think we can gambol around like mountain goats.

It gave Carver an excuse to put his arm around Lucy Balls, though it's far more likely the help proved to be on the other foot, she being thirty years younger!

Her husband was walking with Maizie, listening to her oft-told experience of seeing the wonderful Cypress Gardens on Cinerama, and then her subsequent disappointment on visiting the real thing, which she and Ned made a point of doing on their next visit to Florida. It so often happens that the real thing turns out to be such a letdown, as this was, after the beautiful way it was presented on Cinerama, with girls in lovely costumes, and the boat races, and so on.

When they reached the pool, Carver produced a flask, and they all took turns out of it while they got their breath.

The pool was still surrounded by a sea of dirt and empty cement bags, as well as mounds of gravel and sand, but Gus could overlook all that, with his professional eye, and see it as it would eventually look.

"There she is! And by God, I must say, she's a beauty. Well, she ought to be!"

The workmen had just finished painting one end with light blue paint. The empty cans lay where they had dropped.

"Where does one look for beauty in a swimming pool, Mr. Potter?" Lucy Balls asked.

Gus took her question to be baiting him, but I maintain that she may have been perfectly sincere, and in quest of information.

If Lucy had known (or even guessed) what that excavation, that cement, and piles of gravel, and empty paint cans represented to Gus and myself in dollars and cents, and the end not yet in sight, meaning the landscaping, the paved parking area, and the combination bath and clubhouse, I'm sure she would have been flabbergasted.

"It's a *lovely* spot here, Gus," Hazel Peck said, putting her arm through Lucy's. Hazel was a born peacemaker. "So beautiful with the view of the bay. And these gorgeous old wild apple trees, aren't they heavenly! What wonderful, gnarled shapes they have."

"They're in the way of the sewage," Gus said. "Sorry to disappoint you, Hazel, but they gotta go."

"Hey, Gus!" Carver said. "Why didn't you build one of these fancy free-form shapes while you were at it? Hell, nothing's too good for Contentment Cove!"

Gus minds the heat, especially when his head is uncovered, and I *do* think Carver was going too far with his teasing.

"Look, you goddamn well know what it takes to build a thing like this, construction-wise. Most people don't know a lousy thing about the construction of anything, even the roof over their heads. But I happen to know. It happens that was my business. The way I made my money. Maybe this isn't any free form or whatever you call it, but I say this pool is a beauty, and you can damn well believe I know what I'm talking about."

"A rose is a rose is a rose!" Lucy Balls singsonged. "Isn't that so, Mrs. Peck?"

"Gertrude Stein would have it so, honey!"

Hazel was very well read. It took more than a professor's wife, whose husband probably didn't earn half of the Admiral's retirement pay, to get ahead of her.

"It's a *swimming pool!*" Gus shouted. "It's no lousy rose. Look here, Carver, you got any idea the money it takes to build a thing like this?"

Lucy held out her skirt and twirled around. Men are so susceptible to her type. I imagine she was trying to divert Carver from getting into an argument. "Oh, Mr. Potter, I adore swimming! Let's all go swimming!"

"Oh, for Christ's sake . . ."

But Carver was just the sort to egg her on. If she had suggested flying off to the moon, I expect he would have started flapping his wings.

"Bloody good idea, old girl. We'll jump in and prove the point! Anything to please our lousy host, eh!"

"Righto, Admiral!" She took a long drink out of his flask. It was just fortunate that none of our guests happened to have a contagious disease that afternoon.

That was the moment at which we drove up. Hilly slammed on the brakes so hard that I bruised my shoulder against the door, but she scarcely noticed.

"Lucy, Jules? Come on, I'm leaving. In a big hurry. Apologies, everybody. Gus."

No one heard her. Jules and Maizie turned and waved at us to get out, and in so doing Maizie tripped over a paint can and pulled him down with her. Of course none of them could have been described as cold sober.

It all happened in a split second before we could move. Lucy and the Admiral teetered on the edge of the pool, holding hands, pretending to be about to jump, with the rest laughing and screaming. Except Gus, who kept telling them not to be damned fools.

Then—they either jumped, or fell! Perhaps one or the other lost balance, it wouldn't have been wondered at.

"Oh, look at that pair of jackasses," Hilly groaned, pounding her fist on the steering wheel.

Somehow I scrambled out of the car, and went running to the pool, over the piles of gravel, and cement bags.

Lucy was huddled on the cement floor, with one leg doubled under her, and her husband and Carver leaning down beside her. All I can say about Carver Peck is that he must have been born lucky.

"There's no water in Potters' Pool!" Lucy said, looking up at me, trying to laugh, then she put her face against Carver's sleeve, and began to cry.

"It's her leg, *easy* there."

"Darling, can you let us lift you?"

"What a foolish, damn fool trick!"

"Gus, go telephone for a doctor, quick!" Hazel Peck said, giving him a push.

It hadn't seemed that anything more could possibly happen that day, which only showed how very foolish and one-track we humans can be. Because this was much worse than any of my other little problems.

We could only make the poor child as comfortable as possible, huddling around her to keep the sun off, while her husband held Carver's flask for her to drink. Thank God he had brought one.

It was impossible not to admire her spirit, crumbled down there, in pain as she was, trying to smile, with her eyes brimming tears in spite of all she could do. All when we might have been back on the shady lawn, enjoying ourselves like civilized human beings, instead of there in that blazing hot cement coffin with shoes full of gravel, and the sun beating on our heads.

The doctor finally came, followed by an ambulance from Sutter's Funeral Home. But before they got there, cars were stopping and children were arriving on bicycles in droves, as though the news had been broadcast over television.

I really thought at one point that I should collapse. Total strangers crowded around, asking questions, and giving suggestions, or just staring, until Hazel took charge and shooed them all back. I could imagine what being a freak in a sideshow is like.

"Game girl!" Carver said, patting Lucy's shoulder. "Just hold on a few more minutes."

He was limping from a sprained ankle, but I don't think he even felt it at that point.

Lucy caught my hand and drew me down beside her.

"Mrs. Potter, I'm so ashamed that I spoiled your party this way. Oh, I'm such a fool. I deserve to have broken my neck."

"My dear, the party is inconsequential. We just want to get you to a hospital as quickly as possible. Doctor, where is that ambulance?"

"Any minute now, Mrs. Potter."

"Will you hate me, Jules?" she said to her husband. "Or will you be a Robert Browning, darling!"

She may have been wandering a little, from the heat and the pain, besides which the doctor had just given her an injection. I had never heard Hilary mention any Brownings.

George Pearl leaned over my shoulder, and said, "Haw, haw. Make a beautiful Elizabeth, I must say, my dear."

"Her name is Lucy, George," I said. It wasn't the time for his haws, though, of course, they signified nothing in the way of amusement, but were meant simply the way some people clear their throat.

But Lucy took no offense. "Oh, thank you, Mr. Pearl," she said, smiling at him as though it was any casual, polite occasion.

She looked like a girl sitting there with her full skirt swirled out, and her hair tumbled. Her lashes were wet from crying, and she seemed a wholly different woman from the one I had previously thought of her as being.

"Where's Hilly?" Jules said, looking around in surprise.

I had given her not a thought till that moment.

"She must have gone right on home. She was terribly upset about something. Of course she didn't *know* . . . "

"Will you give her a ring, then, when you can, Mrs. Potter? Tell her I've taken Lucy to the Center City General by ambulance."

Cars had to be moved out of the way for the ambulance, and a path cleared over the rubble for the men to carry a stretcher. Gus had it done in jig time.

Lucy screamed when they lifted her. Carver winced and turned away to hide his face. He was feeling responsible for her accident, that I could see.

As Jules climbed into the ambulance with her, I grasped his sleeve. He turned and smiled, but tears were running down his cheeks. The sight of them just took whatever words there had been right out of my mind, and without a thought I reached and kissed him. It was one of those unexplainable impulses that one sometimes has without any explanation attached.

Back at the house at last, the first thing I did was to call Hilary.

"*No*," she said. "Oh my God, Mina! All right, thanks for calling. Have you heard anymore from the bank?"

"Heavens no, why in the world should I?"

"No, no, no reason," she said, sounding completely unlike herself. "Thanks, Mina. I'll get to the hospital as soon as I can."

As I hung up, it suddenly entered my mind that Gus Junior had never arrived home. It was past six; he should have been back hours before.

Our party guests were still outside, trying to tell Greta what had happened. They were all too excited and wrought-up to think of going home.

That did not pertain to Della, unfortunately. She had gone long since, disregarding my feeble hope that at least she would be in the kitchen to organize dinner, and the clean-up.

But *where* was our son? Gus would be wondering what in the world I was doing so long, but I felt sure Carver and Hazel would help with the guests, so I sat down again and dialed the drugstore.

Dot-Fran's Aunt Lizzie answered the telephone.

"Hathaway's drugstore, Lizzie Colman speaking."

"This is Mrs. Potter. Mrs. Colman, I wondered if my son had been there this afternoon? He drives a dark green Jaguar, one of those foreign cars, you know."

"He's been here all right, and he got Dot-Fran to go off somewheres with him. Don't ask me where, but all I hope is he don't drive the way that young Prestwick over on the island drives that runt of a car he's got."

"My son is an excellent driver, Mrs. Colman. Have no fear on *that* score."

At least my mind was somewhat relieved. He had taken Dot-Fran out for a date, thinking we at home would be taken up by the party, and wouldn't notice his absence. It was not the straight-forward way I should have wished him to act, but I was glad to know he was all right.

I was crossing the front hall, carrying a bowl of ice, a fresh bottle of Gilbey's gin, and a plate of cheese and crackers—Gus was getting terribly hungry—when the phone rang.

"This is Mr. Lascomb speaking."

I sat down, as though I didn't have a thing in the world on my mind beyond listening to Mr. Lascomb. In reality, I could not have remained standing for another minute on pain of my life.

"Why hello, Mr. Lascomb. We seem to be hearing your voice frequently today. What is it that you want this time, Mr. Lascomb?"

"Mrs. Potter, we have sufficient reason to believe that your account has been falsified here. I can speak more plainly than I have been able to all day, for it has been a matter of trying desperately to put our hands on definite proof. Stanley Hathaway is being sought by the state police, Mrs. Potter. We have good reason to believe that he has falsified your account by several thousand dollars. It has been our concern all day to tally your records with ours . . . "

"Falsified our account?" I demanded, unable to grasp his meaning. "But why? Why in the world, *us*? There must be some dreadful mistake."

"Believe me, Mrs. Potter, this has come as a shock to all of us here at the bank."

"My husband and I will leave at once."

"It won't be necessary now, Mrs. Potter, not tonight."

"I assure you it will be for my husband. He will certainly want to see you at once, and ascertain each and every and *all* of the facts."

If the shock had not been so great, I would never have blurted the whole thing out as I did before everyone. But I was very nearly out of my wits at that point.

What a bombshell it was for our quiet little town. Of course everyone understood immediately that Gus and I wished to go up there at once, and urged us to go.

Though Ned Spindle said, "You might as well wait till they catch the poor devil. What good can you do racing up there at this time of night?" Poor old Ned. Maizie certainly had her cross to bear.

We got into the Caddie, without even going back into the house, and were off for Center City, leaving Greta and George to attend to the guests, and also to their own dinner. This latest event had completely taken the thought of food, or hunger, from our minds.

"Don't drive too fast, Gus," I said, right at the start. "My nerves are at the breaking point."

He was relieved to hear what had delayed Gus Junior, but also shared my feeling that our son needed to be spoken to, as we had fully expected him back at the party.

Being, as we were, on the road to Center City, we had no way of knowing what took place at the same time in Contentment Cove.

Hilary was right in expecting Stanley Hathaway to appear at her house.

His car came careening down the lane to the Point very shortly after our conversation on the telephone.

Jules Balls first told me what occurred between them, when we had occasion to meet at the hospital, and so became much better acquainted than heretofore. He turned out to be entirely more congenial and sweet than I had supposed, and Lucy also. So in that respect the accident had at least one favorable result, in enlarging our friendship.

As Jules informed me, it was clear from the minute Hilary saw Stanley step out of his car that he had been drinking heavily. He was wearing a dirty white T-shirt, and rolled-up gabardine pants, while usually he was extremely neat, and he at once demanded that Hilly get in with him then and there and drive to Canada.

"Are you out of your *mind*, Stanley?" she said.

"Maybe I am—I hope to God I am. Come with me, Hilary!"

She took his arm, trying to bring him to his senses.

"Please come, Hilary. You're my only hope."

"Stanley, my dear, listen, *listen* to me, you *must*. The bank is looking for you already. You can't possibly get away. What have you done, Stanley? Tell me. Oh, for God's sake, *tell* me. Stanley, we'll get it hushed up somehow. I'll do all I can, pull strings, anything, I promise."

"You're not to blame," he muttered. "It's not your fault . . . is it?"

"Stanley, I'll go back with you to the bank. We'll *make* them keep it quiet."

"It's too late."

"It *can't* be. We can patch it up somehow."

He lost his balance and slumped to the step, pulling her down beside him, laughing.

It was a nightmare for her, not being able to make him realize the seriousness of the situation. All he wanted was to lie there in the sun, with his head against her shoulder.

"*Stanley*! Sit up! Don't go to sleep. You must *listen*!"

He straightened, wavering. "No, you listen to me! You know how much I make per week at the bank?"

"Oh, darling, I'm not blaming you, whatever you've done, but it's such a damn mess. We've got to set it right."

"It's a mess, all right," he mumbled, falling back against her. "I couldn't face Dad and ask him for any more. He took a second mortgage on our house. And then after . . . after I met you, Hilary," he laughed again, "you know what happened? I began not to give a damn!"

"Stanley, I promise you, we'll straighten it out. We'll pay back whatever you've taken. If the Potters are in on it, I'll *make* them keep their mouths shut."

"I didn't give a damn anymore," he said, almost crying. "You were the only thing I could think about. Or care about. When Beulah nagged me for something, anything, I got it to keep her quiet. I fixed it up *some* way so I could keep her quiet—so I could go on seeing you."

"Oh, what a fool I've been, what a fool, a *fool.*"

"You won't come with me, will you, Hilary? It's all over. It's all over and done with! Right now. Here and now!"

"Stanley, Stanley . . . "

"Here and now, right now!" he repeated, staggering to his feet. "I knew all the time it couldn't be true. I knew you were playing, that's all, just playing."

"No, *no* . . . "

Hilary was almost in a state of hysterics herself.

"Don't say *that.* It's not true. You *know* it's not true. Oh, let me think, give me a minute to *think.*"

"It's too late to think," he said, staring at her. "Don't worry, Hilary, don't worry any more about it. I'm going now."

"Stanley, no, wait—I can't let you go like this."

"It's the only way there is."

She was standing there in a kind of daze, listening to his car driving away, trying desperately to think what she should do, when she heard the state police siren. They had been waiting for him on the main road at the end of her lane.

She started running frantically up the hill after him, up that steep, winding lane. Gus had often told her that she ought to spend some money having it scraped and surfaced, but she only laughed, and said that she had better uses for her money.

But it was just as well that the poor woman didn't reach them any sooner.

Stanley didn't make any try to drive by the police. He may even have expected them to be there.

One of the officers was Leslie Moore, a Contentment Cove man he had known all his life.

"You must be looking for somebody, Les!" he called out to him.

"We're looking for you, Stan," Mr. Moore said. He felt very badly about having to arrest a Hathaway. "God knows why. Somebody must have got a bum steer up there in Center City. You can get things straightened out when you get back up there."

"That's all right, Les," Stanley said. "It's all in your day's work. Look, I got one favor to ask, though—see that somebody breaks this to Dad easy, will you?"

"I sure will try, Stan."

Before either of them could make a move to stop him, Stanley pulled a revolver out of the glove compartment, put it to his forehead, and pulled the trigger.

Hilary heard the shot. She reached the car only a few minutes later, and found him slumped over the wheel with the gun on the seat beside him.

The police were calling over their shortwave for an ambulance. But they didn't need one. It was too late for that.

Our ride to Center City at the same time the tragedy was occurring at the Point was anything but pleasant.

Neither of us spoke for a considerable time. Then Gus said, "Jules Balls could sue us, Mina, do you realize that?"

As I say, subsequently our minds were completely relieved on that score by Professor Balls himself, who never at any time entertained such a thought as suing us for his wife's accident, but we had no way of knowing it then, unfortunately, and to have Gus bring it up added one more to my worries.

It was a lovely twilight, though it was hard to appreciate it at the time. A ground mist rose from the swampland, and frogs were singing. The sky was perfectly clear, and pale, with a thin, bright sliver of moon. When we crossed the river, there was still a trace of sunset reflected in the water.

On the bad curve a mile beyond the bridge, which has a steep bank on one side, strewn with giant granite boulders, we saw lights tilting across the ditch in a peculiar way. The car ahead of us slowed, then pulled to the side and stopped.

"There must have been an accident," Gus said. "Looks as though a car's gone down the bank there, Mina."

"Oh, my goodness, Gus."

"If we could help, I'd stop. But that feller's already stopped. He'll find out what the trouble is."

"Oh, and we might get involved as witnesses. I simply couldn't stand any more, Gus, not tonight."

"Yeah, I know. You've had enough to put up with for one day, girl."

We caught a glimpse of the car, though it was too dusky to distinguish anything about it, other than its being there. There were just those headlights tilted across the boulders. The dreadful thought I had was of someone playing pranks with a spotlight.

Gus reached for my hand. "It's been a lousy day, honey."

"It certainly has, Gus," I said, at the end of my rope. "I just feel as though I've had enough Contentment Cove today to last me a lifetime. I don't feel that I know what to expect anymore. And now this—to find we've been *robbed*."

"It's a lousy deal, a hell of a lousy deal." He coughed, and I knew something serious was coming. "It's possible we've made a mistake, Mina. I'm pretty fed up, and I might as well come right out with it. People are all alike in a little, out-of-the-way place like this. Everything's fine as long as you're new, and handing out money. It's the only reason they want you butting in. Just ask for a little something in return, even a little lousy cooperation, and you start seeing a different face on the picture."

"We've spent *so* much on the swimming pool, Gus, and I don't even know now that it's appreciated."

"Right!" he said. "We're all done spending. Finished and done, here and now. They've got the last lousy cent they're going to get."

"Why would Stanley pick on us, Gus? It does seem so unfair that he picked *us*."

He coughed again. "Mina, I'm going to tell you something I've been keeping to myself."

I hitched closer to him, and he squeezed my hand.

The lights of Center City made a glow in the sky ahead. There was still a trace of sunset, and the radio towers were blinking across the fields like two low red stars. The motels, one right after another on the outskirts of town, were flashing their neon signs. They looked inviting, and bright, against the dusk.

I felt the first peaceful moment of the entire day, no matter what Gus had to tell me. For, after all, we had each other, and our health, which was the most important thing.

Here we were, and though we might be hungry and exhausted from the day we had put in, and though we might be fed up with a good deal that we had not foreseen, in the way of problems, still, it could be worse, a good deal worse. I had Gus, and he had me, minor irritations such as arise between any husband and wife notwithstanding.

"I wouldn't tell you except I think you ought to know the kind of lousy thing we're up against."

"All right, dear. All right, Gus, go ahead and tell me."

"I overheard Ted Hill talking to one of the men, Mina. I overheard him refer to us as . . . as Plus and Minus Potter."

I couldn't even whimper. It was so dreadfully, *dreadfully* disrespectful, and unkind.

"Gus," I said, determined not to break down in any way, shape, or manner over such a mean, ignorant jibe, "Contentment Cove just is not the place I envisioned it to be."

"You're damn right it isn't. You know what, girl, we could sell that place of ours tomorrow."

To hear him say that was as though someone had thrown open the gates of a prison I hadn't realized I was in. Why had I gone on pretending for months that Contentment Cove was what I had thought it to be, rather than what it was?

Yes, we had been disappointed, perhaps even tricked, and the brave thing to do was admit it, admit our mistake and chalk it up as all in a lifetime. That was all we *could* do, when we were the sort who looked and hoped for the best always, and then so often were disappointed. We expected too much!

In the case of Contentment Cove, we had been all too ready to see what we wanted to see, instead of what was really there. It was just one of life's many setbacks, which all of us are heir to, the best we may try. Only for us, this happened to be a very costly one. We had been well paid for our generosity, and not kindly, or in kind!

Mr. Lascomb unlocked the door of the bank from the inside as we came up the steps. There was only one dim light on, so that the grilled tellers' windows along both sides, and the octagonal, stand-up writing desk in the center had an unfamiliar, gloomy look.

"Well, Tom, this is a hell of a note!" Gus said.

Mr. Lascomb looked at us very strangely.

"Gus, Mrs. Potter, I . . . I have to greet you with more bad news."

He was perspiring, though it was quite cool, even chilly inside the bank. "Prepare yourselves, please, Mrs. Potter. I've just received word from the police—they contacted your home—your son has had an automobile accident, he and a young lady."

"Gus *Junior*?"

"It happened only a short time ago. You must have passed it on your way here, in fact. They've both been taken to the Center City General. Your son has a broken jaw, I think; beyond that I don't know, Mrs. Potter."

It was over an hour before we were allowed to see Gus Junior, and then only a glimpse to let him know that we were there, and everything was being taken care of. The poor child started to cry when he saw us, though he was barely conscious from all the sedation.

Dr. Porter Pratt, whom we had had summoned as soon as we arrived (he was attending some affair at the country club and came straight to the hospital in his tuxedo, which looked so odd, being a style of dress I had never connected with that part of the world), reassured us that he was not in danger. His jaw was badly broken, and he had a dislocated shoulder, and several broken ribs, as well as severe bruises over his entire body.

It was bad enough, goodness knows, but I could only thank God he was alive. I broke down myself when I left his room and the sight of that poor bandaged, aching head, with the tears welling into his eyes when he saw us standing there.

Dr. Pratt himself gave me an injection, and took us into a private room nearby, where we might stay, rather than in the public waiting room.

"Er, Doctor," I overheard Gus say to him, "when can I see Miss Hathaway? We want her to have the best care money can buy, you see to that."

"Miss Hathaway has a broken left arm, and a badly cut right arm and shoulder," Dr. Pratt said. "There was considerable loss of blood, but I think you could look in on her."

They were just leaving the room, when Hilary came bursting in past them, looking in a far worse state than I myself was.

"Oh, Hilly, dear," I began to cry, in spite of all best intentions.

"Is she badly hurt?" she demanded. "Oh, Porter, thank God, you're here. Have you seen her? For God's sake tell me how badly that child is hurt?"

"Calm down, calm down, Hilary," Dr. Porter Pratt said, putting his arm around her. "She has some bad abrasions and a broken left humerus, but she'll be fit as a cricket in no time."

Hilary covered her face, and began to shake. Hysterics were not to be wondered at, considering what she had just been through, though of course I was unaware of all that had happened heretofore, and thought at the time if she could just break down and have a good natural cry, she would be better off.

Dr. Pratt nodded to us over her shoulder, and practically carried her out, and closed the door.

It didn't come to me until they had gone that she hadn't inquired about Gus Junior. Perhaps it discloses a small nature, but I have never been quite able to forgive her that.

It was over a year before I heard from Hilary again, after Dr. Pratt took her out of our room that day. That was in the form of a view card from Prince Edward Island, forwarded to us in

Bermuda, where we were spending several months, with *Holiday Greetings* scrawled on it, and signed Spencer and Hilary Wister.

Professor Balls had told me of her reconciliation with her husband, and I most certainly hoped for her sake that it turned out to be permanent.

So that day finally came to an end, like any other. Gus and myself remained there in the hospital that night, thanks to the kindness of Dr. Porter Pratt.

The state police told us what had happened. A trailer truck crowded Gus Junior onto the shoulder of the road, where his wheels skidded in the loose gravel, causing him to lose control, and to go sliding over the steep embankment. The Jaguar was wedged between two boulders, with neither Gus Junior nor Dot-Fran able to get out or even to move.

There are nights, even now that it is all long past and gone, when I wake up shivering to think that the car might have caught fire.

They could see the lights of passing automobiles, but were completely helpless until someone noticed their headlights and stopped to investigate. Gus Junior was not able to speak or cry out.

I imagine it is not too hard to understand why we sold our Contentment Cove home, and moved to this lovely spot on Lake Michigan. Though we were loath to leave for many reasons, hating to give up our many true friends (though naturally we shall always keep in touch), our view of the broad Atlantic, and our mammoth fireplace, built from our own beach rocks.

Still, there were many memories better left unsaid, many disappointments, which could not forever be overlooked.

I'm sure we are all three going to be very happy here in our new home. Gus is constructing a fieldstone fireplace in our ninety-foot living room, which will take a six-foot log. He says his previous experience at Contentment Cove stands him in good stead.

Later, we shall perhaps erect a flagpole near the junction of the roads on the edge of our property, and landscape a pretty little green, where ceremonials can be held, such as Memorial Days, and Fourth of July observances. It seems little enough that we can do for our friendly, kind neighbors.

We have named our lovely home here Contentment Cove, showing that we harbor no regret—live and learn! And I must say that our sunsets over Lake Michigan, through our tinted picture window in the living room, take off their hats to none anywhere, including those of the Atlantic Ocean.

The Town

Spring always seems a long time coming in New England. But in March the sun is beginning to warm, and it's time to pull the evergreen boughs from the perennial flower beds.

They leave a thin trail of dry spills across the lawn, and burning with their fierce crackling blaze on a foggy day, with the bell buoy sounding its melancholy whoo-whoo, *the smell of the sea, the wet thawing woods, the spruce smoke and its dense white cloud floating across the picket fence, announce the end of one season and the birth of another as no calendar can.*

A few more sunny days and clumps of veronica, iris, Red Emperor tulip bulbs, yellow butter balls long imprisoned begin to sprout spindly shoots reaching for the light.

All about the Cove, fields are burned in March. On each still evening, heavy and damp with dew, fires glow across the heathland, on the island, where caretakers have begun their season's work, in the blueberry barrens behind the new Consolidated School, and in the vacant lot beside the branch of Guarantee Trust.

Burned grass turns green early, and burned fields bloom bright with paintbrush and buttercups and white-faced daisies. Some claim that burned fields turn to bushes, others claim not.

In spring, the fishermen who frequent the bays and inshore ledges set their traps again, and on each clear morning, in the first fresh light of the rising sun, the near sea is dotted with them, and comes alive with the putt-putt *of their outboard motors.*

The new family in the log cabin close to the water complain bitterly that they are awakened before sunrise day after day, by lobster boats only a few yards offshore. But this is a matter beyond the jurisdiction of the selectmen, and the new family finds the dawn hours of a fisherman's day an implacable opponent, dictated by the windless sea.

Who before has ever minded the erratic, friendly putt-putts of daylight? It is part of waking, or of sleeping. It is like groping to the window in a dark night hour and seeing a neighbor's bright reassuring light across the street, like waking from an unwelcome dream to hear a car pass, ordinary, droning, recognized, bringing you back from a friendless land to your own safe bed, to the Cove, and home.

In another month, the road to Center City blossoms with wild pear, wild cherry, wild apple; the hackmatacks turn a delicate, joyous green.

But whatever the season, there is the sky above Contentment Cove, and the sea surrounding it, blue in their infinite variety; there are islands, the sea ledges looming along the horizon; there is the town itself, caught in the fingers of the coastline.

A chosen land.

10/1/07 Paid Book 12.76